RANGER MCINTYRE: UNMENTIONABLE MURDERS

 This Large Print Book carries the
Seal of Approval of N.A.V.H.

RANGER MCINTYRE: UNMENTIONABLE MURDERS

JAMES C. WORK

THORNDIKE PRESS
A part of Gale, Cengage Learning

GALE
A Cengage Company

Farmington Hills, Mich • San Francisco • New York • Waterville, Maine
Meriden, Conn • Mason, Ohio • Chicago

Copyright © 2018 by James C. Work.
Map of Rocky Mountain National Park copyright 2018 by James C. Work.
Glossary of words are included at the back of the book.
Thorndike Press, a part of Gale, a Cengage Company.

Thorndike Press® Large Print Historical Fiction.
The text of this Large Print edition is unabridged.
Other aspects of the book may vary from the original edition.
Set in 16 pt. Plantin.

LIBRARY OF CONGRESS CIP DATA ON FILE.
CATALOGUING IN PUBLICATION FOR THIS BOOK
IS AVAILABLE FROM THE LIBRARY OF CONGRESS

ISBN-13: 978-1-4328-4485-1 (hardcover)

Published in 2019 by arrangement with James C. Work

Printed in Mexico
1 2 3 4 5 6 7 23 22 21 20 19

RANGER MCINTYRE:
UNMENTIONABLE MURDERS

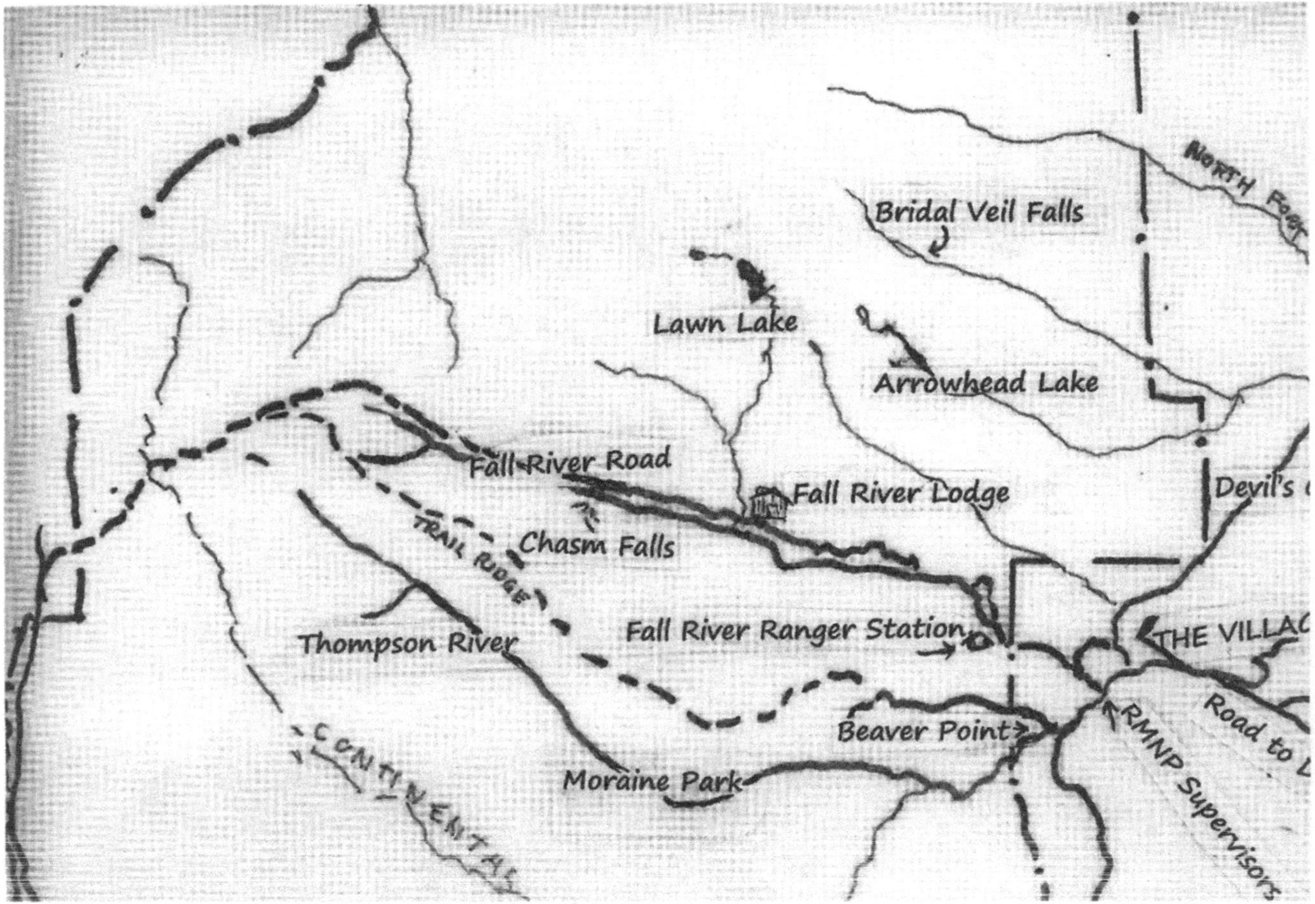
NORTH FORK
Bridal Veil Falls
Lawn Lake
Arrowhead Lake
Fall River Road
Fall River Lodge
Devil's
Chasm Falls
TRAIL RIDGE
Fall River Ranger Station
THE VILLAG
Thompson River
Beaver Point
Road to
RMNP Supervisors
Moraine Park
CONTINENTAL

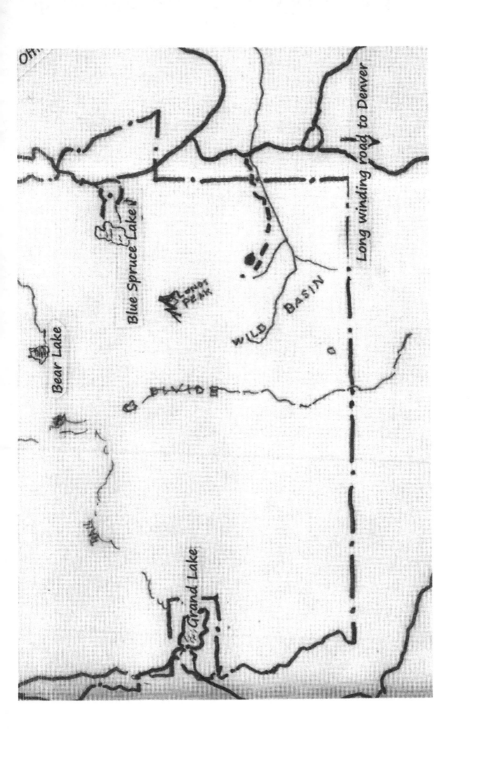

CHAPTER 1

"Good morning, Miss Killian," the waitress said.

"Good morning, Hazel. How are you to-day?"

"Very fine, thanks. Looks like we're in for another sunny day, doesn't it? Sleep well?"

"Like a log. The nights are so much darker than in the city. And quiet. But for some reason I always seem to wake up hungry."

"I think it's the mountain air. Seems to give everyone a good appetite. Will you have the served breakfast, or the buffet?"

"Just the buffet, I think."

"I'll charge it to your room number. Your ranger is already here."

Doris Killian had already taken notice of "her" park ranger smiling at her while he was helping himself to sausages and scrambled eggs from the sideboard. She returned his smile and went to draw herself a cup of coffee from the urn. She drew a cup for him as well, seeing that he had his hands full — a plate of sausage and eggs in one, a plate of cinnamon rolls in the other.

"How do you feel about dead bodies?" he asked as they put their cups and plates on the table and sat down. Both of them liked the window table with the view of the mountains and the village.

"I prefer them alive," she said. "Although I suppose dead might be interesting."

"I need to drive up to Chasm Falls this morning," the ranger said. "A tourist found a dead guy in Fall River."

"What was he doing up there?"

He offered one of his cinnamon rolls. She waved it away.

"Fishing, according to Jamie Ogg. There's this deep pool at the base of the falls with some fine trout in it. You have to be there at the right time and use a good-size fly, maybe a #10 or #12 Black Gnat. At the pool under Chasm Falls I like to use a Gnat, with a Royal Coachman on a dropper, maybe two feet up the tippet. Jamie said it looked like the tourist had been using worms on a weighted hook. Worm fishermen. Live and let live, I guess. Anyway, this tourist snagged something and there's this dead guy floating around in the pool, under the surface, you know."

An alarm buzzed in his brain, warning him that he was babbling like a teenage sport trying to impress a cute girl on their first date, but he couldn't help it. He was afraid that if he didn't keep talking she might finish her breakfast and leave. Of course, on the other hand, if he kept on chattering the way he was she might leave even before finishing her breakfast. It represented a very serious quandary to Ranger McIntyre, since to him one of the truly worthwhile pleasures in life was sharing a leisurely early morning breakfast with an attractive woman.

"What I meant was . . . what was the dead guy doing up there?" she said.

"Oh, the dead guy? Well, he wasn't doing anything. He was dead. It was the tourist who was fishing. Early this morning. Worm drowners seem to think they need to be on the river by sunrise."

"How did he die? Was he killed? Was it an accident?"

"I don't know."

"Who was he? Do you think he might have washed down the river? Did they find a car? How do you think he got there?"

"Jamie didn't say. He phoned from the lodge and said we have a dead guy at Chasm Falls. I suppose if Jamie thought we had a murderer running around the park, he

11

would've mentioned it. Would've told me to bring a gun. Something like that."

"You don't carry a gun?" she asked.

"Not usually, no. Hardly ever need one. Most of the time carrying a gun is a darn nuisance. They're always in your way. You go to reach into your pants pocket, you need to either lift your holster or slide it out of the way."

There he went, babbling again. But he couldn't help himself. She kept looking at him with those moist nut-brown eyes like she was taking in every word.

"Sometimes you bend over and the gun butt jabs you in the ribs," he continued. "Every evening after carrying it around all day you need to wipe it down. Dust, rust, fingerprints. A gun can be nothing but a nuisance, especially when you hardly ever have to use it. Say! These scrambled eggs are awful good this morning! They've got little scallions or onions or something chopped up in them."

"Fingerprints? On your gun?"

"Not much of a problem up here in the mountains where there's no humidity. But anywhere humid, you leave a damp finger mark on a gun's frame or barrel and, in a few days, there's a rust spot there. I think these little green things are green onion tips.

12

They give the eggs a nice taste, don't they?"

"Let's back up a little," she said. "Why did you ask me how I feel about dead bodies?"

"Oh. Well, like I said, I need to drive up there."

"As soon as you've eaten enough breakfast for two men?"

"Right. You sure you don't want this last cinnamon roll?"

"Thanks, but no. You're not in a hurry to find out what happened?"

"I don't think our dead guy will begrudge us a bite of breakfast. And he sure as heck isn't going anywhere. And he has Jamie with him, because Jamie's a ranger and that's his job. Well, he's an assistant ranger, anyway. Jamie might have everything figured out by the time we get there."

"We?"

"Right. I thought you'd like to come along. Unless you manage to find a car to rent and you planned on doing something else today."

"You want me to come along? To view this dead person? Is that how you show a girl a good time?"

"Not usually!" And the ranger laughed.

He had a nice laugh, a rich baritone chuckle. When he laughed, it made little

13

crinkles at the corners of his eyes.

"No," he went on. "You said you came to Rocky to take photographs of waterfalls. If you want to drive up there with me this morning, I could show you Chasm Falls. If you don't have a car yet, that is. And if you wanted to come along. It's a doozy of a waterfall. You see, Fall River comes meandering along across a long and level moraine, in and out of the trees. At the edge of the moraine it strikes a granite ledge and drops forty or fifty feet down a narrow cleft in the rock and into an ice-cold pool about half the size of this dining room."

He felt like he was babbling again.

"With a dead body floating in it," Doris added.

"I hope not. Jamie should have fished him out by now. The park service ambulance might even be there before us. They might have taken the body away already."

"I'd need to change," she said, raising her skirt two inches to show him that she was wearing heels and dark silk stockings.

"Okay," the ranger said. "You do that. I'll have another cup of coffee. Maybe another sausage."

"Do I have time to finish my breakfast?"

"Oh, sure. Take your time. Read the newspaper. Did you see this article? President

14

Harding mentioned our new National Park in a press conference last week. See, right here on page three? 'Rocky Mountain National Park will one day be as important as Yellowstone,' he said."

"Only maybe more dangerous?" she asked. "People plunging over waterfalls?"

"Nah. Yellowstone, it has those boiling mud pots for people to fall into. And an overpopulation of bears. They like to eat campers. RMNP is as safe as kittens, except like you said when people go over a waterfall. Or drive their car off into a canyon. Last summer, a hiker tried to walk up to an elk and got himself gored. Can I bring you more coffee while I'm up?"

"Thanks, no. Maybe an elk pushed your dead guy over the waterfall."

"That's an idea. I'll round up all the elk and interview them."

There was that baritone chuckle again.

"I'm finished here," Doris said. "I'll go up to my room to change while you have another cup of coffee and think up more silly things to say."

Two miles out of town they reached the end of the asphalt paving where blacktopped Highway 34 became a two-lane gravel road. The little Model A pickup truck bounced

15

along at a steady pace, the motor chugging a happy note. The mountain air was chilly, especially whenever they entered a stretch of deep forest shadows. It came in around the windscreen and made her shiver.

"Can I close this window?" she said over the noise of the engine.

"You can try," he said. "Maybe you'll have the magic touch, but it's been stuck for a couple of weeks. Haven't been able to slide it closed. You okay over there?"

"Just swell," she said.

She kept her boots planted firmly on the floorboards up next to the firewall, her legs keeping her body braced, her arms cradling the Kodak. Her other camera was in the rucksack tucked behind her legs, an arrangement that made her legs virtually immobile. She could hear her tripod rattling back and forth in the bed of the Ford behind her and prayed that it wouldn't bounce out onto the road.

"I was thinking about your name," the ranger said.

"What about it?"

"Well, Killian. And cameras. I got to thinking about it last night after you went to . . . after you retired for the evening. There was a Major Killian who took pictures in the Great War. He came to our

16

airfield once. One of the boys flew him over enemy lines to take aerial photographs. I never saw any of his pictures."

"You were a pilot?" she asked. "In the war?"

"Briefly. I flew a Nieuport 28. The war was about done with by the time I had finished flight training in Texas and got over to France."

"I see," she said. "Major Killian was my father. The army assigned him to make photographs of battlefields, equipment that had been destroyed, injuries, corpses, anything like that. They wanted to study his pictures and build better ways of killing people."

"Kinda gruesome for him," the ranger said.

"Yes. At least he was lucky enough to come home alive. But he was changed. All that death. And having to record it all on film. It affected his mind. Plus, those damn Germans had to go and use mustard gas. Whoever invented mustard gas ought to be shot! Father inhaled it over there and it wrecked his lungs. I know it's what killed him. Damn war. Damn governments. Pardon the language."

"Think nothing of it," he said. "Tell you what, let's find something more cheery to talk about. Hey! Here comes the Fall River entrance station! Miss Killian, waterfall photographer, welcome to Rocky Mountain National Park, one of the newest national parks in our fine nation and one of the most spectacular. We want you to enjoy your stay."

"You stole that line from the brochure back at the inn, didn't you?"

"Maybe I wrote it for the brochure," he said.

"Did you?"

"No."

The entrance station consisted of a rustic log cabin on one side of the road and another log building on the opposite side. Between them a trussed roof also made of heavy logs straddled the width of the roadway. A red octagonal sign in the middle of the road said STOP. The ranger drove on through.

"Now we're in the National Park," he said. "My territory."

"Weren't you supposed to stop at the entrance?" she asked.

"No need," he said. "There's nobody on duty."

"Who's supposed to be on duty?"

"Me."

His boot jammed the clutch pedal down and he shifted into second gear. The Ford's engine labored importantly to climb the long rising curve to the top of the moraine.

"It looks like you could live there. I noticed a cabin up the hill behind the entrance, I mean."

"That's what it's for. The government provides me a luxurious two-room cabin complete with running water, which means you run over to the creek and get it."

"But you live at the Pioneer Inn boarding house."

"Sometimes. Their breakfasts are better than mine."

"What if your supervisor or someone needed you? What if they came to the entrance station to find you?"

"Well, there you go."

She was still concerned about her tripod falling out of the truck. Whenever they went over a bump in the road she heard it bang against the bed.

"Maybe I should stop and take my tripod out of the back of your truck," she suggested over the sound of the engine. "I could put it behind the seat?"

"Can't stop on this steep hill," McIntyre said. "If we did, I'd have to back all the way down to the bottom and take another run at it. Besides, I don't think there's room behind the seat for your tripod."

"Why not?" she said. "What's back there?"

"My fishing rod case and my creel."

Why not a picnic lunch? she thought. *Maybe the unfortunate dead guy wouldn't mind waiting while she and the ranger took pictures, did a little fly fishing, and had a nice lunch. Gee, if only they had brought a badminton set maybe they could set it up and play a little badminton after lunch.*

She was beginning to suspect that this park ranger didn't take his job too seriously. Letting civilians ride in a government vehicle. Carrying a fishing rod on duty. Driving past a stop sign. But at least he had the look of a responsible ranger. Oh, yes. In every inch of him he was a ranger. He could model for the Rocky Mountain National Park brochure. Take the flat hat, for example. That hat was becoming the symbol of the National Park Service and he wore his with a tiny tilt forward, giving him a serious but kind of cocky look. His dark green coat — a "tunic" they called it — was clean and recently pressed, as were his tan jodhpurs. His knee-high boots, laced from toe to top, showed a light coating of dust but had been polished to a military shine.

"Speaking of names," she said.

"What about names?"

"What do people call you? Besides 'Ranger

McIntyre,' I mean."

"Mother called me Grayson," he said. "But nobody else calls me that."

"What do they call you instead?"

"Tim," he said.

He pumped the clutch pedal twice and tugged the shift lever down into low gear. The Ford growled and lurched and went on climbing the curve. Steam rose from the radiator cap.

"We'll need to stop up ahead at Beaver Meadows for radiator water," he said over the engine noise.

"Fine," she replied. She needed to "stretch her legs," as they say. Oh, boy, did she need to stretch her legs. As . . . they say. Too many cups of breakfast coffee. He took a water bag from the back of the Ford. Seeing the question in her face, he pointed across the road toward the forest.

"Girls to the north," he laughed. "Boys to the south. Them's the rules in backcountry."

Here was another thing, she thought.

This park ranger, Timothy Grayson Mc-Intyre, had no qualms about allowing a defenseless female to venture alone into the deep, dark forest, probably inhabited by bears and cougars, to find a log or boulder where she could . . . as they say . . . in

21

privacy. That wasn't the worst part. The worst part was that when they resumed their drive, they hadn't gone more than two miles when they came to a massive two-story tourist lodge complete with stables, a trout pond, and a coffee shop. And public toilets. He might have mentioned that they were ten minutes from a toilet before she went off to hang her little bare derriere over a log in the woods.

"Fall River Lodge," he announced. "Rooms by the night, cabins by the week. A lady named Minnie March owns the place. You ought to stop in and meet her sometime. You'd like her. She makes a mean rhubarb pie."

"I suppose you'd know," she said.

He seemed not to hear that.

"Widow lady. Mike died three years ago. They built a first-class place, though. There's even a hydroelectric generator for electric lights. This is where we turn off."

They had come to a junction where the main road began a long curve up into the forest while another road veered off, crossed the mountain stream, and took them past Fall River Lodge. A half mile beyond the lodge they entered a sunny grove where the pristine white aspen trees were nearly two stories tall. She wished she could stop and make a photograph; the aspen were like Grecian columns with the late morning light edging down through the leaves. It was a photographer's dream. But they drove on; at the far edge of the aspen grove the truck rumbled across a log bridge where another mountain stream came burbling and churning over the boulders and fallen logs.

"Beautiful!" she said over the engine noise. "And the road is smoother!"

"They did a good job of grading it along this stretch," he said, "but it gets rougher up ahead where it begins to slab up the side of the mountain. And it's almost a sixteen percent grade. You'll need to hang on."

Hang on to what? she thought. *And with what? I already have finger cramps from holding onto the camera. What's "sixteen percent" and what did he mean, "slab"?*

The sixteen percent grade included three hairpin turns with a panoramic view two hundred feet straight down to the river. Doris found herself holding her breath and leaning over as if the pickup would topple down the precipice if she didn't keep her weight pressed against the uphill door. What on earth had ever given a surveyor the idea of making a road that not only seemed to go straight up but hung on the edge of a cliff? McIntyre called it the Devil's Cork-

23

screw. She didn't begin to breathe again nor did her white knuckles relax until they reached the top of the corkscrew and drove out into another flat valley, this one suspended high above the Fall River canyon. The ranger stopped, set the parking brake, and got out to pour water into the radiator.

"If she starts to roll back," he called to her, "just put your foot on the brake pedal!"

"Oh, jolly good. Government vehicle or not. If this thing begins to roll backward I'm jumping out. If the darn door works."

"There they are," he said, pointing.

Below them, beside the stream, two men were standing over a figure covered with an olive drab army blanket. Ranger McIntyre seemed in no particular hurry to examine the body. He seemed more interested in giving Doris a tour of Chasm Falls.

"Might want to bring your Kodak," he suggested.

And shall you bring your fishing rod? she thought. *Maybe the poor dead guy could loan you a Black Gnat or a Royal Coachman.*

"This steep trail leads to the top of the falls, if you want see the view from up there. But be careful, because it's slippery from the mist. And it's a long ways down. Or if you don't want to go up there you can take

24

the trail down along the stream. There's a vantage place below the pool where you get a good view of the waterfall. For pictures, I think most people go down there. Where those men are, see? From there you can look up the gorge between the rock walls with the waterfall above you."

"For the time being," she said, "I'll stay with you."

"What've you got here?" asked Ranger McIntyre.

The very boyish-looking young man in a ranger uniform was looking past McIntyre at the attractive woman behind him.

"Ah," McIntyre said. "I nearly forgot my introductions. Miss Killian, this boy in green is supposed to be my assistant ranger, Jamie Ogg. Jamie, meet Miss Killian."

She reached around McIntyre to shake the boy's hand.

"Assistant?" she said. "What do you assist with?"

"We ain't exactly figured it out," said young Jamie. "Mostly I stay at the entrance station or else I go and do whatever Tim tells me. Except usually there's nothing to tell me to do. Sometimes I take a horse and go on patrol up and down the hiking trails. I like that. We have lots of hiking trails to keep an eye on."

"Tell me about this dead body," McIntyre said. "Know who he is?"

"Name's Snyder, Ernst Snyder," Jamie replied. "We got his wallet here. Oh, and here's his five-day fishing license. Found it in the pocket of his shirt."

McIntyre looked at the license. The wallet and license were both dry.

"At least we know he was right-handed. See that signature? And where he wrote his address? Was he wearing a watch? On the left wrist?"

"He was," Jamie said.

The other man coughed to let them know he was still there.

"Oh, sorry!" Jamie Ogg said. "Ranger McIntyre, this here is Mr. Blackman. He's the one who found the body."

"Glad to meet you," Blackman said, shaking hands with McIntyre.

"You found the body this morning?"

"Yeah, I came out to do a little early fishing . . . me and the wife are staying at Fall River Lodge . . . and I got up there at the top of the falls, looking for a likely trout hole up there, you know, and what do you think I find?"

"I don't know. What?"

"A pile of clothes. Coat, pants, shirt, vest,

26

hat. Shoes. All nice and folded and in a pile with the hat on top. I look around, see? First thing I thought is that their owner is having himself a bath in the stream. Well, sir, I went out to the lip of the falls up there and I look over the edge and there's this guy floating facedown in the pool. Just drifting around in the water with the current. 'Round and 'round. Wearin' nothing but his underdrawers."

"We been talkin' about it," Jamie Ogg volunteered. "We figure what happened is he must've been fishin' that nice quiet pool up there at the top of the falls. You know how the stream flattens out and makes a long calm stretch before it goes over into the waterfall? We figure he dropped somethin' up there. Maybe his rod, maybe his creel. Or maybe he was standin' at the head of that calm stretch changin' a fly and dropped his fly wallet in the water. Maybe whatever it was floated over the falls. We ain't found any of them, rod, creel, fly wallet, nothin'. He strips off his clothes, see, to climb down there and wade into the pool and retrieve whatever it was. But first he looks over the falls to see if he can spot his gear in the water, and bango! He leans too far, loses his balance, maybe hits his head, and ends up in the stream."

"Except why," McIntyre asked, "why take off everything if he was going to climb down to the pool? I agree it makes sense that he might have dropped something and it went over the falls. But what did he do, strip and climb down here but leave his clothes up there? That part doesn't make sense."

Doris Killian watched as the ranger drew aside the blanket and knelt down to examine the body. McIntyre made notes in his pocket notebook, then methodically turned the unfortunate Mr. Snyder one way and the other in order to examine both sides and the back. Apparently satisfied that he had seen everything there was to see, the ranger pulled the blanket back over the body and stood up. Without a word to anyone he walked to the government pickup truck and returned carrying his fishing rod and a small tackle box.

Well, she thought. *It looks like our ranger has done his duty and needs a little relaxing time with his fly rod.*

McIntyre tied his heaviest tippet to the end of the fly line and selected his largest wet fly, adding a couple of split shot to make it sink. After studying the flow of the current and the way the falling water boiled and rolled and churned, he began to make long, graceful casts of the line out into the pool at the base of the waterfall.

"Awful deep out there," he called back to them over the pounding of the waterfall. "Freezing cold, too."

"Fall River," Jamie Ogg told Doris. "It starts up there on the Continental Divide six, maybe eight miles from here. Comes straight outa the snowfields, which is why it's really ice cold."

"You mean 'literally' ice cold?"

"Yeah, really."

More minutes went by. Doris unfolded her camera to take a few scenery pictures. The ranger made cast after cast before he felt a subtle resistance in the line. He raised the rod tip to set the hook, reeled in, and found his hook had lodged in the cork handle of another fishing rod. McIntyre examined the fly rod with curiosity, made a note in his notebook, and went back to fishing. This time his catch turned out to be a wicker creel complete with leather harness. He put it in the grass next to the rod.

"Jamie!"

"Yessir?"

"Make a detailed sketch of these things and put them in your patrol car. Don't change them in any way. Take them back to the station and put them in my office."

Doris came up behind the two rangers.

"What's going on?" she asked.

"We might need a coroner on this one," McIntyre said.

"Why?"

"The fly reel. It's rigged for a right-handed man. But not the creel. It's hooked up backwards for a right-hander. And it shouldn't be hooked at all. The strap that goes around the waist, it's fastened. Tidy, like his pile of clothing. Interesting. I'm thinking about the depth of the water, too."

"What about the depth?"

"Two things," McIntyre said. "One, from up there on the lip of the waterfall you can't see the bottom of the pool. If he dropped his rod and creel over the falls, accidentally, but saw where they landed and stripped to dive in after them, he wouldn't have known where to dive. And, unless he was really dumb, he sure as heck wouldn't dive from the top of the falls not knowing where the bottom was. He'd come down the trail and wade out into the pool. But why would he undress himself up there before walking down? And would he do it barefoot? Look at the sharp rocks on the path, not to mention the pine needles and roots and such. From the condition of the soles of his feet I'd say he's a man who never went barefoot. As cold as the water is, he couldn't have stayed in it more than a few seconds. I'll bet you won't find any willows or saplings cut down, either."

"What?" Jamie Ogg said. "Why?"

"You lose your rod in the pool. Wouldn't you cut yourself a long willow branch and fish around for it? But our Mr. Snyder stripped down to his underdrawers, stacked his clothes neatly, climbed down the path barefoot to the base of the falls, and dove in after his equipment? Seems fishy to me. No pun intended. Anyway, we need to make notes and sketches before the ambulance boys come and take the body away, and before any more people come to mess up the scene."

Doris had an idea.

"Would pictures help?" she suggested. "I could make photographs of the pole and the fish basket. And the corpse."

"It's a fly rod, not a 'pole,' and that 'fish basket' is called a 'creel.' But I'd like that, yes! I'd appreciate it. Some photos could save a lot of time, for sure. If you don't mind. I can ask the park service to pay you for film and developing."

She returned to the truck and brought back the large camera and the wooden tripod with steel-pointed legs. Jamie Ogg helped her assemble the equipment while

31

Ranger McIntyre climbed to the top of the falls in order to have another look around. When he returned, he was carrying the pile of neatly folded clothes with the shoes on top.

"Ambulance is coming," he announced. "Hear it?"

The ambulance driver was in high dudgeon, which Ranger McIntyre exacerbated by pointing out that the ambulance should have been there an hour ago.

"Damn thing!" the driver snorted. "First it boils over before we get to Endovalley. We stopped and put water in the radiator, and we almost made it to the top of the sixteen percent grade when she stalls out with a vapor lock."

Doris thought she smelled a whiff of alcoholic breath while the driver was talking. Surely a man wouldn't take a drink in the morning, especially while driving that precipitous mountain road. And with the Prohibition on, too.

"That's what happens when you drive a Dodge," Ranger McIntyre said. "The Ford, it has a more dependable fuel pump."

After he and Jamie helped the driver load the dead man into the ambulance they scouted the area again in case they had missed anything important. Mr. Blackman was still standing around as if he was unsure whether he was allowed to leave.

"Good of you to help us out, Mr. Blackman," McIntyre said. "If you'd write your name and address in my notebook, I'll send you the final report. If you'd be interested."

"Sure," the man replied. "Let me have the notebook."

"By the way," Ranger McIntyre said, "you didn't come up here by horseback, by any chance?"

"No. I hiked up from the lodge. Along the river trail. It's shorter than walking along the road. I hiked back the same way to phone the ranger station. Anyhow, I never learned how to ride a horse. Why?"

"Fresh hoofprints up there near the stream where it goes over the falls. Probably doesn't mean anything. Horses can stray away from the corral at the lodge and wander up the valley. Maybe Mr. Snyder was riding a horse. Or maybe somebody took a morning ride before our victim went over the falls. If he did go over."

All during the drive back to the village, the ranger stayed in a quiet reverie. Doris looked at him several times but didn't want to interrupt his thoughts with any idle questions or chitchat. He was thinking hard about a serious issue; no doubt he was working out solutions to the riddle of how that man had ended up naked and floating in the river. It wasn't until they were less than a mile from town before she got up the nerve.

"You seem awfully quiet," she said. "Mind if I ask what you're thinking about?"

"Lunch," he said. "Meat loaf is today's special at the Neetasapin Café. You hungry?"

A week went by. At the Pioneer Inn, the way the perky photographer and the good-looking ranger had breakfast together each morning gave the staff something to titter and gossip about. Two additional guests arrived that week: Mr. Snyder's brother and cousin, who had come from Illinois to bring his body home. As they told Ranger McIntyre, it couldn't have been anything but an accident. Ernst Snyder had no enemies, except for people who generally resented anyone with a German name and a German accent.

The war, you know.

McIntyre handed over Ernst Snyder's cash and possessions from his room at the Fall River Lodge. The brother and cousin agreed with McIntyre that it was odd how he had undressed down to his underwear and had either waded or dove into the freezing water, but he was dead and they needed to arrange for the local mortician to embalm the body and ship it home. McIntyre asked to keep the fishing equipment a while longer, and the brother agreed. McIntyre would send it to them later.

So that, it seemed, was that.

Park Supervisor Nicholson paid a visit to the ranger station to see the "evidence" and to ask why his ranger had kept it. Not that keeping it looked suspicious, but it was McIntyre and it was fishing equipment. McIntyre wasn't there, however. Nicholson was a bit annoyed to discover that the assistant, Jamie Ogg, was running the entire station while Ranger McIntyre loafed around in the village. He told the ranger as much when he met up with him. Unruffled by the supervisor's rebuke, McIntyre continued to bivouac at the Pioneer Inn where he could enjoy breakfast and morning chats with Miss Doris Killian.

"I still do my day's work," he told Nicholson. "And admit it: wouldn't you rather share fresh cinnamon rolls with a young lady than share soggy thick pancakes with Jamie Ogg?"

McIntyre was more interested in the girl

than in the cinnamon rolls, but he didn't tell Nicholson about it. However, he was somewhat stymied, and admitted the same to himself, when it came to figuring out how to spend more time with her, how to work up to the point of hand-holding and maybe kissing. He caught himself daydreaming about it. One evening he happened to overhear guests at the inn talking about a new movie film they had seen in Denver. His mind conjured up an image of himself and Doris sitting in a movie house holding hands in the dark. Maybe with his arm slipped around her shoulders.

"I'll be leaving tomorrow," she said one morning. "Time for me to stop sightseeing and start selling my story. I need to return home and try to make some money."

The ranger's eyebrows clenched in a look of disappointment. If it's possible to pout with one's eyebrows, that's what McIntyre was doing. What about the kissing and hand-holding, the walks in the mountain evenings?

"Did you take all the pictures you'll need?" he said, hoping she hadn't.

"I made views of Chasm Falls, Alberta Falls, Calypso Cascades, and Ouzel Falls. That should be enough for a photo layout.

I'm planning a magazine story. However . . ."

"However?"

"Well, I don't want to jinx my new idea by talking about it, but I think I could do a book! Wouldn't that be swell? If I can find a publisher. I've been studying my map of the park and it shows dozens and dozens of waterfalls. I'll bet most of them are picturesque. My idea is to come back next summer and explore them for a book. The waterfalls of our new National Park, that sort of thing."

"Sounds like it would make a book people would buy," he said, already wondering if he could wangle enough time off during the summer months to take Doris to those waterfalls. Some of them would need to be overnight trips. He was imagining a campsite in an alpine meadow with a view of a cataract and little lake with trout in it. He imagined a campfire in front of the tent, two people feeding sticks into the flames and talking away half the night, alone in the mountains with each other. *There's your trouble, Timothy Grayson,* he thought. *When it comes to women you're mostly imagination.*

The following morning McIntyre sat at the window table as usual, eating all alone as he watched the bus driver load Doris's bags and tripod into the baggage compartment. There went his chances of inviting her to go to Denver to see a film. There went the fantasy of the two of them camped out at Bridal Veil Falls.

Two weeks went by before the mail carrier handed McIntyre a large envelope showing Doris's return address. It contained the photographs she had taken of the Chasm Falls corpse, along with a quick note saying, among other things, "see you next summer!" A cheery little p.s. said *"Lady Traveler's Companion* wants to buy the picture story!!!"

He tossed the packet on his desk, leaned back in his swivel chair, and let himself daydream about next summer. In his mind's eye, he could see again the tent and campfire beside the trail at Bridal Veil Falls. Maybe he'd try to figure out a way he could afford to buy one of those Baker tents, large and comfortable, the kind that has its front open to the campfire. She would take photographs of him frying trout in front of the tent. It would be an idyllic mountain camp with perfect weather and no responsibilities and no blanket-covered corpses; Ernst Snyder's poor dead white drowned body would be forgotten. Little did McIntyre know . . . had no way of suspecting . . . that events of the winter were to change every-thing. The photos Doris had made of the corpse at Chasm Falls would send both the photographer and the ranger down a much, much different trail.

CHAPTER 2

He loved this part of the job.

The routine stuff was all right, patrolling trails and answering visitors' questions and doing what was needed to "preserve and protect" the wilderness. However, solving problems was the real meat and drink to McIntyre's mind. Give him a set of perplexing details or bewildering evidence to sort out and he was a happy man. In the midst of the hell and carnage of the war, it was problem-solving that had brought him moments of mental calm: his assignment with the Army Aero Squadron was to pilot his Nieuport biplane over German units and see if he could figure out what the enemy troops were up to. Up in the clear sky, far above the clamor of battle with only the sound of his engine and the wind in the wing struts he could soar like an eagle, leaning out of the cockpit to study vehicle tracks, gun emplacements, supply roads, and the size and orientation of trenches and revetments. On a pad strapped to his leg he sketched the details until he understood the entire picture; back at the aerodrome he would tell the commanders the location of the enemy troops, their movements, and the strength of the units.

A forest fire presented a similar exercise in logistics, figuring out where the blaze would flare up next, where to turn it, where to construct a fire line to stop it. When an amateur climber got stuck on a mountain cliff and it was up to the rangers to pack up their ropes and slings and dash to the rescue, McIntyre saw it as a challenge in physics and problem-solving.

He smiled at a memory. Something that happened last November. He had ridden Brownie to a remote cabin in Wild Basin in order to arrest a woman trespasser squatting in someone's cabin. She had also poached deer in the park and out of season. The job was straightforward: he would ride to the cabin, arrest the woman, make sure the cabin was locked and secure again, and take her to the county sheriff. However, as McIntyre reached the cabin a tremendous snowstorm broke loose over the mountains. Dark masses of clouds bulged up over the Arapaho Peaks and collapsed into Wild

41

Basin in wet, heavy snow. The woman was glad of his company, even though he was there to arrest her. She took the news of her arrest with good cheer, saying that it would be warmer in jail and the food would be better. Meanwhile, she could think of worse things than being snowbound with a nice-looking ranger.

She and McIntyre were stuck in the cabin for two days and two nights. Luckily, she had collected plenty of firewood. The cabin was also well-stocked with quilts and blankets; McIntyre slept comfortably beside the fireplace even though the woman said that the bed in the other room was wide enough for two.

Among the other things that the owner kept in the cabin was a jumbo-size picture puzzle. Even six month later McIntyre could still see that jigsaw picture, all the pieces spread out on the floor in the firelight. He and the woman worked on the puzzle for a couple of hours or more, their two heads nearly touching as they sat cross-legged and bent over. After a time, she began to yawn and stretch. She remarked about being too warm there by the fireplace. McIntyre replied in monosyllables.

"Yeah." "Okay."

He was looking for one particular piece of

puzzle, the one shaped like Louisiana.

The woman went to bed.

McIntyre smiled at the memory. It had been a challenging puzzle. A picture of a range of mountains with a village in the foreground. Lots of empty sky, white snowfields, that sort of thing. A mental workout.

He put the memory away and took up his magnifying glass to examine the Ernst Snyder photographs. He had already noticed that they weren't in sequence: the numbers printed on the back indicated that four pictures of the corpse were missing. Probably discarded for being blurred or too dark.

Doris's pictures included the pile of clothing, which the ranger had carefully kept the way it had been found, but the photos didn't show much. It looked as if Mr. Snyder had stood near the trees at the top of the falls and methodically stacked his clothing. Apparently, he folded the trousers and put them on the ground, then the jacket, shirt, and undershirt. The socks were inside the shoes, the shoes on top. Very logical, very orderly. Very German.

After taking off his clothes and folding them, what did the man do? Either dove off the falls into the pool thirty feet below or walked down the path, barefoot and in his undershorts, and waded in. If he dove from the top of the falls, that was probably when he hit his head; the local physician, who doubled as coroner, found a wound that had bruised the skull, although he declared it death by drowning because he found water in the lungs.

McIntyre studied the body closely with his magnifier. Doris Killian and Jamie Ogg had made sure to turn the victim in order to have photos from every angle. Some of the angles were quite revealing, where the underdrawers had gapped, which could be another explanation of why she had decided not to send all the photos. The missing photos probably showed the victim's privates. Using the magnifying glass, McIntyre saw a very interesting bruise across Snyder's back. Very interesting, that bruise.

McIntyre was still looking at that bruise and trying to account for it when the station door opened and Jamie came in.

" 'Morning, Cap'n!" he said cheerily.

"Morning yourself. Come over here. Take this glass and look at this photo. Is that a bruise on the guy's back?"

Jamie looked. "Could be a bruise," he agreed. "Noticed it when we turned him over. Kind of a long one."

"C'mon, let's take a walk out back."

McIntyre led the way around the ranger station and searched under the pine trees until he found a fallen branch.

"Stand on that rock there," he told Jamie. "With your back to me."

Jamie stepped up onto the rock. McIntyre raised the pine branch. In slow motion, he pretended to strike. He stopped the branch when it reached the back of Jamie's head and frowned.

"Hmm," he said. "Not quite right."

He made the same experiment from several angles before seeing the solution.

"Left-handed. Holding it left-handed changes everything. Now it matches the shape of the bruise in the photo."

"Let me try it on you," Jamie said. "I'm left-handed."

They switched places. Wielded by a left-handed person, the branch would leave a bruise up across the shoulder and a head wound like the bruise on the dead guy.

"That does it," the ranger said. "Come on back to the station."

The photos were still spread out on top of the clutter of paperwork. McIntyre always swore that there was a desk under there, somewhere. Supervisor Nicholson was of the opinion that no one had ever seen the desk, at least not the top of it.

"Look at that long bruise. It starts at the top of the left shoulder blade," he said. "See how it lines up with where his skull got cracked? He either slipped while standing at the top of the falls, fell over, landed on his back on something in the water, like a floating log, or . . ."

"Or he was standin' right on the edge and somebody came up behind him and whacked him," Jamie said. "Somebody left-handed. Over he went. Down into the water. Drowned."

"Right. And you're left-handed. Where were you the morning Snyder was killed?"

"I was here. I was fixing myself breakfast. I got a witness."

"Who's that?"

"Brownie. I took her some fresh hay and a can of oats. Now what do we do?"

"You're going to stay here and man the station. I'm going back up the river to Chasm Falls."

"If the supervisor or the chief ranger comes by, what should I tell them?" Jamie asked. "They'd want to know about this, I'm thinkin.' "

"Ask them if either one of them is left-handed, and what they were doing that morning. You can tell them I went fishing,"

McIntyre said.

"That's what they think you do all day anyway," Jamie protested. "You know you're never gonna earn yourself a promotion if you don't start taking the job seriously."

"There you go," said McIntyre, putting on his ranger hat and heading out the door.

"Dear Doris,

Thank you for sending the photos. They are a help but I am afraid they point toward it being murder instead of accident (or suicide, which officially is ruled out). It is all quite the puzzle. I scouted Chasm Falls to see if maybe he had fallen over the falls and hit a heavy log with his back but found no such log. And nobody would have reason to drag such a log out of the water and hide it if you see what I mean. I searched the area for a thick broken tree branch that could be a club but found nothing. Hard to tell one branch from another. But thanks to your photo we think he was hit from behind while standing at the lip of the falls in his undershorts. Question is, why? Oh, and I don't think he was fishing either.

One other thing interesting is those

hoof marks. The livery boy at Fall River Lodge says a woman asked to have a horse saddled and waiting for her at first light that day so he got up in the dark and did it and then went to the kitchen and when he came back the horse was gone. Boy can't remember her name if she even gave it. Can't describe her except to say she was uppity. Paid cash. When he came back from leading a trail ride at noon the horse was in the corral with saddle still on it. One hoof mark looks like another, so there's a dead end.

Well, you would not know the park now. The aspen leaves and chokecherry leaves have turned color and there are bright colors all over the mountains. Much less water coming down the river. Car traffic is also less, but on weekends too many people stop in the middle of the road to look at yellow aspen. Don't know why they can't park and hike instead but that's their business.

One good thing about this murder business, my supervisor keeps saying he'd like to transfer me to Yosemite or Yellowstone or somewhere but he can't as long as I'm investigating this death. The victim's family wants me to keep looking into it too, so if you come back next summer it looks like I'll still be here. I'll save you a cinnamon roll.

Your Breakfast Companion,

Tim McIntyre"

"Dear Ranger McIntyre (or should I say Tim?),

Thank you for your letter. I am very glad to learn that my photographs were some help to you, and I wish you a speedy resolution to the case. Murder, you say? My, it sounds like a terrible and horrible business. I hope you will let me know how it all comes out.

I have cheerful news! I wrote you that a magazine agreed to buy my pictorial story about the RMNP waterfalls; now the same magazine wants another such story next summer, with different water-falls. The book idea is still alive too. I am looking at a map of RMNP and thinking I might hire a horse and camp-ing outfit and visit some of the waterfalls named for birds. Ouzel Falls, Bluebird Falls, Finch Lake Falls, and so forth.

This might give you a laugh: thinking of camping next summer, I have pur-chased a revolver! *And* I have been tak-ing shooting lessons! It is a .32 Smith &

49

Wesson revolver, quite a handy little weapon, and I'm becoming rather proficient with it.

Back to topic, the magazine offers to release copyright on my waterfall series and a book publisher is interested in having me do an actual picture book, once I have more waterfalls to add to it. Isn't that wonderful? On top of that, the developer/printer is interested in selling my prints in his shop. And I have found another man interested in some of my pictures but I can't tell you about it except that he will pay *very* well. All of which means that I'll have plenty of money to travel back to RMNP next summer for an extended working vacation. I may even have enough to buy you a nice dinner somewhere, unless you'd rather eat cinnamon rolls, ha ha!

Missing the Mountains,
Doris Killian"

"All quiet."

The telegraph message from army headquarters had seemed unbelievable. Incredulous pilots and mechanics had crowded around to look at the piece of paper. The war was over?

"All quiet."

Hours before the telegraph had brought the news, the French aerodrome pilots, their American counterparts, the ground crews, and the civilian workers had already taken notice of the silence; no artillery, no bombs exploding in the distance. No rifle shots. Just an eerie quiet everywhere.

Winter brought down the same pervasive hush of silence over Rocky Mountain National Park, like a widespread white blanket of stillness. It was as if the Granite Mountains themselves were asleep beneath the snow, breathing quietly, conserving strength for the springtime to come. Cottages were boarded up to stand dark and empty in the freezing air; tourist lodges were shuttered, their dusty hallway floors echoing only silence. Ranger McIntyre was ordered to move his things into the entrance station cabin, which he would have to himself now that Jamie Ogg was off to a semester of college. McIntyre was to stay there and monitor the Fall River quadrant of the park.

Some days one or two cars would come through his station, sometimes none at all. After each snowfall, the snowplow operator would come to clear the road and might stop at the station for a cup of coffee and a chat. Major Nicholson, the RMNP supervisor, was a visitor every Monday like clockwork. McIntyre was glad the supervisor was so regular: it meant he probably wouldn't be visiting on any other day. Which allowed McIntyre to put on his skis, take his fly rod, and ski along Fall River up to certain beaver ponds. Unless the temperature dropped to below zero and stayed there for a week there were always openings in the river ice; if a man dropped a weighted nymph into one of those holes he might catch himself a trout.

Going out on patrol was almost as boring as staying on duty in the station. He would put the skis in the truck and slowly drive up and down the roads watching for anything that needed attention. If he spotted snowshoe tracks or ski tracks, for instance, he might follow them on foot and see where that particular winter adventurer had gone. Once it turned out to be a poacher. It was clear from the evidence left behind that he had killed and skinned a deer and had packed out most of the meat. Probably done by moonlight. According to the cuts on the hide, the blade of the poacher's knife was dull and had nicks in it. The snowshoe tracks showed where the rawhide webbing had been patched.

McIntyre was relatively certain who the poacher was. The deer meat had gone to the poor guy's wife and kids. When the ranger wrote his daily report all he said was that he had come across the remains of a young buck deer, probably a victim of a "mountain lion or other predator."

Two or three times a week he drove into the village to pick up his mail and enjoy a late breakfast at the café. He and the postmaster had a marathon chess game going next to the potbelly stove in the mail sorting room.

Ernst Snyder's brother wrote to McIntyre on behalf of Snyder's wife and family to thank McIntyre for his help. According to the brother, Ernst's body had been examined by a doctor before they buried him — Ernst Snyder, not the doctor — and the doctor confirmed that Ernst had suffered a blow to the back of his head and across his shoulder. The doctor was of the opinion that the head trauma would have been sufficient to stun him, perhaps render him unconscious. So, as McIntyre had suspected, it was a case of homicide. He had been hit on the head by a rock or weapon and then probably drowned. Who had the opportunity and motive to do it? McIntyre began to reconstruct the scene in his imagination as if it were a picture puzzle.

Snyder had been there in the woods, probably in the evening or early morning. No one at the lodge had seen him leave, unless it was the mysterious woman who had taken out a livery horse at first light. McIntyre's best guess was that Snyder had started hiking up Fall River looking for a good place to fish, had lost track of time, had ended up two or three miles upstream, and had found himself at the base of the falls. From there the most natural thing for him to do would be to follow the path to the top of the falls for the view. Everyone who stopped for the view of the falls seemed to want to scramble up the rocks and see where the water went tumbling over the edge.

Someone else had been up there, possibly the woman who rode the horse. Someone who had a reason to club Snyder across his back. Why was he in his undershorts? Either the attacker found Snyder already in his undershorts or else Snyder had stripped down while the assailant was there. There was no way he could have been stripped after going over the falls into the pool: the neat stack of clothes was dry. *Maybe,* McIntyre thought, *maybe I should be trying to figure out who had the opportunity to be up there at Chasm Falls, that woman in particular. Maybe I'll stop at Fall River Lodge and have a look at their guest register.*

The thought of going into the dark chill

of the boarded-up lodge gave him a shiver. McIntyre didn't mind winter in the mountains. In fact, he enjoyed the peace and quiet. But a closed-up building in the winter was a shivery, dreary place to go. Even carrying a Coleman lantern, which gave off some heat, it would be chilly as an icebox in there. One good thing, he had all winter to do it; he could choose a day that was sunny and warmer. Most of the owners of hotels and lodges that closed down for the winter would leave keys in case of emergency, either at the supervisor's office or the nearest ranger station. If Minnie March had left a key to the Fall River Lodge office, maybe he could find the lodge's receipts and copies of the bills they gave guests, and they might show who had hired a horse from the livery.

Meanwhile he would perform his daytime duties and use his evenings to tie dry fly patterns and varnish his bamboo rods, read books, and assemble one of the picture puzzles he kept in the station closet. Whenever a sunny day came along and the weather warmed up above freezing, he would take the mare, Brownie, out for a ride and maybe work at teaching her more equine tricks. Jamie liked training Brownie, too. They taught her to retrieve a hat or rope

55

or tool from across the corral. They taught her the command "break it up," at which she forced her way between two people to separate a fight. She could kneel, lie down, open a door. Jamie had even taught her "bite!" — which meant she was to take a person's arm or shoulder — gently — with her teeth and not let go.

Winter's boredom days didn't come without some problems. Water froze in the bucket, the firewood ran out; a skier got lost and they found him again; the pickup truck wouldn't start unless he draped a tarp over the engine and put a pan of hot coals underneath. February teased people with a dry thaw and a chinook that evaporated the snow from the meadows, but then March retaliated with a three-day wet snowstorm that broke trees and sagged the roof of Brownie's pole shed at the ranger station. After a soggy, snow-blanketed March came the longer days in April when the ice covering the river began to break and crumble, when snowbanks in the meadows began to recede and a few venturous wildflowers apologetically opened yellow faces toward the returning sunshine.

Winter's grip weakened in May and all the bustling preparations for summer began. There were the entrance station windows to clean, log buildings that needed a coat of linseed oil, visitor outhouses that had been leaning askew ever since the deep snow of January and needed to be braced upright and given a good whitewash. With only three men on the maintenance crew, much of the springtime maintenance fell to the rangers but McIntyre didn't mind. It was good to be outside in shirtsleeves and working, good to know that spring was coming and bringing with it new people to hike the trails and picnic in the meadows and photograph the snow-tipped peaks. And maybe photograph the waterfalls. He was especially keen to have Doris Killian come back to look at waterfalls.

CHAPTER 3

The hired horse was saddled and waiting as the liveryman had promised. All that remained was to strap on the canvas saddlebags. One saddlebag contained the folding camera, extra film, a lap robe, and two swimming costumes, one for men and one for women. In the other bag was a light jacket, a lunch, a thermos of lemonade spiked with sodium oxybate sleeping powder, and a hunting knife. With the compact telescoping tripod strapped on behind the saddle, everything was ready.

Preparation and planning. Every detective novel stressed the importance of preparation and planning, like the Sherlock Holmes books in which the villain overlooks one small detail. Things such as buying the sleeping powder in tiny quantities over several months, studying maps of the National Park, and lifting names from the telephone directory to use as aliases when hiring horses and renting rooms. What the detective novels did not describe, however, was the inner thrill of those preparations. In the simple procedure of testing whether coffee, tea, or lemonade was better for hiding the taste of sodium oxybate there was a rush of blood to the brain. It made the hands tremble. The thrill was repeatable, too. Sharpening the knife, buying the swimming costumes, purchasing extra film . . . each and every act was a little moment of intense excitement.

The thought of the money was nearly as exciting as were the preparations. It could not become a career, that much was certain. No, this enterprise would earn enough to finance a new start in a reputable, legitimate occupation. A little sacrifice, a little danger, a great deal of quiet excitement and then settling down to manage a little shop somewhere.

A two-track dirt road from the livery led into a huge moraine meadow more than a mile across where tall grass and low willows hid a meandering trout stream and ended in a parking area. From there, one could choose from three different trailheads. Depending upon which trail they chose, hikers and horseback riders could go to almost any lake, stream, or mountain peak in the area.

Luckily, the parking area in the moraine meadow was empty when the victim arrived. A young woman on horseback riding up the trail toward Cub Lake. A young woman, slender and lively. She was awfully photogenic and she was riding alone. It would require only a few minutes to overtake her. The trail showed no earlier hoofprints, meaning that there would be no one on the trail ahead. The valley and meadow looked deserted all around. The victim and the situation were ideal, as if what was going to happen that morning was meant to be. It made the heart pound with excitement.

The young rider's name was Varna and, no, it was not an intrusion at all. In fact, she would be delighted to have company to talk to while riding up the trail. As it turned out, she liked nothing better than to talk. A great deal, and practically nonstop. She was from Pasadena and she had traveled to Rocky Mountain National Park all by herself "in order to spend time away from things, you know," because she had important decisions to think about, decisions about changing jobs and getting married, well, maybe. If she got married she might have to give up working, but she didn't want to, but anyway she simply needed to take herself away from Pasadena in order to think things through. She felt daring and emancipated out here in the Rockies, well, newly born. It was exciting and new to be able to go riding on her own like this. More women should try it, going alone into nature and practicing self-reliance.

"It's a little scary being alone out here in the real wilderness. But I've got a gun I keep in my bag."

She patted the oversized shoulder bag hanging at her side.

"They told me I shouldn't have a gun in the National Park or that a gun had to be 'sealed' or something before you bring it in, but nobody will know. It's not like I'm going to shoot any animals, after all. Strictly for protection. You won't tell on me, will you?"

All the way across the meadow and on into the forest and she was still talking. She described her parents and their house, the college she had attended and the automobile she had bought with money from her very first job. But she hadn't driven her car all the way from California, of course; she rode the train to Denver and took the commercial mountain bus to Estes Park.

The trail continued through the pines and around the shoulder of the mountain to Cub Lake. For the most part, it followed the meandering creek, making detours in order to bypass a rocky gorge or dense stand of trees. About halfway to the lake, at the highest point of one of the gorge detours, they noticed a very faint, virtually unused track going off to the left. It was not an official trail, more like a game trail, but it seemed to head in the right direction.

"Where do you suppose that little trail goes?" Varna said.

"Well, this map isn't very detailed but it looks like it goes toward Cub Lake. Hey, we're new adventurers, remember? Let's find out!"

"It will be like that poem!" Varna said. "Have you seen it? That New England poet wrote it. About a road not taken. A road less traveled by, he called it."

"Let's take it! Lead on!"

The path turned out to be an old hiking route to Cub Lake, long abandoned. It was very steep in places as it twisted its way up the ridge and looked unused except by deer and elk. The going was rough; the horses had to carefully pick their way up the loose, narrow track where at times there was barely room for them to pass between the trees.

Difficult as it was, the scramble over the mountain was well worthwhile. On the far side of the ridge it broke out of the forest into a grassy meadow where a disused campsite overlooked the lake. The place hadn't seen campers for years; meadow grass had grown over the fire pit and a bed of soft moss had spread over the sitting log. Birds twittered from the trees. Waves made little lapping noises at the lake's edge. All was still and peaceful. And most importantly, secluded.

They dismounted; Varna stood on tiptoe to stretch her slender body, reaching her arms toward the blue crystal sky as if trying to embrace it. The mossy sitting log caught her attention and she went to it, patting it like a hotel guest trying the mattress.

"What a huge tree! This ol' trunk is nearly wide enough to sleep on. At least as wide as a cot!"

"It's perfect. Exactly what I need. Will you take care of the horses?"

"I'll tie them over there with the long cords, the way the livery boy showed me."

"Good! When you've done it, come sit on the robe with me and have a sandwich. I've got lemonade as well."

And apples. Varna munched happily away and sipped at the cup of lemonade. She kept talking, exclaiming about the scenery and asking questions but scarcely waiting for answers.

"Hey!" she said, interrupting herself. "I remembered something! Didn't you say the mossy log was what you needed? What do you need it for? Don't tell me you want to take it home with you!"

It was time to open the other saddlebag and take out the Kodak.

"Promise you won't tell?"

"I do promise."

"Sure?"

"Cross my heart."

"I sell photographs. It's how I'm able to afford trips to the Rocky Mountains."

"Oh! Like postcards of the scenery!"

"Yes. I've sold views of mountains. But they didn't bring very much money. There are too many other amateur photographers wandering around the mountains taking their own views of every rock and peak and lake. No, I'm doing something different. I'm specializing in outdoor pictures of men and women. That's why I rode up here today. I've been scouting locations for 'certain kinds' of pictures. And this place will be ideal! Absolute privacy, beautiful background. Tomorrow I can start looking around the lodge, maybe the village, for a young woman to model for me. But don't tell anyone. Promise? If a rumor were to circulate that I'm looking for a model I might be mobbed with applicants."

"Model?"

"Yes. Every girl seems to want to be one. They see the girls in the magazines and tell themselves that they could be models, too. But they're usually too heavy or don't look very graceful. In swimming costume, you know. But I'll find the right one. I'll pose her on that huge log. That's why I said it was perfect. Can't you see it? A cute girl with bare legs, on the log. With the lake sparkling in the distance? And another photo over against that smooth boulder. I think I'll have her lean back on the rock, one leg bent. She could do another pose at the edge of the lake there, like she was going to wade in."

"And a girl simply comes up here and poses for you? Just like that?"

"Oh, sure. I pay her for her time and trouble, of course. She might also get a royalty afterward, depending on what a magazine or postcard publisher is willing to pay. She might make a nice piece of change."

Varna's eyes were beginning to blink rather often. Her face looked a little flushed. The powder in the lemonade was starting to take effect. The drug was working slowly, but that was fine. First would come a high rush of energy and wild enthusiasm, followed in about an hour by a deep sleep.

"What kind of swimming costume?" she said. "I mean, modern or old-fashioned? The old-fashioned ones can be quite cute, really."

"Oh, modern! I'll show you! I brought one along. I've got several more back at the lodge. I'll hold it up for you. No sleeves, see? The arms are totally bare. And it's a nice navy color, with these white stripes across the inset that covers the, uh, the . . . bosom. This hem would come about mid-calf on a girl. Oh, and here's another thing! I'd forgotten that I packed it."

Varna looked at the rubber thing. She blinked again and frowned uncomprehendingly.

"A swimming cap?"

"Yes, but! This is a French model. The importer said he'd supply caps for advertising photos. The advertising pays very good money, of course! I'll ask my model to show off the cap in a couple of pictures. This French style of bathing cap is called a 'casquette.' To put it on you pull it clear down over your face and turn up the rim in front like a darling blue cloche. Fun."

"Your photos . . . are to sell swimming costumes and these casquette things?"

"Partly. If I take them to a publisher who does catalogs. I won't try to fool you, though: I take my pictures as cheesecake. There's a rich market for photographs of girls in skimpy outfits. One of my buyers pretends to sell a catalog of swimming attire, but most men buy it for . . . other purposes."

"Purposes?"

"Men like to look at scantily clad girls. Bare legs. You'd be surprised what they find exciting. The more flesh in the picture, and the more unusual the picture, the more they pay. Nudes can be worth a fortune."

"You can always find models like that? I mean, at the lodge like you said?"

"Every time. Maids, waitresses, receptionists. There's always one who finds the idea of modeling cheesecake very thrilling. Sometimes they say they'll do it without even being paid. I give them free prints of the pictures if they want. To show their friends. Back at the lodge I'll find a girl who has a day off and who has nothing else to do. I'll bring her up here and we'll spend a day doing various poses and shots. This will be a perfect location, isn't it? So private! It's kind of exciting to be so private, don't you think? In fact, I think I'll take a couple of view shots before we leave."

She began setting up the tripod and camera, which took a few minutes. Everywhere, literally in any direction, postcard opportunities presented themselves. Thrusting rough granite crags with tatters of snow still clinging in the crevasses, fir trees in darkly shadowed clusters with their spear tips soaring into a pure sky, the field of grass and flowers and of course the lake with its little waves twinkling under the sun.

Varna stood up. She was a young woman and unable to resist the impulse to pick up the blue swimming costume and hold it against her body to see how it would look. Her eyes danced and sparkled like the little waves on the lake. Her bosom rose and fell with each breath. She wondered why she was breathing rapidly at the daring idea she was having. Not realizing how the drug was amplifying her pulse, she told herself it was only an effect of the high altitude.

"Why couldn't I do it?" she said.

Of course. As planned.

"Wouldn't I do? As a model, I mean?"

"Hmmmm?"

Feign lack of attention. Peer into the view-finder instead, pretend to be framing a photograph of the scenery.

"Hmmm?"

"Let me be the model!" Varna was practically dancing with excitement. "Let me!"

"Oh. Well, I suppose we could try it. If you're sure. I want you to know what you're letting yourself in for, though. If I sell the photos to my usual buyer, there'll be many, many men looking at your image. With lust in their faces, if you know what I mean. Sure you want to do that?"

Varna was already fumbling at her shirt buttons and looking around for a place to disrobe in order to change into the swimming costume.

"How about behind that pair of trees over there?"

Varna practically ran to the trees, loosening her shirt as she went.

It was an opportunity to open the girl's rucksack and find the gun she mentioned. Sure enough, there it was. A slick little .22 Colt Woodsman. An automatic. When she pulled back the slide to see it if was loaded a cartridge flew out and disappeared somewhere in the deep grass. The ammunition clip was full. The safety latch was on the wrong side for a left-handed person, but no matter. It seemed a good idea to hide the gun in the camera saddlebag. For safety reasons.

Varna stepped out from behind the trees, ready to be a photographer's model in swimming costume. She stepped daintily across the pine needles, covering her bosom with one arm and looking very shy. Before long, though, she was smiling broadly into the lens, posing for picture after picture with the lake or the forest in background. Stretching the tight rubber casquette over her hairdo proved challenging, but she managed to tug it down clear to her chin before folding the front part up to look like a cloche.

As the shutter clicked, her poses became more and more coquettish. Some could have been called daring. It didn't take long to exhaust the first roll of film.

"Shall I sit on the log now?"

"I need to load a fresh roll of film first. But now that I've seen you pose, I'm not sure the log makes a good prop for us. For a swimming motif, I mean. No, the swimming costume won't go with the log at all. But after you put your clothes on, I think I'll try a picture of you on the log. Wearing your hiking clothes. You know, as if you had been on a hike and lay down there on the log to rest. Seems more natural with clothes on, don't you think?"

Varna seemed disappointed. She even tugged one shoulder of the swimsuit to show a bit more collarbone. Her eyes had lost a little of the shine caused by the sleeping drug. In a few more minutes she would be confused.

"I think I have nice legs," she said. "Don't you?"

"Very. Yes, nice indeed. Say! I'll tell you what might work, if you won't be embarrassed."

"Oh!" Varna said. "Yes, please!"

"Well . . ."

"Please."

"I don't want to embarrass you."

"No, please. I promise! Cross my heart!"

"Well, what if we got your clothes and brought them over here and folded them neatly and put them in a nice neat pile right next to the log, with your boots next to them. We could use them to compose a kind of still life, see?"

"What about me? Where would I be?"

"Well . . . don't be embarrassed, now. In this set of pictures, you could be lying on the log. Like you were resting. Only . . ."

"Only what?"

"You're only wearing your knickers. And

nothing else."

A long silence.

Very long.

Without a word Varna tiptoed back to the private spot behind the trees, a bit unsteady on her feet. She stayed there quite a while. Maybe she had dropped off to sleep. But she reemerged, hugging a neatly folded pile of clothes to her chest with one hand, carrying her high hiking boots in the other hand, wearing nothing except a pair of satin knickers with lacy frill around the legs. And the rubber casquette. She moved like a person in a trance as she arranged the clothing and the boots neatly beside the log. She lay down on the log and stretched out. With her nude back cushioned on the cool moss she gave a long, deep sigh of breath and she was asleep.

It was easy, very easy.

Several pictures of the sleeping girl, several different angles, and it was time to pull the rubber hood down over the nose and mouth and hold it tight. Her legs and arms jerked a few times, her head thrashed weakly from side to side, and it was done. It was done. All that remained was to tug the casquette off her head and snap more pictures. With the hair loose and disarranged, very provocative. Finish the roll of film. Adjust the knickers to show more flesh, take another roll of photos. Pose the cute little body this way and that. Plenty of daylight remaining, lots of time to clean up the site and return the horse to the livery. Varna's horse could be led down to the main trail. Once it was on the main trail, it would take itself home, like all good livery horses.

It seemed a shame to leave all that pale flesh to be burnt by the sun. The robe would cover the body. It would be as if Varna had been taking a nap in the nude and had felt a chill. Had felt a chill and had covered her bare body with the robe. Perfect. The film was "in the can" as the movie makers said when they were satisfied with what they had done. In the can and ready to make a lot of cash. As for the thrill of it, that was the extra added benefit. The thrill tingled every inch of the body and the brain, like being drunk or taking dope but without the fuzzy head feeling. It left the heart racing, the eyes wide, the palms of the hands damp. Wonderful.

CHAPTER 4

Those who fish with worms and salmon eggs subscribe to the belief that fish bite best in the early morning, before sunrise, which is why those people leave their warm beds while everything is still dark outside. With little more than a cup of coffee for their breakfast they go to the river and stand shivering in the cold, trying to impale a fat slimy worm on a sharp hook without stabbing their shaking fingers.

Flycasters, on the other hand, do not believe there is any need to be up and on the river at the chilly crack of dawn. In fact, the best part of a good day of fly fishing lies wholly in the imagination, in the enjoyment of a warm breakfast while mentally picturing the perfect spot, a river pool where a large unsuspecting trout is lazily feeding on floating insects. After a bite of scrambled eggs, the dry fly enthusiast might be seen holding the fork aloft in the attitude of a

74

perfect cast. Even while tying a fly, wrapping the hook with thread and feathers until it becomes a Royal Coachman or Ginger Quill or Black Gnat, the dry fly purists are "on the river" in their minds, imagining that one perfect cast into that one ideal eddy or rill.

It was Ranger McIntyre's day off and he would have it all to himself. While shaving and dressing he pushed everything else out of his mind and thought only about a certain fish that lurked in Curry's Rapids of the Thompson River, a heavy old rainbow trout that would begin to rise and feed around noon.

McIntyre would begin his morning with a leisurely breakfast at the Pioneer Inn, where he could be ninety percent sure of running into Doris Killian now that she was back for a second summer's visit. After a pleasant hour with her he would drive to Curry's Rapids, where he wanted to test a few of the artificial dry flies he had tied during the winter. His usual table was available, the one by the window overlooking the village and the mountains beyond the village. Not wanting to seem as if he was lying in wait, he went to the buffet sideboard where he helped himself to a wedge of egg and bacon casserole and a brace of pancakes. Hardly had he begun to pour syrup on the first pancake when she walked in. She was dressed in glossy hiking boots, tan jodhpurs, and a white shirt with a thin black necktie, the image of a magazine ad for Silk Facial Soap, a modern young woman radiating health and vitality. McIntyre's heart made a jump and a thump and he knew that his day off was going to be fine. Except for one problem. The dilemma could lie in deciding whether to spend the day with Doris or with the rainbow trout in the Thompson River. The trout might have to wait.

The decision as to how he was to spend his day, however, had already been made. The desk clerk followed Doris into the dining room with a message: the ranger needed to come to the reception desk and take a phone call.

"Hello?"

"Tim? This is Jamie. I'm up here at Stead's Lodge. We've got another one."

"Another what?"

"Dead body. This one's at Cub Lake."

"When? What happened?"

"Late yesterday. One of the livery horses came back without its rider. Young woman, name of Varna Palmer. The boys figured she'd turned her horse loose to go home by itself, but the desk clerk checked her room and she hadn't slept there either. At first light this morning they rode out to take a look around. She'd told them she wanted to ride to Cub Lake. Anyway, there she is at the lake. Dead and cold."

McIntyre looked through the doorway back into the dining room and gave a sigh. Doris looked wonderful sitting silhouetted against the window. Made a man want to do nothing but stare at her all morning. Another sigh of resignation escaped his lips as he turned back to the telephone.

"Okay, Jamie" he said. "Here's what to do. Tell Stead's livery guy to saddle up a couple of horses. Go to the kitchen at the lodge and have the cook make a few sandwiches for us. Oh, and you'd better ask Stouffer for a couple of gas lanterns and maybe a couple of flashlights in case we're up there late. Next, phone the trail crew shack and tell them I want two men to carry the body out from Cub Lake. They'll know what to bring, a litter or stretcher. Tell everybody not to disturb the actual scene of death, too."

"Tim," Jamie said, "there's another thing. Butch told me . . . Butch is one of the guys who found her . . . they found her like we found that guy at Chasm Falls last summer.

Clothes folded up and stacked all nice and neat, body wearing nothing but underpants. Lying on a log."

"Nothing but her underpants?"

"That's what he said."

"And the clothes? Stacked in a neat pile?"

"That's right."

"Damn."

"You want me to go up there to the lake, Tim?" Jamie asked.

"No, I guess you'd better take charge of the entrance station. Is one of the livery guys still with the body?"

"Yeah. One came down to call us, one stayed there."

"Right. I'm on my way."

Back at the window table the ranger polished off his breakfast. Between bites he told Doris about the phone call and the discovery of another dead person in the park.

"Your pictures last summer," he said, "those were helpful. I'm going to stop at the station and grab my own Kodak, but I wondered if maybe you'd . . ."

"If I'd bring my camera and come along with you? To see another dead body?" she said. "You do need to come up with an outing that isn't as gruesome. I mean, it's terrible to think about. A girl lying dead. And alone, back in all those mountains. Awful. But going with you sounds more interesting than what I had planned. And if my photos might help, well, sure."

This is typical, McIntyre thought. *Story of my life. I have a day off to go fishing. Along comes a chance to take a hike with an attractive young woman, maybe to a secluded stream where brookies are waiting to be caught. Instead of that, I take her to see a dead body. Again.*

Nuts.

At Stead's Lodge on the edge of Moraine Park, Butch had the horses saddled and packed with blankets, food, and lanterns.

"How did you happen to find her?" McIntyre asked.

"We rode up the Cub Lake trail, me and John, looking for her," Butch explained. "After the horse came back with the saddle empty. She mighta turned it loose, sometimes people do that, but when her room hadn't been slept in we figured she'd mighta been thrown or somethin' like that."

As he spoke, Butch pointed across the wide moraine to where a long, dark mountain ridge made a formidable wall to the meadows. He moved his finger like a pointer as if they could actually see the trail snaking its way up and over through the heavy for-est of spruce and fir.

"Toward the top of that last pitch on the Cub Lake trail we saw these here hoofprints goin' off the trail. They led up a little ol' abandoned track that nobody uses anymore. Almost a game trail. Tracks showed how two horses had gone up there, and not long ago. Funny thing, though, those same two sets of tracks came back down, too. Looked like the two horses come down with each other. We saw the two sets of tracks and figured she'd ridden back down the trail. Didn't seem to be any use in going on up to the top of the ridge but it's a good thing we done it, anyway."

"That's where she is?" McIntyre asked. "Up that old trail?"

"Yeah," Butch said. "You know how the main trail brings you around to the north-west side of the lake. Where the camp site is? This game trail I'm talkin' about, it brings you out directly acrost on the other side of the lake. Heavy timber over there on that side, you know. Except for this little open place where people used to camp."

"I think I know the place," McIntyre said. "There's a good fishing spot near there."

"How come is it," Butch asked, "that you know all the good fishing spots in the whole damn park?"

"Part of my job," McIntyre said with a smile.

"Quite a job you got. There's another thing kinda puzzles me," Butch said.

"Such as?"

"Those other hoofprints. That second horse. All of ours are accounted for, see? Seven went out that day, but the other six was couples from the lodge. Plus, those people didn't go the direction of Cub Lake. Two rode up to the pool and four went up the Fern Lake trail."

"Maybe that second horse came from Barrow's stable down the road?"

"Maybe. Yeah, I guess it could've. By way of the river trail it'd only be another mile, maybe mile and a half. Still kinda weird that whoever was on that horse didn't see the dead body when they was up there at the lake. Didn't report it, anyway. Weird. Know what I mean?"

Over two hours later McIntyre and Doris rode out of the trees and into the private little clearing. The lonely spot could have made a setting for a children's fairy tale with its meadow of deep green grass framed in shadowy pines as it sloped down to a blue mountain lake where a dancing breeze

81

rippled the surface into twinkling diamonds.

The stable hand waved to them. The body lay on a log near the edge of the clearing, covered with a car robe.

"Let's tie these horses out of the way," McIntyre said. "If you don't mind I'd like you to look at our deceased with me. Maybe you can see details I might miss. You know, from a woman's perspective. If it won't bother you to look at a corpse. We ought to look for any sign that she might have been . . . you know? Or anything that'll tell us what she was doing here?"

The hostler walked up to them while they were picketing the horses. He was a little embarrassed to see another woman, but visibly relieved that Ranger McIntyre had showed up. Not a comfortable thing to do, being left alone to stand guard over a corpse out in the wilderness.

"I'm John," he said, offering a handshake.

"McIntyre," the ranger said. "This is Doris. She came along to take photos for evidence."

"Glad t' meet you. The body's right over here."

John led the way to the log. When Ranger McIntyre reached down to take hold of the blanket the hostler turned red in the face

82

and stepped away to see if the horses needed his attention.

Ranger McIntyre gently raised the edge of the car robe and folded it down until it covered only the groin area. There he lifted it and both he and Doris looked underneath. The dead girl was wearing a pair of knickers with lace trim, but otherwise the pale body was bare. The knickers were clean, no stains, no blood, and they hadn't been torn or twisted in any way. McIntyre put the robe back the way it had been; Doris unfolded her camera and took two photographs to show how it had been arranged.

"You suppose she was sunbathing?" McIntyre said. "She looks peaceful. It's like she deliberately took off her clothes and lay down there. I don't see any bruises anywhere. Even her underpants don't look like they've been disturbed."

"It doesn't seem like sunbathing to me," Doris said. "There's no sign of suntan lotion or oil. And you know how you burn in this mountain air. And she's not wearing any sunglasses. Or protection on her hair. No, I don't think she was sunbathing at all."

"Maybe she went swimming in the lake," McIntyre said, "and lay down here to dry off. Except then I'd expect to see dirt or moss on her soles or between her toes, some sign of her being in the water. The main question is how did she die, whatever she was doing up here. I don't see any marks on her body at all. No blood, no wound. Nothing."

"You're right," Doris said, winding a new roll of film into her Kodak. "She wasn't strangled or there would be neck bruises. As fair as her skin is, you'd see finger marks if she'd been strangled. I don't see any. As you said, there's no wounds of any kind, unless they're on her back."

"She didn't thrash around," McIntyre said. "The moss isn't torn up, there's no scuff marks on the ground, no sign that she was held or tied up or anything. It's as if she just laid down, covered herself with that car robe, and died. That's how it looks. She might have died of heart failure, except young women in good health don't normally do that."

Doris took two photos of the ground next to the log, to show that the grass hadn't been disturbed.

"What about her clothes?" McIntyre said.

"What about them?"

"Well, you're a woman. Let's start with the puzzle of how she got out of her clothes. When you, um . . . when you . . . dis-

84

robe . . . is that how you'd stack your clothes? I mean if you were outdoors like this. Maybe you're thinking of going swimming in the lake, for instance. With nobody around. You see what I mean? I guess I'm wondering if she stacked them or if it was somebody else who did it. Did she come across this private place by the lake and decide to take her clothes off for some reason? All on her own? Or did somebody help her undress, if you know what I mean?"

Doris laughed at his discomfort. He was trying to visualize a female disrobing beside a mountain lake and it was embarrassing him. For a forest ranger who fought raging fires, engaged in shootouts with poachers and moonshiners, arrested drunken drivers, and confronted illegal campers, he was certainly shy when it came to "woman things." Clean-cut, good-looking, and now adorable. Wow.

She would have to help him with his visualization.

"Let's see," she said. She set her camera on the log and moved her hands over her own body in a pantomime of undressing. "I guess I would take off my jacket first, like this, or if I was carrying it in my hand, I would fold it in half and put it on the ground. That way it would keep the other

85

stuff dry. Next, I'd probably take off my belt and put it on the stack along with my neck scarf. Only I'm wearing a necktie, of course."

"Yeah, of course."

McIntyre was trying not to look at her as she went through the motions of stripping. Instead, he kept his eyes on the dead girl's pile of clothing. Doris was enjoying his embarrassment.

"Now what. Hmmm. I guess I would need to sit down to unlace my boots and take them off. And while I was sitting there I'd strip off my stockings, too. I wouldn't want to walk in these pine needles and dirt in stocking feet. I'd get pine sap and stuff all over them."

"Hold it there," McIntyre said. He examined the ground. He opened his own camera and made two pictures of the clothing pile.

"You said you'd sit down to unlace your boots and take them off. That means there ought to be marks in the duff where your bootheels dug in. Should be at least a couple of indentations from the heels. I don't see any such thing anywhere around here."

"Well, anyway," Doris said, smiling to see that the ranger was still blushing. "Next, I would stand up and take off either my shirt

86

or my riding pants, like this. Are you watching? If I knew I was going to stack my clothes I would take off the jodhpurs first because they're the heaviest and should go on the bottom. I'd remove my shirt next. Fold it, put it on top. Like she did, see? Now imagine I'm standing here wearing nothing but my little silk camisole. Except that she was wearing a two-piece underwear outfit. Mine is all one piece. She removed her brassiere. If it had been a camisole like mine, at this point she'd be totally bare. Does that do it for you?"

McIntyre was suddenly aware of how warm the bright mountain sun had become. His face felt hot like he had been bending over the stove. He decided that he needed to pick up the dead girl's rucksack and examine it. It contained ordinary things, a pocket knife, a cheap little box camera, a wrapped lunch from the lodge kitchen, a compass. And two scarves. The rucksack was also giving off a very faint but familiar scent. He raised one of the scarves to his face and smelled it.

"John!" McIntyre called. "Can you come over here?"

The hostler had made himself scarce so he wouldn't need to watch the examination of the nude body.

"Take a whiff of that scarf," McIntyre said, handing the scarf to him. "What's it smell like?"

John took a whiff of the cloth.

"Gun oil?" John said.

"That's what I thought," McIntyre said. "Those dark spots, I think they're oil stains."

"How would you know it was gun oil?" Doris asked.

"The odor. Gun oil smells like bananas and vanilla. I think our dead lady carried a pistol in her backpack. Wrapped in this scarf. Probably loaded."

"And how would you deduce that her gun was loaded?"

"No cartridges in the rucksack. I'd be willing to bet we wouldn't find any ammo in her trouser pockets, either. They're all in the gun. My guess would be that she had little or no experience carrying a firearm or else there would be a box of extra cartridges and probably a leather holster. Only a nervous beginner afraid of guns would load one and then wrap it in a scarf to keep it safe. John, I tell you what: while Miss Killian takes photos, why don't you and I spread out and make a search. We ought to look around once more before the trail crew arrives with the litter. We're looking for a gun or anything she might have dropped.

Like a hat. I haven't seen her hat. And watch for scuff marks or dents in the ground where she might have sat down to take her boots off. And hoofprints of that other horse. Although with our own horses and all, I guess it won't do much good to look at hoofprints. But we don't want to overlook anything that would help explain how she got undressed and how that car robe got here and who spread it over her. I don't think she did it herself."

As Doris was setting her tripod, McIntyre noticed another detail. He had been wondering about small indentations in the ground near the corpse, like the sharp point of a climber's pickaxe or alpenstock might make. Now he saw that the steel points on Doris's tripod left those same little marks. Maybe the hypothetical second horseman had discovered the naked body. He set up a tripod like Doris had, made photos of the corpse, covered it with the car robe, then slipped away before anyone else showed up. A shiny gleam caught McIntyre's eye and he bent to pick it up. It was a .22 brass cartridge half-hidden in the grass. Brand-new, untarnished, the lead bullet still in place. Unfired. McIntyre unfolded the magnifying glass on his pocket compass and examined the cartridge closely.

"Hmmm."

Continuing the search, the ranger's next discovery was a woman's hat lying on the ground behind three tall ponderosas that would shield the spot from the lake and the clearing. The pine needles and duff showed that someone had sat at the base of one of the trees. There were deep heel marks, too. This was where she had removed her boots, hidden from the clearing.

"Find anything?" John asked, coming up behind him.

"Found a hat. Plus, signs that somebody sat here behind this tree. See those heel marks? Out of sight of the clearing. Hidden. What does that suggest to you?"

"That she came back here to pee, maybe? Or this is where she took her clothes off?"

"Why come here?"

"Well," John said, "because . . . oh! I get-cha! Come here to not be seen! Means maybe somebody else was in the clearing, huh? There was another out there and she didn't want them to see her. She come back here outa sight to undress."

"That's the way I read it," McIntyre said. "Here, what do you make of this? I found it in the grass over there a ways."

John took the .22 cartridge and looked at it. He shrugged.

"Looks brand-new," he said. "Hasn't been laying there very long."

"Use this magnifier on it," McIntyre suggested.

"Still nothing. What am I supposed to look for?"

"Was it ever chambered in a gun, do you think?"

"Oh. I see what you mean. Sure, now you say that. Look at this shiny little scratch here on the lead where the bullet slid into the chamber. And this here little mark on the rim of the brass, that's where the extractor grabbed the casing. Little marks, but they're there. I got a rifle that does the same thing, leaves a mark like that. This shell was chambered in a bolt action rifle and then they ejected it without pullin' the trigger. Or the gun was an automatic, like a pistol. A revolver wouldn't leave those marks."

"Okay," McIntyre said. "Good. That lines up with what I was thinking. Now imagine you're out here in the forest and you come across an automatic pistol or a rifle. Or maybe you're snooping in a backpack you've come across and you find a gun. You pick it up, right? Natural thing to do. After picking it up what do you do?"

"Well . . . I open the bolt or I pull back the slide to see if there's a shell in it. See whether it's loaded or not. It's the first thing most people would do, check the chamber for a live round."

"And what happens if there's one there?"

"If there's a shell in the chamber?" John said, "Well, when I pull back the slide it flies out. Or when I pull open the bolt, in case it's a rifle. I see what you mean. A cartridge comes flyin' out and it lands in the grass where I can't see it."

"Right," McIntyre said. "The way I got it figured, that poor dead girl had a gun in her pack over there by the moss-covered log. She came over here behind these trees to take off her boots and undress herself. There was a second person here, otherwise she wouldn't have come behind the trees to undress. Meanwhile that same second person opened her pack, found her pistol, checked to see if it was loaded. When that person left here he took it with him. Any way you look at it, there was somebody else here besides her. Unless you think she might've shucked the cartridge out of the gun herself and then threw the gun away. Which makes no sense, does it? No, there was another person here. And they didn't report the body, maybe because they were the reason for her being dead and naked."

■ ■ ■ ■

Doris and McIntyre had finished taking notes and photos by the time the trail crew boys arrived. Gently the boys lifted Varna and turned her over for two additional pictures of her bare back; her fair skin showed no signs of anything unusual, other than impressions from the moss and a few insect bites. The boys carefully wrapped her in a blanket, wrapped the tarp over the blanket, and strapped her to the canvas stretcher.

"Are they going to carry her on that stretcher all the way back?" Doris asked.

"Sure. To the trailhead. Three miles, give or take. They've probably got a truck or the ambulance waiting there."

"I would've thought they'd use a pack-horse."

"Listen, those boys are trail crew. They can hike all day at three miles an hour wearing sixty-pound packs and carrying axes. When they were building a footbridge up at the pool last summer they manhandled logs that must've weighed two hundred pounds each."

Neither Doris nor McIntyre said much as

they rode back to the lodge. Doris watched the way the ranger sat in the saddle with his back perfectly straight, the reins held loosely in one hand, his eyes calm and his flat brim hat set square to the world. *What a swell picture he would make,* she thought. McIntyre broke the silence a few times; however, his mind was preoccupied with the puzzle, a picture puzzle with crucial pieces missing. Like the missing gun. A missing witness. A missing cause of death.

A housemaid at the lodge helped Ranger McIntyre and Doris pack Varna's clothes and personal items in her suitcase, which he would keep at the ranger station. Doris and the maid also helped him make a thorough search of her room. Neither the housemaid nor the cleaning lady had seen a car robe among Varna's things. In fact, neither of them had noticed anyone at the lodge having a car robe such as he described. Most people would leave theirs hanging on the robe rail behind the front seat of their car. They might use it for a picnic, but there was no reason to bring one into the building.

"There's another jigsaw piece that doesn't fit. Who brought that car robe all the way up to Cub Lake? Did she take it up there herself?"

Back in the village McIntyre dropped Doris off at the inn before he reported to the National Park supervisor's office where Dottie helped him find the phone number for Varna's family. The sister who answered the phone reacted with shock followed by choking and deep sobbing. When she was able to speak again she said that she would tell the family. They would need to arrange for someone to take a train to Denver and bring Varna's body home for burial.

After performing his examination of the victim, the village doctor agreed with the conclusion in Ranger McIntyre's report: "cause of death unknown, possibly suffocation." The body was removed to the village icehouse where a windowless wooden chamber served as a morgue.

The following morning McIntyre ate his breakfast slowly, but Doris didn't show up. Maybe she had gone for a long hike and had left early. Or maybe she was just sleeping late. Well, he said to himself, he couldn't sit around drinking coffee all morning and waiting for a girl. There were things to do, beginning with meeting the sheriff at Supervisor Nicholson's office

On his way to the S.O. the ranger stopped at the camera shop to see if Kaplan had been able to develop the death scene photos overnight.

"These are grim pictures," Kaplan said, spreading the prints out on the counter.

"Yeah," McIntyre agreed. "Grim's the word. Really grim. Did Miss Killian bring her film in to be developed?"

"Not yet, no."

"I see. I'm glad you had time to develop these, anyway," McIntyre said. "I appreciate it. The ones from the dead girl's camera don't show anything useful. It was a long shot, but I hoped she had taken a picture of whoever was up there at the lake with her. Anyway, thanks for getting to it this soon."

"To tell the truth," Kaplan replied, "I had nothing else to do. Business has been slow, for summer. Only sold one camera in the past couple of days. Some film and chemicals. One woman came in for special film but I didn't have it."

"What woman was that?"

"I don't know. Prettyish kind of woman. Talked like a college professor. Aloof, if you ask me. She wasn't young. Spiffy clothes, expensive-looking. She had the kind of camera you oughta buy for yourself, Ranger. Why don't you trade me that old folding pocket model of yours and I'll order you one like hers. It's called a twin lens reflex.

Makes sharp images. Film is 4×4 in her model, nice large negatives. All special order, the film I mean, but worth it. With a camera like that you could sell pictures to these calendar companies. As much as you travel around the mountains, you could probably make good money taking view pictures. Maybe that's what the snooty woman was doing, taking pictures to sell. I didn't ask her, but maybe that's what she was doing. Like I said, I didn't ask. Maybe I should've. Maybe whoever buys her pictures might be interested in some from me."

McIntyre was studying the photos arranged on the counter.

"Look at that," he said, pointing at one of them.

"What about it?" Kaplan said. "It's a close-up of a dead girl's head. Grim, like I said before."

"Look at the hair. I should've noticed that before. It's all mussed up and matted down. But she's wearing lipstick and rouge. Even the eyebrows look groomed, see? Whatever messed her hair up, how come didn't she fix it? Wouldn't a woman fix her hair if it looked like that, even if she was alone?"

"Don't know," Kaplan said. "Maybe. Maybe you'd know the answer yourself, if you spent more time looking for a wife and less time with your fly rod. You can't marry a fly rod."

"A fly rod's a lot easier to handle. But listen, I can't stand around discussing women all morning. I'm late for a meeting. If anybody asks you to develop any pictures connected with this death, let the supervisor's office know about it. That would include any photos of the Cub Lake area in general. And any pictures with young women in them."

At the supervisor's office McIntyre hung his flat hat on the coatrack, straightened his tunic and necktie, ran a hand over his hair, made sure his boots weren't dusty, and entered the inner sanctum. The sheriff was already there.

"Nice that you could find the time to join us," the supervisor said. "I hear you've been busy taking tourist ladies to fishing spots."

"There's a reason for that. I'll put it in my report," Ranger McIntyre began. "You see, what happened was . . ."

"Put it in the report," the supervisor interrupted. "The sheriff needs to talk to us about this death. The family phoned Doc and asked him to examine her again. Doc still thinks maybe she was somehow suffocated. And from what Ogg tells me . . ."

"Jamie already reported to you?"

"He thought I might like to know the details. Me being the boss and all. I didn't figure to have your report until the Killian woman went home or the fish stopped rising. Anyway, the dead man's family rang up the sheriff. They asked him to investigate, but the only way he can operate on federal land is to have a police counterpart from the NPS. Here's how it's going to be. I'm bringing in two more men, a couple of summer hires from the Grand Lake side of the park, to man the Fall River gate. I'm taking you off the visitor accommodation paysheet and putting you on law enforcement. Shine up your badge and start wearing your gun. And on your way out, be sure and pick up a pad of citations so you can ticket people for littering and speeding."

"Yessir."

"Speaking of guns. The girl's brother confirms that she owned a pistol, a .22 Colt Woodsman automatic. He's mailing the serial numbers as soon as he can find them."

"What's the procedure from here?" McIntyre asked.

"I think we oughta check the crime scene again," Sheriff Crowell said. "Search up and down the trail in case anybody dropped anything. I think we'd better make up a list of people who might've been at the lodge or at the livery and maybe saw her. Anybody who might have seen anything. If they've checked out and gone home, have the reception desk give you their addresses and we'll contact them by phone or write 'em a letter. I'd be willin' to bet we'll find somebody who was looking out a window or walkin' out to go fishin' and saw something."

"I'd like to talk to the other liveries," McIntyre said. "I might find out who was on that second horse."

Supervisor Nicholson studied McIntyre's face.

"Including the Mills Creek Stables? Thinking of spending some time there, are you?"

"I thought I might."

"Mills Creek where a man can be down in those willows and nobody can see him fishing for brookies where those good deep holes are?"

"Maybe, but . . ."

"Find your gun and strap it on, Ranger. Leave the fishing equipment home. If I see you carrying so much as a fly rod, I'll transfer you to Death Valley. You find out how these fatalities happened, and do it quick and quiet. We're a brand spanking new national park and we do not need to be seen as a bunch of layabouts who let some maniac wander around killing off visitors while we're stalking trout or sparking young ladies."

Ranger McIntyre walked out of the supervisor's office, got into his pickup truck, and drove to the Fall River entrance station. Jamie Ogg wasn't too pleased to learn that he would be doing all the "touristy work" while McIntyre spent his time investigating crime, not until he learned that the supervisor was sending two summer temps to replace McIntyre.

"Two men to help me," Jamie said. "Boy, that will be a change!"

"You'll be in charge," the ranger said. "I'm counting on you to keep them busy. Maybe take advantage of the extra help to do maintenance around here. Make a rotation schedule for keeping one man on the entrance gate most of the time. Nicholson thinks too many people drive through here without buying a park's pass because there's nobody at the gate to stop them."

"Sure, of course," Jamie said. "And where are these two men going to sleep? One can bunk in with me, I guess. The other'll need to share your cabin."

"They can both have my cabin," McIntyre said. "I plan on staying at the Pioneer until this job is done."

"Better breakfasts?"

"There you go. Need to keep up my strength."

"What's wrong with my pancakes?"

"There's too many of them."

The ranger's next job was to drive up Mills Creek and talk to Paul Barrow, owner, manager, hostler, swamper, groomer, and honey wagon driver at Mills Creek Stables. In short, he was the only one who worked there. Being one of those out-of-the-way places it didn't attract anywhere near as many customers as did the lodge liveries; the lack of business, however, wasn't the only reason that Barrow ran his stable alone. The fact was that Barrow was a hermit, or would have been one if he didn't need money for groceries and tobacco. He couldn't put up with other people, and by the same token nobody could stand working for him. If he wasn't blatantly ignoring you he was belaboring your ears with denunciations of politicians, preachers, and people in general. He hated blacks, Mexicans, Germans, bankers, and just about anybody from Iowa. He lusted after every woman he saw, regardless of size, shape, or color, but didn't understand them and didn't want anything to do with them.

McIntyre found him shoveling horse manure into the honey wagon, getting ready to haul it to the honey pile back in the aspen grove.

"Now that Washington has officially declared this to be a national park," McIntyre told him, "we'd rather you didn't pile your horseshit where it can leach into the creek. Park policy. Don't spoil the natural surroundings."

"Oh yeah? Well why don't you go tell Calvin Coolidge to come out here and show me where he wants to put the shit. Goddamn politicians, make it illegal for a man to buy himself a damn drink. Now they think they can tell a man where he can pile horseshit. Whatta ya want?"

"You heard we found a dead woman up at Cub Lake?"

"Whatta ya think, I done it? I heard she was naked as a plucked hen, too."

"That day it happened, do you remember renting a horse to anybody? In fact, I'd like to know about anybody who hired a horse that entire week."

Barrow guffawed and flicked a piece of horse manure off his sleeve.

"Now y' think one of my horse customers

103

killed her? Or maybe you think I done it. I guess anybody'd throw horseshit in the creek'd strip a girl necked and kill her."

"No. I think it's possible that somebody rode one of your horses up there that same day. There were two sets of tracks. I need to know who was up there besides the dead lady."

"What'd the print look like?"

"Come again?"

"Follow me."

Barrow led McIntyre to the corral, where he walked up to the nearest horse and lifted one of its hooves to show the bottom of the horseshoe. Right next to the toe caulk a deep X had been filed into the steel.

"I mark mine," Barrow said proudly. "Y' run a place like this, once in awhile y' gotta go lookin' for livestock what strayed loose. I make that mark so's I can tell my own. Ain't gonna spend time chasin' no damn livery stock from some damn lodge for 'em. I bet y' didn't even look close enough at them tracks t' see. That's the trouble with the government hirin' you guys for rangers just because you was in the war. Got no trail sense."

"I'll go back and see if any of the prints are still there. Meanwhile, you recall who rented horses that week?"

Barrow dropped the hoof and leaned against the horse. He took out "the makin's" and slowly, carefully rolled himself a cigarette. He borrowed a match — although he probably had one of his own — and stared off toward the creek as if he were peering into the far distant past. McIntyre knew better than to rush the man.

"Wellsir," Barrow said at last, "there was a family with two kids. Weren't too good riders, but that ain't my concern. That fella that runs the camera shop in town — can't never remember his name. Sounds like the name of a damn German."

"Kaplan. Van Kaplan."

"That's the duck. I got his name writ down in my ledger. Anyway, he rented that chestnut over there. Rode up to Mills Glacier to take photographs, at least that's what he said. One, maybe two days before they found the dead woman. There was a honeymoon couple with a tent outfit, too. They took two saddle horses and a packhorse for three days. Said the ground was too hard to sleep on but I reckon one of them spent the night lying on the other one, if you know what I mean. Probably her on him, the way women are these days."

"Who else?"

"Only two. A snooty female all on her

own, and a man with no hand."

"Tell me about them."

"You know, Ranger, I got to thinkin'. My business ain't what it oughta be. Here I am, a good string of horses, situated on a real nice fishin' creek. Folks can rent one of my horses here and purty quick be headin' down nearly any ridin' trail in this valley. But they all want t' ride out of them fancy lodges. Don't know I'm here, most of them."

"And?"

"Well, I was thinkin' maybe you rangers could put the word out. When people come through your entrance stations, I mean. Tell 'em 'hey if you're wantin to ride horses, there's this good livery over on Mills Creek.' "

McIntyre got the message. One hand washes the other. Favors in return for information.

"I could look into it," the ranger said. "I could tell the boys. If you had some brochures or postcards made we could put them in the rack at the gate. That's how the hotels do it. Okay?"

"Okay. Maybe I'll talk to that camera shop whatshisname. Kaplan. Him as makes postcards. Maybe he'd trade horse rides for cards. But whatta you want to know?"

"I'll lay it out plain for you, Barrow. But

106

don't you let it go any further. The thing is, I think somebody killed that young lady up at Cub Lake. And I'm starting to think that whoever it was followed her up there. Either they happened to spot her riding toward the Cub Lake trail and followed her, or else they were hanging around the trail junction waiting for somebody — anybody — who looked like they were headed up into that valley alone. Whichever it was, two horses went up the trail that morning and two horses turned off on the same track to the lake and two horses came back down. Leaving one dead body behind."

"And you're askin' me . . ."

"Where the second horse came from. The victim's horse came from Stead's, I already know that."

Barrow rolled another cigarette. The deep frown on his forehead probably indicated that he was deep in thought. After smoking the cigarette halfway down, he spoke again.

"It'd figure to be one of mine. You're right about that. Your killer could've got a horse here from me and headed up onto th' moraine. From there he'd ride acrost to the Thompson River trail. From there it'd be maybe a ten-minute ride to that trail junction. But you got a problem with your theory."

"Which is what?"

"That horse didn't come from me. I told you. The camera store guy went out that day, or maybe the day before, I don't exactly recall, but he come back by way of the Boulder Ridge trail. That one-handed guy never said where he went, but he couldn't hardly manage the reins with his one hand, let alone kill somebody."

"Which hand?"

"Huh? I guess he was missin' his right hand. Lemme think. Yeah, the right one. Probably a war casualty."

"And the woman?"

"Snooty, like I said. Foreign accent. Sounded kinda like one of those damn Germans, but I didn't mention nuthin' about it. Maybe Italian or New York. Hell, they all sound alike. Real uppity, you know? But cash money talks loud enough, if y' know what I mean. But she couldn't be the one y' want neither."

"Why is that?"

"For one thing, money. I mean money. The boots, ridin' pants, fancy jacket and hat, all of it top quality stuff. Tailored. You people think I'm a dumb ridge runner who never knew about stuff, but fact is I know quality. Partly why I'm here, 'cause of bein' tired of livin' around snoots like that.

108

Anyway, she had this expensive-lookin' camera box and a little short tripod. Hell, Ranger, she even had her a custom-built leather rucksack. Polished leather, like a suitcase with shoulder straps. Never saw anything like it. She says something about heading toward the glacier for photos — she said 'pho-toe' in that accent of hers — and scribbles down her name in the ledger but I can't read her handwritin' and pays me cash. My question is why the hell would somebody with lots of money kill anybody?"

"When she came back, which way did she come?"

"Didn't see. It was late and I was busy closin' down. Tossin' hay to the horses, I heard noise, turned around, and seen her puttin' her stuff into her car. The horse she'd rented was okay, hadn't been run hard or nuthin'."

"Anything else? Was she short, tall, brown hair, blond, skinny, anything like that?"

"Like I said, what I mostly seen was her money. Average build, I guess. Average height. Dark hair, but I think it was a wig."

"What makes you think that?"

"When she took the horse and was ridin' off outa here. I was lookin' after her, y'know the way y' do with a woman walkin' away. Only the horse give a kinda jounce and her hat slipped t' one side and I'da swore all her hair slipped with it."

Ranger McIntyre took down the description of the mystery woman's car — plain, black, two-door, nothing unusual about it — and went his way. Crossing Mills Creek on his way back to the main road, he saw a trout rise in the glassy surface of the water behind a beaver dam. But he only sighed deeply, thought about being reassigned to Death Valley, and kept driving.

CHAPTER 5

Things were going perfectly. It is what comes of good planning. If one makes plans carefully, takes advantage of every situation, success becomes inevitable. Discovering the inconspicuous cabin among the trees was the example. Originally, the purpose had been to scout the network of trailheads to find the ones most likely to attract a solo rider. Or a lone hiker. A tent hidden under branches could serve as a sort of base camp, a camouflaged nook in the forest. On the map draw a circle encompassing two, three trailheads; reconnoiter within the circle for ideal hiding place.

What should appear, however, but a small miracle in the shape of a narrow dirt track leading to a fenced property in the heavy woods off at the edge of the broad valley! There was a simple wooden sign nailed to the gate post:

"Wigwam Lodge. Cabins."

Alice Reader, owner and operator of

Wigwam Lodge, claimed to be well known throughout the area. By her own admission, she was the first woman to homestead anywhere around here and was the last woman anyone — particularly a man and even more particularly any government man — would want to mess with. Kept to herself, minded her own business. Most of the time the damn park service didn't remember she was here and the rest of the time they acted like they didn't care. There would come a day, and she knew it, damn it, when they'd either buy her out or burn her out or just run her out because that's how they operated. Now that this National Park was starting to look like a going concern any private land inside "their" boundary would be seized sooner or later. No damn doubt about it.

Until that happened, she'd hang on. Rent her cabins, run her trap line, maybe rent a horse to a tourist now and again, and she'd make out okay.

What about these cabins? Was there one available?

"Hell, available's what I got the most of. C'mon. I'll show you what they look like."

The assortment of dark log cabins in the tall old ponderosas looked like a scene from a Black Forest fairy tale. Each one was a different shape and size. Each was hidden in its own isolated nook among the trees. Alice Reader led the way to one that didn't even have a proper outhouse, merely a wooden seat spanning a hole in the ground. A rusty coffee can perched atop the pile of dirt that had come from the hole. A screen of tree branches provided some privacy. Inside the cabin, a bed with mattress, a squat two-hole cookstove, a rickety little table with two equally rickety chairs. For a nightstand next to the bed there was a wooden box that, according to its label, once contained DuPont dynamite. Another dynamite box was nailed to the log wall above the stove to serve as a kitchen cupboard.

"Wash basin's on the bench out back," Alice explained. "Bring it inside if you want, I don't care. Cut your own firewood with your own axe. I don't loan mine. There's a creek off through the trees that way," she pointed, "water's good. Cold as hell, but good. Piss in the forest, crap in the privy hole, and toss in a can of dirt when you're done. You supply your own blankets and I'm not responsible for chiggers, lice, or bedbugs. There's a frying pan and saucepan hanging on the wall and plates and spoons and such in the DuPont box. Be sure you

113

leave 'em clean when you go."

"What about a horse?"

"I got one you can use. I'll find y' a saddle. I'll keep her with the others or else you can keep her back of your cabin. I guess I could let y' borrow a long picket rope. Or y' could collect branches and build a pen out there. Hell, you can keep her in the cabin with you if you want to. I don't care."

"How much?"

"Cash up front, horse included, no question asked, forty bucks the month."

"Forty."

"Take, leave it. I don't care. Down to the village y' can stay in the Livingstone Hotel and pay eighty, for crissakes."

It was ideal. It was even more strategically located than the original plan. Private, protected, convenient to three trailheads. Even the road into the place was hard to see from the main road and the car could be parked out of sight next to the cabin. Yes, it would do. It would do very well, indeed.

No names required, no questions asked. No neighbors. Perfect.

The morning sky was endlessly deep and columbine blue, a perfect day for horseback riding. Perfect for sightseeing in the park, and perhaps . . . perhaps . . . "photography." No rush on the photography, no hurry. Pick exactly the right hiker or horseback tourist for a model and choose just the right moment and place. That was the secret. Take your time and choose carefully.

However, a candidate did present himself early in the day and he was almost ideal. He was a blond with very white skin, a vigorous young man. He was hiking across the moraine meadow, heading for the Juniper Lake trail, which would take him to timberline, where he hoped to do some mountaineering. It was obvious he knew what he was doing, with the long coil of rope over his shoulders, the full backpack, and the Bavarian alpenstock he carried. His muscular pale body would make interesting pictures. But he looked too strong, too athletic, and altogether too heavy to manipulate easily. Besides, the place and timing were not ideal; a hiker came along while they were talking about the beauty of the morning and the thrill of being alone in the mountains. A witness. No sense taking chances. So it was goodbye. Exchanging a casual wave the young blond went his way again, striding along the trail to remain forever oblivious to the fact that he had narrowly escaped a fate far different than any he could have imagined.

It was too bad about the pale young man. Merely thinking about stripping him made the hands and heart tremble with pleasure. However, there had been the fun of thinking about it. Taking the photos was an anticlimax: thinking about it was the real thrill, the long build-up, the lovely tension all along every muscle when you were being the predator, then seducer and villain. She had thought about using a photo studio, a private and safe place to tease or seduce the subject into disrobing. However, to do it out in the open where there was risk of discovery, that was where the excitement was.

On the Cub Lake trail a fat young woman on horseback was quite tempting. She might be easy to drug. The abandoned trail to the lake and campsite clearing was nearby. Like the blond youth this young lady had nice pale skin that would show up beautifully against a weathered log or mossy boulder. She was definitely chubby; the oily little weasel who bought photos for his "French" postcards had said that nudes of chubby young women sold very well. Very well, indeed. Very profitable, he had said.

"Of course, we can't just order up a dead nude to our specifications, can we? We —

116

that is, my man who does the printing, and I — are pleasantly amazed that the authorities let you take as many photos as you have. Once the European 'market' discovers them, you'll probably find yourself wealthy. I am amazed at how easily you've persuaded the park police to take photographs. Clever. Extremely clever. If it is true. If you even asked permission. If they even know you've done it. Which is none of my business."

One side of his lip curled in a leering smile. The problem with his all-knowing sneer was that he didn't know quite as much as he thought. He didn't need to know that the park rangers knew nothing about the photographs she was selling for lewd postcards.

"For our purposes — our legal purposes, in case a conscientious citizen should report our photos to the district attorney — the story is foolproof. You are an anonymous photographer who is paid in cash for crime scene documentation pictures. You may not even be the one who has taken them. You may have, shall we say, intercepted the negatives. We don't actually know whether the pictures are of deceased nudes or models posing as such. Nor how you came to have them. We merely buy them from you as potential 'curiosity' photos and sell them to clients who have 'special' tastes in photographic art."

"Judging from the amount of cash you give me, I would say we're all doing well."

"Maybe the park police will call on your talents again the next time they have an accidental death. Our clients are eager. And will pay virtually anything for authentic photos. Such art is not to my taste, of course. But I say if the market exists, a businessman would be a fool not to take advantage."

It might prove worthwhile to accompany the fat girl as far as the next trail junction, to chat, to size up the possibilities. The "possibilities" could almost be called exciting. The young woman's naiveté, her happy enthusiasm for being outdoors and on her own, the way her endowments bounced and jostled on the saddle. How much sleeping powder would it take to make her look like a corpse? Twice the previous dose? The real question, however, lay in the locale itself. Go back to Cub Lake again? Very dangerous. Too many people visited the primary campsite on the far side of the lake, at the end of the main trail. It would take only one curious hiker with binoculars, or a wandering fisherman, to queer the whole

118

operation. Plus, to use the site at the end of the abandoned path would be like returning to the scene of the crime. It might give the rangers something to go on. No, Cub Lake wouldn't do. It would look like a pattern. It would look like a pattern and everything depended upon the appearance of randomness.

"I seem to have forgotten my canteen and lunch!"

"Oh, dear!" the chubby girl said. "You're welcome to share mine. I always seem to pack enough food for two."

"No, I really couldn't. It's less than a mile to the lodge. I'll trot back for it and catch you up before long."

That would do. There was no lunch at the lodge, of course, no connection with the lodge at all. And there would be no catching up. It was an excuse to turn back and take another trail in hopes of finding someone else. Someone alone. Someone photogenic. If not this morning, tomorrow would do just as well. Do not rush, no matter the temptation. Don't make mistakes, don't create a pattern.

When he stopped off at the inn in the village for lunch, Ranger McIntyre discovered Doris at the window table. Ordinarily he would have eaten at Gerry's Chili Palace, where the meals were cheaper. Life-threatening, maybe, but cheaper. On Fridays, however, the inn had clam chowder. And freshly baked bread. McIntyre couldn't resist either one.

"Haven't seen you in a few days," he remarked as he sat down. He automatically straightened his placemat and arranged his silverware in a neat row on one side. He liked all his tools under his right hand when he ate.

"That's right," Doris smiled. "It has been awhile. Nice to see you again." And she really meant it, because it was nice to see him again. He had such a wonderful, open face. Such warm brown eyes.

"I've been busy," the ranger went on. "This murder case. The S.O. put me on the enforcement division payroll. Seems like every day I have to check up on a report of an illegal camp or some tourist thinking he saw smoke from a moonshine still or something."

"You call him the S.O.? Tim! Is that a nice way to refer to your boss?"

His laughter was wonderful. It made Doris wish that she knew a joke to tell him to make him laugh again. Even the waitress turned to see what was funny.

"Supervisor's Office," he explained. "Kind of a general term for the National Park Powers That Be. Everything that goes wrong around here is blamed on the S.O., sooner or later. Anyway, where have you been hiding yourself? Are you getting good waterfall photos?"

"No, not really. As luck would have it, the day after you and I rode to Cub Lake I had a telegram and had to go back to Sioux City. An emergency, you know. Caught the express out of Denver."

"I wondered what happened to you. I asked at the desk, but all they knew was that you said for them to hold your room and you took off. I came around to see about having your pictures developed."

"Oh, no! I hope you didn't need them right away!"

"Not as it turned out. The ones I took came out good enough. More or less proved that she hadn't been strangled, shot, stabbed, or clubbed to death. Called the family's doctor again and he'd gotten a second opinion from another doctor. They agree it looks like suffocation, but don't know how. I'm still thinking it's murder. Whoever did it was apparently strong enough to pull her head back and put something over her face to cut off her air

121

supply. He did it so quick that she didn't have time to struggle. At least that's the way I see it."

"How awful," she said. "The thing with the pictures . . . I still had the rolls of film with me when I got to Sioux City. I took them to the man who usually develops my film and makes prints for me. He said he'd send them express when they're ready."

"Maybe he could use that new airmail service!" McIntyre laughed again. "Have you heard about it? You can mail a letter from Denver and it'd go to Omaha or Kansas City by airplane. And those mail pilots fly night or day, all kinds of weather. Don't know how they do it."

The bowls of chowder arrived, steaming hot and brimming with chunks of potato and clam. Doris opened up the napkin that was keeping the bread warm and broke off a piece for each of them.

"Anyway," she said, "this family emergency delayed my waterfall project. I only have about two more weeks of vacation time left."

"That reminds me," McIntyre said. "I never did hear what kind of office work you do. How you manage a month off, I mean. I'd love it if the park service gave me a month off, especially during fishing season."

"Mine is a dull and boring story. I'm one of those gals who works for her relatives. An uncle of mine is in the real estate business with law cases on the side. He has two girls to do the stenography stuff, but I run errands, talk to renters about their grievances, drive around looking for properties he could buy, that kind of thing. He's usually glad to be rid of me for a month. He hired me to be his Girl Friday, but he says that so far I've only made it to Tuesday."

"Can't believe anybody would want to be rid of you for a month," McIntyre said, cooling his spoonful of chowder by blowing on it.

"Why, Tim McIntyre!" Doris said. "Are you trying to flirt with me? I'm shocked!"

"No, you're not, and yes, I am. Eat your lunch. Are you off to take more pictures today? I don't know where you could go. It's too late to be starting out on a long hike, with the day about half gone. Alberta Falls, maybe, unless the road crew has the Bear Lake road torn up again. I'll sure be glad when that road project is finished."

"I hate to tell you this," she said, "especially now that you've started being all flirty. But you won't be seeing me for a while. Three, four days, maybe a week. You see, I've decided to relocate to the Wild Basin

123

area. I found a lodge there, very reasonable. I doubt whether the meals will be as good, but it seems comfortable. And will save me miles and miles of driving."

"But that's all the way over in the Little Thompson River drainage! Takes nearly two hours to drive there from here. Plus, I hardly ever have a reason to go to Wild Basin. There's a man on the ranger station there that I've never met, it's that remote."

"Now, now," she said. "No whining allowed! I'll be back here before I have to go home. We'll go for a ride or find a place to have supper together. Okay? But if I'm going to have enough photographs for my project, I need to be where there are plenty of things to take photos of. My map of the park shows at least a dozen named waterfalls in Wild Basin. Lots of them sound interesting, like Ribbon Falls and Confusion Cascade."

"Ribbon Falls is really a creek that runs down over a slanted boulder maybe fifty, sixty yards long. In the right light, like early morning, it looks like a silver ribbon. And Confusion is exactly what the name says it is. When you first see it from the trail . . . it's a small creek . . . it looks like it's flowing one direction. When you come around the corner in the trail it looks like an entirely different cascade. When you leave the trail and walk up to it, you see it falls into a narrow slit in the rocks. It emerges again where you wouldn't expect it to."

"See? That's why I'd want to stay there and make day trips to waterfalls."

"I guess you're right. I had hoped to take you to Bridal Veil Falls, though."

"Maybe we'll have time after I'm back from Wild Basin. Or it might be a good excuse for me to come back next summer! But about my pictures of that poor dead girl . . . will you be needing them? Shall I have the desk give you the package when it comes for me? It should be in the mail next week."

"No, I guess I don't need them that bad. I've got other leads to look into. Provided I have the time. I'm awful busy issuing parking tickets and handing out fines to people for feeding jelly beans to chipmunks."

"Tell me about more about it," she said, offering another chunk of bread torn from the warm loaf.

"About what? Jelly beans and chipmunks? Not good for the chipmunks. Or any animal. For that matter, they probably aren't very good for humans, either."

"You're in a humorous mood today. I meant tell me about your leads in the case

125

of the dead girl at Cub Lake."

"Well, for one thing there's this mysterious woman in a wig. Then there's a guy with one hand, I need to find him. He might be a witness. And the camera store guy, Kaplan. He might have been in that area about the time the murder happened. And a horse that came from nowhere. Somebody rode a horse up to Cub Lake the same time the girl was killed. They vanished, horse and all. I think I'm looking for a fast trail rider, if you want to know. Strong, able to overcome the girl without a struggle, and a fast trail rider. Possibly using a more expensive camera than most of us could afford. Now that I think of it, you might be the person I'm looking for! Hey! Case solved! Now you'll have to stay in town. Maybe I can prove you also killed Mr. Snyder. Although, I do have another theory that says Jamie Ogg might have done it. Because he's a southpaw."

"Congratulations!" she laughed. "Two murderers and both of them right under your very nose!"

"Thank you, thank you. Nothing to it, really. But all kidding aside, I'm certain that somebody else rode a horse up there and either killed our victim or found her lying there. Whoever it was rode back down the trail fast enough that nobody, not the hostlers or anybody, saw him. It's like the Chasm Falls case; we've got hoofprints, some witness that nobody saw, and clothes neatly stacked. The similarity is almost eerie. It's as if we've got a killer who goes around killing people and making neat piles of their clothing."

"I suppose while I'm gone you'll be visiting stables and liveries looking for a phantom horse? And good fishing spots?"

"Now you sound like my supervisor. He thinks all I do is fish. But I'll be busy. There's a half-dozen stables inside the park boundary alone and I should check all of them. I'll be cleaning horse muck off my boots twice a day for a week."

"Such fun!" Doris said. "And poor little me, I'll be eating lunch beside a beautiful waterfall in Wild Basin. Maybe I'll take a fly rod along with me. I can come back and tell you how the fishing is."

"Now you're being just plain mean," he said.

She leaned closer, near enough that he could smell the scent of her powder.

"While I'm there in all that solitude," she whispered, "I might take off my clothes and sunbathe."

"Nobody likes a smart aleck," McIntyre

said. "I might have to come all the way up there to arrest you for feeding the mosquitoes. Let's get serious a minute, though. While you're roaming around out there, you keep in mind what happened to the Chasm Falls guy from last summer. And that poor girl at Cub Lake. You keep that gun of yours handy. Don't talk to strangers."

"Rangers?"

"Strangers, wise guy. Especially anybody who offers to ride along with you or wants to share a campsite. Anybody who asks you a lot of personal questions. And double especially a woman in a dark wig or a guy with one hand missing. If you spot either one of those, you hurry the heck out of there and report to the Wild Basin ranger. Don't take any chances. At anything suspicious, make a run for it. Don't wait until it's too late. Nobody will hear you if you yell for help."

"Yessir." Doris made a mock salute. "Understood."

"I'm serious. And another thing, if you're at a lake or stream and have an urge to take your clothes off and go into the water, don't do it."

"Why! Timothy G. McIntyre! I'm shocked! Are you thinking naughty thoughts?"

128

"No," he said. "People swimming naked frightens the trout. Takes a week before they calm down enough to rise to a dry fly."

With the afternoon half gone, McIntyre decided to begin his investigations in town. However, it took all of his willpower to tear himself away from Doris Killian. He wanted to run and catch up with her like a lovesick little boy scampering after pinafores and pigtails. But duty spoke to him. Duty, and the threat of being reposted to Death Valley.

There were two livery stables in the village proper, one on the main street and one at the edge of town. The young swamper at the first stable remembered a man with one hand.

"He asked if we ever trucked our rental horses up to the National Park. I told him no, that mostly our customers use the south trail out toward Devil's Gulch. That seemed to interest him. Tell you the truth, Ranger, it kinda made me shiver the way he rubbed the horse we were standin' next to. You know how a person might rub their hand over a horse's flank, kinda absentminded? Only he done it with that stump where his right hand used to be. Gave me the heebie-jeebies."

"Did he hire a horse?"

"No. Said he'd think about it, though. Seemed interested in the Devil's Gulch idea, asked if it was a lonely place. You know, not many people? He went across the street and up to the camera shop. I seen him go in. That's the last I saw of him."

The owner of the camera shop remembered the man with one hand, too.

"Bought four rolls of film for his Model 17," Kaplan said. "And he asked about a gadget."

"Gadget?"

"Said he had two cameras, didn't have them with him. The Model 17 and another one but he didn't know the model number of that one. But he said he was interested in finding a self-timer for one of them."

"Self-timer?"

"Yeah. It's a little clockwork thingamajig. You attach it to your camera and set it for anywhere up to about sixty seconds and it clicks the shutter. That way you can be in your own picture, see? Good for those family shots. I didn't have one. He said he used to have one but lost it in the mountains. He wanted to buy another one."

"To use one of these self-timers," the ranger said, "you'd need a tripod, right?"

"That would be the best way. A tripod, or a way to prop the camera up to take the picture. Like your pocket camera, it has that little leg that folds down in front and you can set it on a table or a flat place. You could do it that way, but a tripod would be best."

McIntyre was remembering the sharp indentations he had seen near the body at Cub Lake. And he wondered exactly where in the mountains the one-handed man had lost his timer. And exactly what he had been taking pictures of.

CHAPTER 6

"That's an interesting fly rod you've got there."

McIntyre turned, startled at the voice behind him. He hadn't heard anyone forcing himself through the willows or wading along the river. When McIntyre saw who it was, however, he was no longer surprised. "Nick" Nicholson had not always been tied to a desk as Rocky Mountain National Park Supervisor: in his youthful prime he was one of the best outdoorsmen in America. One of his hunting pals said he had seen Nicholson creep up on a sleeping elk, a full-size, magnificent animal, and touch its flank. Tired rangers who fell asleep during business hours might wake to find one of Supervisor Nicholson's calling cards tucked into their shirt pocket. He was a famous hiker; rangers swapped stories of being worn out from trying to keep up with Nicholson on a marathon hike through the Rockies. His treks were legendary for distance and speed.

"What's it do? Come apart in five sections?" Nicholson said. "Mine's only got three."

Caught. McIntyre was caught red-handed with his secret weapon in his hand.

Supervisor Nicholson was out of uniform. He was carrying a fly rod. He had a wicker creel slung over his shoulder.

"I guess you got me," McIntyre said. "What's it going to be? Reassignment to Death Valley? Or Yellowstone? Please don't say Yellowstone. I hate the stink of those mud pots. The winters up there are killers."

"Relax, McIntyre. Tell me about this fly rod of yours."

"I made it myself. You've already figured why it has five sections to it. Makes it short enough that I can take it apart, put it in my rucksack, and nobody needs to know I've been fishing."

"Maybe you come fishing in order to think about these death situations?"

"Right."

"In a way, your investigation will be enhanced by some fishing and relaxation?"

"Sure, that's it. Efficiency. Plus, if I catch trout for my supper or breakfast it saves a trip into town to eat."

"Me, I come out here to forget about the

office," Nicholson said. "Forms, letters, requisitions, directives from Washington, those weekly updates they send me for the S.O.P. manual. Drive a man crazy."

"Anything in the standard operating procedures about where to pile horseshit?" McIntyre asked.

"What?"

"Never mind."

"I thought you mentioned horseshit. Anyway, I was looking for you. Figured it would be faster to hunt for you on the river than wait for you to come to headquarters. I remember this used to be a favorite spot for you and . . . sorry. I shouldn't have mentioned her. Painful memory."

"Yeah," McIntyre said. "We used to come here and catch little brookies for breakfast."

"I had a long letter from the family lawyer for the Ernst Snyder family," the supervisor said, "the man who died last summer? At Chasm Falls?"

"What did their lawyer have to say?"

Supervisor Nicholson stripped out what looked like thirty feet of fly line and flicked a graceful cast into a swirling eddy across the stream. A trout came up and nudged the dry fly, but avoided the hook.

"The family wants more investigation. Going through the deceased's effects they

134

found a surprise. A packet of love letters. It seems that Ernst had been having a torrid love affair, at least three years of summer rendezvous with a woman. Family never knew anything about it, but the letters made it clear that whoever she was, she expected Ernst to meet her at Estes Park. Or else. In her letter she more or less threatened to expose the affair if he didn't show up. And show up he did. As we know."

"They think she did it?" McIntyre said. "Murdered him?"

"The lawyer wants to find her and talk to her about it. Here's how it works. We investigate within our jurisdiction, which means finding out if she entered the park, whether she stayed at one of the lodges or cabin camps, when she left. And who the hell she is. We give that information to the sheriff and he finds out where she lives."

"And I'm going to do that instead of being transferred to Yellowstone?"

"Right. I want you to examine all the records of the entrance stations, talk to anybody who was on duty, interview the lodges and livery stables and restaurants, anywhere she might have been. We can assume that we're looking for a woman traveling alone, a woman attractive enough to have an affair with a man, probably one who

135

has enough money to be on vacation. If she didn't come on the bus, she had to have a car. Maybe one of the gas stations serviced it and would remember her. It's a long shot, but long shots seem to be a specialty of yours. Speaking of long shots, how is your new friend Miss Killian, anyway?"

"Do we have a name for this woman? Initials on the love letters, maybe?"

"Nothing. Ernst was careful. She was, too. The letters were signed 'me.' He destroyed the envelopes and flattened out the letters in a folder. In order of date. Very neat and tidy."

"Like that pile of clothes at Chasm Falls."

"Right. All we can tell from the letters is that she was here last summer and she threatened to expose the affair."

"Okay," McIntyre said, starting to reel in his fly line. "I'll see what I can find."

"There's one more thing. The family got around to opening the box of Ernst's personal effects, the stuff Jamie collected and sent to them. He enclosed a note telling them about the rod and reel and creel, but they don't think the equipment belonged to him. But that's not to say he couldn't have bought new equipment when he got to Colorado. Maybe somebody at the lodge can remember seeing him with a fly rod. Or

136

maybe the outfitter's store remembers selling it to him."

"I'll ask around."

"What do you have on?" said the supervisor, pointing at the dry fly on the end of McIntyre's line.

"Royal Coachman. A number 12."

"Why don't you make a cast over that eddy. He didn't like my Rio Grande King."

Orders are orders. McIntyre stripped off thirty feet of line and made a perfect roll cast into the river eddy. The dry fly floated lightly on the rounded swells, drifting naturally atop the margin where the stream's current rubbed into the calmer water. In the wink of an eye the stream's surface seemed to explode as a lunker went for the Royal Coachman, carried it into the air in a beautiful flash of arching energy, then dove again for the bottom.

"Holy cow!" Nicholson blurted. "Set the hook! Set the hook!"

McIntyre needed no instruction. With him it was pure reflex for his left hand to haul back on the slack line to set the hook deep in the fish's jaw. From that point on the fight between man and trout would become a delicate dance, the man making no mistakes that would let the trout snap the thin line, the trout using instinct and strength to do exactly that.

McIntyre raised the tip of the rod experimentally, to feel the weight of the fish, and the fish instantly replied by making a run for the main current of the stream. It stayed on the bottom and went upstream, swimming strongly.

"I can't bring his head up!" McIntyre shouted while starting to move upstream, following the fish, keeping the tension bending the tip of the fly rod.

"Must be a German brown," Nicholson said. "That's how they run when they're hooked!"

Five minutes later on a sandbar fifty yards upstream, McIntyre had the exhausted trout in the landing net. Supervisor Nicholson came up to the ranger as he was gently releasing the heavy brown trout back into the water.

"Good one, huh?" the supervisor said.

"Too good to keep," McIntyre replied. "A trout with that kind of fight in him, you don't kill him."

"Where you goin' this morning in case we need you?"

Jamie Ogg was helping McIntyre hitch the horse trailer to the back of the RMNP pickup truck.

"Later on, I expect I'll be either at Stead's ranch or Canby's Stables. First, I'm going to pay a visit on our friend Leon. Leon Counter?"

"You gonna finally shut down his moonshine still? Shouldn't you take a couple of us with you?"

"What still are you talking about? Officially, we're not aware that he even has a moonshine still. I'm just going to talk to him, that's all. Just talk. While I'm gone, you and the summer temps could cut those weeds around the flagpole and the buildings. And restack your firewood. Looks like a bear or a coyote tore into it. Probably looking for mice."

Brownie sniffed at the oats in McIntyre's palm and obediently followed him to the trailer. It was a game they played: the ranger pretended that he wasn't going to put her in the trailer, that he had simply wanted her to have a handful of oats to eat. For her part, the mare sniffed the oats and pretended she didn't know he had a halter in the hand that he kept behind his back. She pretended that she hadn't heard the rangers hitching the trailer to the truck. Truth to tell, she didn't mind walking up into the trailer; usually it meant they were going someplace more interesting than the corral behind the ranger station. By hesitating and balking, though, she got the oats.

Leon Counter's place squatted high on a nondescript ridge. His bulge of mountain was ordinary and hardly anyone ever noticed it, especially against the backdrop of the magnificent Front Range of the Rockies. The park service should have evicted him by now, seeing that he had no deed or title to the land and it was part of the National Park. His dwelling was something McIntyre termed a "three-half-house": half dugout, half natural cave, and half brush pile. Two paths crossed over the ridge, game trails used by deer and elk and bighorn sheep; otherwise there was no trail anywhere near the place, nothing to interest a tourist. Or, more to the point, a law officer. Leon was a moonshiner and a squatter on government property and almost any other ranger would arrest him. McIntyre, however, discovered that Leon was an asset to the district and did more good than harm. The hermit had foiled three poachers on his own and had reported numerous others. He had helped McIntyre round up a couple of pothunters looting an Indian campsite over the brow of the ridge. One morning after a lightning storm, he reported spotting a forest fire, which the fire crew was able to extinguish before it spread.

In effect, Leon Counter was the ranger's unofficial and unpaid deputy on Tuxedo Ridge, keeping an eye on an area that was not on any of the rangers' patrol routes. Whenever McIntyre paid Leon a visit, he turned a blind eye to the wisps of smoke and steam emitting from the jumble of boulders near the dugout, and paid no heed to the odor of hot mash and alcohol.

The principal feature of Tuxedo Ridge was that it had no features. It was an uninteresting place. Except for one thing: if a man with binoculars stood on the treeless saddle of the ridge he could look down into Moraine Park in one direction, into Tuxedo Park to the east, and could see considerable stretches of the Fall River valley. It was a nearly ideal location for a fire lookout, should the park ever decide to build one.

"It's funny you'd ask," Leon said in response to McIntyre's question. And he added "How ya, Brownie?"

The moonshiner cradled the mare's head in his arm and stroked her nose.

"This flat hat forest cop been treatin' you okay?" he said. "Givin' you plenty of oats?"

"How come you say it's funny?" McIntyre persisted. "That I'd ask, I mean."

"Oh, about seein' anything peculiar? C'mon and take a stroll over to the saddle and I'll show you."

When they got to the open ground beyond the trees, Leon pointed down at Moraine Park in the distance.

"Couple days ago. I'm here watchin' for a guy who was comin' up from town, see? Maybe a customer, maybe none of your business. Down there on the meadow near the river I can see somebody on horseback. Kinda tiny from here, but it was somebody on horseback all right. See where the trails split off? Y' can see the one comin' from the lodge and where it splits. It splits again a little further on. I got my field glasses and while I'm waitin' and watchin' for my visitor this horse rider moves out into the willows by the river and over to that first trail junction. After a few minutes he goes back where he started. Next thing I see is him riding to the other junction. Stays there awhile. Kept doin' that kind of stuff for maybe a hour, maybe two. I figured it was you and Brownie lookin' for somethin', or waitin' for one of your hardened criminal tourists to be took into custody for litterin' or somethin'."

"What happened to him?"

"Well, nuthin'. Like I said, he kept goin'

from one trail t'other. My visitor showed up and I seen the horsebacker go back into the willows headin' for the north slope of the moraine and that's all I seen."

"And this wasn't a few weeks ago, but a couple of days."

"Yup."

"Could the rider have been a woman?"

"Now that you mention it, maybe. Couldn't tell from here."

"You know what, Leon?" McIntyre said. "That's a lot more interesting than you'd think."

"Glad to help. That all you came for?"

"Yes. Wanted to know if you'd seen anything. Nobody crossing the ridge, that you know of?"

"Not a soul nor a body neither."

"Maybe you heard we had what might be a murder," McIntyre said. "Up at Cub Lake. I think whoever did it is long gone by now, but you might keep your eyes peeled when you're out and about. Could be somebody out here killing people."

"Aw, Ranger!" said Leon Counter. "Are you worried I might get myself murdered? That's real nice of you."

"I'm not worried about you. I'm worried that if you got killed, there wouldn't be anybody watching the fire under your whiskey still. If you got killed it could get loose and start a forest fire and burn down the National Park."

"And without a park you'd be outa a job?"

"Let's say I'd be sent somewhere where the fishing isn't too good."

McIntyre felt that Brownie needed more exercise. Therefore, instead of riding straight back to the truck, he thought they might go on down the ridge and have a look at the spot where Leon had seen that lone person riding back and forth. There had been an afternoon rain, which would spoil any chance of finding hoofprints, but it wouldn't hurt to look around. Besides, riding helped him think. Maybe not as much as fly fishing or a good breakfast, but being in the saddle did have a way of focusing the mind.

The trails showed plenty of tracks, both horse and human, but none that meant anything to the ranger. He reenacted the scenario that Leon had described, riding Brownie back into the willows a ways, riding out as if to intercept someone coming up a trail. If the mysterious horseman had been waiting for a victim to come along, he had certainly chosen a strategic setup. The rider would have been able to see anyone else on a trail anywhere in the wide, flat valley. McIntyre spotted several mule deer and a small herd of bighorn sheep, and at a considerable distance. Seeing a human on horseback or someone hiking along one of the trails would be simple.

The ranger rode back into the willows and came out again, this time pointing Brownie toward the Cub Lake trail. Again, anybody riding or hiking along that trail would think it was just coincidental to meet a horseman coming from one of the stables downstream. There would be an exchange of greetings, "hi, how you doing, nice day, where you headed" and all that. It would be natural for them to ride side by side for a while. The murderer would have to be alert in case a witness happened along, but then it would be simple to break off, make some excuse to turn back.

Imagining the location as a picture puzzle showing a killer stalking a girl named Varna, McIntyre could see pieces fitting into place. The killer waiting, the girl coming along, the casual meeting, the ride up into the forested mountain toward the lake, the suggestion they take the unused trail . . . but how was she killed? That piece was missing. And the motive, that was missing as well. And how she came to take off her clothes, of course. Three missing pieces.

After the murderous deed had been done, the killer would come riding back down the same trail, leading the livery stable horse as far as the moraine meadow where it would be set loose to return to the lodge on its own. Those puzzle pieces matched perfectly.

McIntyre clucked to Brownie and the mare started into an easy trot across the long meadow and up into the forest. They overtook a hiker who heard them coming and stepped off the trail to let them pass; he probably wished he had a camera ready, for the sight of the mounted ranger with his flat hat and his high boots, his tunic and pistol belt, the horse in a high-stepping trot would make a splendid photo for the folks back home.

Sure, McIntyre thought. *Sure. Victim and killer ride into the trees, riding along, talking, becoming acquainted. Very natural. They come to the game trail that goes over the hill. Killer says it would be fun to find out where it goes, and presto! He's got the victim off the main trail. Before long he has her cornered at the lake. And alone. She doesn't suspect a thing. That's got to be how it worked.*

But how the hell did the killer manage it with Ernst Snyder? Evidently the girl was talked into undressing, or else she was drugged and stripped. Or forced at gunpoint. But Snyder, how did he end up with his clothes off? Was he drugged, maybe held at gunpoint? McIntyre imagined a jigsaw piece showing a gun pointing at Ernst Snyder, forcing him to undress and jump over the falls. It almost fit the picture.

At the crest of the hill, Ranger McIntyre dismounted and dropped the reins to the ground to let Brownie browse the grass. He took out his pocket notebook and read through his notes about the Snyder death, in case any details had slipped his mind. Neither Varna nor Snyder showed any signs of being tied up, beaten, stabbed, or shot. Except for the bruise on Snyder's back and the head wound. In both cases the clothing was neatly stacked nearby, leading to the inference that both victims intended to go into the water. However, one body was found at the bottom of the falls with his clothes up at the top, while the other body was lying dry and clean at a campsite with her pile of clothes nowhere near the lake's edge. McIntyre had done his share of skinny-dipping, but couldn't remember any time when he left his clothes in camp. Always kept them near where he was bathing in case somebody might come along. And he had never folded his clothes into a neat stack. He hung them on any handy tree limb or bush or else draped them across a rock. Only as a last resort would he put his clothes on the damp grass. It was possible, of course, that the murderer had folded the clothes after killing the victims. Tidying up, as it were.

"Well, dammit!" McIntyre said aloud.

Brownie looked up with meadow grass dangling from her mouth. She had heard the ranger use the word so many times that she often thought it was part of her own name: "Whoa Brownie Dammit."

"We should have checked for finger-prints!" McIntyre told the mare. "Finger-prints! Maybe on a buckle or on a piece of polished leather like a belt or boot. Any fingerprint other than the victim's would mean somebody else handled those clothes, see?"

Brownie winked one eye and went back to her browsing. No idea what the man was talking about. Whatever he was saying didn't include "go," "dammit," "oats," or "ride," and therefore had nothing to do with her. Like "whoa up." Sometimes he shouted "whoa up" as if it was supposed to mean something to her. Brownie sent a shiver down her flank — the equine equivalent of shrugging her shoulders — and continued browsing.

148

McIntyre's notes from the interview at the camera shop included the words "self-timer," which now reminded him to make another careful search of the murder scene. The one-armed man had told Kaplan he lost a self-timer.

Self-timer. Those tripod marks in the ground. Maybe . . . maybe it was Varna who had a camera on a tripod. Maybe she had a self-timer, took off her clothes to take her *own* picture. But why would a girl do that? Okay, assume she had her reasons. She would stack her clothes very neatly because she was methodical. A methodical person is the sort of person who would seek out a very private setting in which to photograph herself. She would bring the car robe and tripod and self-timer. When she undressed she would put her clothing in a tidy stack. The pictures were self-taken and then the camera and tripod vanished and then she was killed before she could get dressed again. It was a different puzzle picture but it almost made sense.

There still had to be a second person. How did that person come to be there? Maybe the killer didn't ride along with her after all. Maybe he followed her at a distance so she didn't know she was being followed and he hid in the trees and watched the photography session. Maybe he watched while Varna took pictures of herself in her underpants and lay down afterward to fall asleep on the log in the warm sunshine. Maybe she had the car robe with her and covered herself up so she wouldn't sunburn. The killer could have come sneaking up out of the trees and smothered her. He made more pictures, took the camera, tripod, film and all, and rode away. Her horse probably followed his down the trail. That's what a livery horse would do, if it wasn't tied up.

But there was a problem with this version of the puzzle. If it was the one-armed man and if he took Varna's photography equipment, why would he ask Kaplan at the camera shop about a self-timer? Maybe he only wanted Kaplan to show him one in order to learn how the gadget worked. McIntyre made himself a note to have Jamie contact Varna's family and find out if she kept any records of her camera equipment. Receipts with serial numbers, that kind of thing. Since she kept the receipts for that Colt Woodsman .22, she probably kept her receipts for other things as well.

McIntyre picked up Brownie's reins and put his boot to the stirrup. He hadn't found any additional physical evidence, but he was nonetheless pleased with his day's work, for he had come up with a good workable scenario for the murder at Cub Lake. His next step should be to find the man with one hand missing and see if he had a camera that didn't belong to him.

I'll check any stores that sell film, McIntyre thought. *While I'm at it, I'll ask at the grocery. Wherever the guy is sleeping, he needs to buy food.*

At the same time, he would need to be figuring out who Ernst Snyder's lady friend was and whether she might be the snooty one with the expensive taste in clothes. Who she was and where she was.

She seems to have plenty of money, McIntyre thought. *Money and style. I need to start by asking at the more expensive hotels and lodges and see what I can find out. If she checked into the Livingstone or one of the other lodges they'll have a registration card with her home address and her automobile registration number.*

McIntyre put the notebook back in his pocket. First thing tomorrow, he would begin looking for more pieces of the picture. However, he knew from experience that he shouldn't stop thinking about other possible versions about what might have happened at Chasm Falls. He wouldn't want to focus on one particular hypothesis until he had more facts. He needed facts. Right now, though, what he needed was a good supper. He took a look at the sun's position and calculated that he and Brownie would be back at Fall River in time for the evening rise. Maybe he'd catch a couple of trout and see if the cook at the Pioneer Inn would fry them up for him.

The next morning, he took a little extra care in brushing his uniform and wiping his boots before going downstairs. He thought about Doris all through breakfast, looking at the empty chair across the table. The waitress heard him let out a little sigh and asked if she could bring him a bromo. He didn't have much of an appetite — two slices of scrapple, two fried eggs, and a pancake were enough — and when he had finished he decided to have only one more cup of coffee, which he would take out to the porch to enjoy in the cool mountain air. As luck would have it, however, he had no sooner selected a chair when a pair of vacationing matrons came chirruping up to him. One was holding her box Brownie camera in both hands like she was making an offering of it.

"Oh, Ranger McIntyre! We're glad we found you! Would you mind if I took your picture standing next to Betty? For the folks back home, you know! They'll be thrilled to know we stayed in the same inn as a real ranger!"

Sure. Part of the job. Dutifully he put his coffee cup on a table and stood next to Betty with his arm around her shoulders. He had to lean down a little, since the top of her head only came about as high as the breast pocket of his tunic. Betty then took charge of the camera and snapped pictures while the ranger stood next to her companion.

Later on while he was walking toward the livery stable by way of the camera shop, he was accosted again. This time it was a farmer from Illinois who wanted a picture of his wife and kids standing next to a real honest-to-god ranger. McIntyre had a friend who was a Mountie with the Royal Canadian Mounted Police, out of Calgary, and he said it happened to him all the time.

"It's like those characters in London, the palace guards," the Canadian said. "People see a ranger or a Mountie in uniform and they can't resist asking him to pose for pictures. I bet they'd never think of going up to a New York cop and asking him to pose, would they?"

At the camera shop, Kaplan couldn't add

153

anything to what he had already told Mc-
Intyre about the one-handed man. The man
had told Kaplan he used a tripod. He said
it was difficult to hold the camera with one
hand. Otherwise he was just an ordinary
man dressed in ordinary clothes. Didn't say
where he was staying. Kaplan didn't know
whether he had a car. He didn't know the
man's name, either.

"Tell me," McIntyre said. "When you sell
a camera, you keep a record of the serial
number?"

"Of course. Some of the manufacturers
even require me to mail the numbers to
them, along with the name and address of
the buyer. See that card file by the cash
register? Every camera's listed in there.
Date, name of buyer, price, serial number,
everything."

"You think most camera stores do that?"

"Sure. They'd be stupid not to. Suppose a
client comes in with a broken camera, some
part that failed. Wants me to fix it for free. I
look it up and if it's one of mine, sure. But
if I didn't sell it, I'll need to charge them
for the fix."

"Okay. Well, thanks, Mr. Kaplan. If the
one-handed man comes in again, maybe you
could let me know? Maybe leave a phone
message at the Pioneer Inn. Or call the park

154

office. They always seem to know where to find me."

"Will do."

McIntyre walked across the street and up the block to the livery stable to see if the hostler remembered anything else about the man with one hand.

"As a matter of fact," the hostler said, "he was here again this morning."

"Driving? Did he have a car?"

"No. He was walking. I got the idea he's lodging here in town. Anyway, he wanted to know if he rented one of our horses, how long it would take to ride to somewhere that was really secluded. You know, a remote place people don't go to."

"What did you tell him?"

"I told him since the stable's in the middle of town, our trails aren't secluded. More like public paths. Most of our customers take the guided trail ride with one of our wranglers. Either that or they maybe ride up Boulder Creek a ways. In the case of your man with one hand, I told him I thought his best bet might be to head east from here along Thompson River and bushwhack his way up Mount Pisgah. Nothing but forest there. Of course, it's dry as hell, no creeks or lakes up there, which is why nobody goes there. Or, I told him, if it was

155

me, I might go north on the Devil's Gulch road. I'd cut west at Little Creek and follow it up into Black Canyon. You know that country. A man could go up Black Canyon, maybe cut across the high ridge to Arrowhead Lake."

"But he didn't rent one of your horses?"

"Nah. Said he might come back another time when he could plan an early start. Said he needed to go to the store and buy groceries."

McIntyre thanked the hostler and walked up the street toward the village's only grocery. It must have been his day to be a walking advertisement for the park service: halfway to the grocery store he was accosted by another pair of vacationing ladies. This time they were schoolteachers and they had a Brownie camera with them. Each one had to have her picture taken beside the tall ranger in his uniform.

At the store, McIntyre found his favorite cashier/owner on duty.

"Hi, Mabel," he said.

"Well! Look who's come down out of the woods! My Murphy will be glad to know you're here in town."

"I don't see him anywhere. What's he doing, cutting meat in the back room? Or have you got him stocking shelves?" McIntyre asked.

"Oh, lord no! That'd be too much like work for Murphy. He's got a terrible allergy to it, you know. And it is a lot of work, making sure the shelves are stocked all the time. We've thought of going back to the old setup and forget about this help-yourself kind of store. It's lots easier to have customers come up to the counter and ask for what they want and you hand it to them. Anyway, to answer your question, Murphy's not here. He's gone up to the National Park to poach government fish. I think he went to Beaver Meadows. That's why he'd be glad to know you're here in town."

"Mabel, you're terrible. But tell me now: has there been a man in here this morning, a man with only one hand?"

"Has been, and is. Wasn't he among the canned goods a minute ago? I'd say he's over there in the baking goods now."

"Hand me one of those shopping baskets, will you?"

Mabel lifted a wire basket over the counter and gave it to McIntyre. He moved toward the baking supplies, grabbing a few items from shelves as he went to make it look like he'd been shopping.

The man was there, kneeling down to look

at the bags of cornmeal on a bottom shelf. McIntyre pretended interest in a high shelf. He took down a box, put it back again, and gave an audible sigh that caused the one-handed man to look at him.

"Never can remember," McIntyre said aloud. "Thought I'd bake some biscuits. Can't remember if it's baking soda you use, or baking powder."

The one-handed man stood up.

"Powder, I think," he said. "But I'm not much of a baker either."

"You, too, huh?"

"Sometimes there's a recipe on the flour sack. Or on the baking whatever box. Try looking on the back of that Clabber Girl can there. Maybe there's a recipe."

"Good idea," McIntyre said, reaching for the can. "Thanks. You a visitor in our fair city? Haven't seen you around. Not that I'm in town that often."

"Yes. Trying to escape the rat race, if you know what I mean. Matter of fact, maybe you could help me figure out where I should go."

"Sure," McIntyre said, tapping his finger on his badge. "It's part of my job. National Park Service."

"Right. The uniform gives you away."

McIntyre laughed.

"What can I help with?"

"Isolation," said the man with one hand. "I want to rent a horse and find a really remote spot where I won't see anybody else. Maybe a little lake, or a mountain top with a view. I'd like to be alone and I'd like to take pictures. Problem seems to be that I'd have to have a trailer to haul a horse to the right trailhead. Or else hire a horse from one of those expensive lodges in the park. But I can't afford it. I'm staying in a room I found in a private home. Over on Riverside Drive."

"Let me think," McIntyre said. "I wish I had one of our park maps with me. Anyway, north of town you'll find Devil's Gulch road. If you take that road to Glen Haven, that's a little settlement about eight or ten miles down the canyon, you'll find a livery stable. Reasonable prices. From there you could ride up the North Fork to either Lost Lake or Deserted Village. Old mining town that failed. Or instead of driving down to Glen Haven you could turn off before the road starts down the canyon, which is maybe two miles out of town, and drive into the Maguire Ranch. They'll rent you a horse and you could ride to Bridal Veil Falls, maybe beyond that up to timberline."

"Sounds good."

"Or, if you don't mind hiking, both of those are good for a one-day hike," McIntyre suggested.

"I walk to work all the time, back home," the one-handed man said. "Back in Chicago. When I can find work, that is. Nobody in the damn town will hire a one-hand man."

"Then you could hike if you wanted to," McIntyre said. "You'd be surprised at the number of people who sit in an office all year and then think they can come and do a ten-mile climb up a mountain. But if you're used to walking you should be able to hike to Bridal Veil Falls or Arrowhead Lake with no problem."

McIntyre kept up the pretense of shopping by taking things from shelves, putting most of them back. If this man was the killer, he was certainly a cool customer. McIntyre watched how the man kept the shopping basket hung on his stub arm as he took down cans of soup or boxes of cereal and read the labels. The stub could explain how Varna was killed. It would be hard for a one-armed man to strangle a victim, but it was conceivable that a strong man could hold her down with the stub arm and smother her with the other hand, maybe using a jacket to suffocate her with. Or a car robe.

160

"How do you like Chicago? To live in, I mean."

The one-armed man snorted.

"Hate it. I'm only living there because of the government. My wartime disability. I have to take any job the veterans' office tells me to take."

"At least you can walk to work," McIntyre said. "Me, I either live at the ranger station or have to drive every day. Funny, huh? A ranger who has to drive everywhere he goes?"

"I gotta car. Don't use it much. Damn traffic."

"I heard it's easy to move around in Chicago without a car," McIntyre said. "A guy told me there's good trains, busses, streetcars."

The one-armed man snorted again and slammed a can of soup into his shopping basket.

"Never use 'em, those streetcars" he said angrily. "They're full of those damn women who wear short skirts and call themselves flappers. They reek with their damn perfume, always rubbing up against a man on crowded trolleys, always laughing at other people, staring at people. Where the hell are the good women? Not that any decent woman would be seen dead with a disabled veteran, but they all wear these little short skirts and stupid high heels and those goofy buckets on their heads and they talk all the damn time. I'd rather walk."

"Can't be that bad," McIntyre said.

The two men had worked their way back along the shelves to the front of the store. It was time for McIntyre to either check out or find an excuse to stay.

"Hah. A lot you know," the man with one hand said. "You live here, where there's lots of country. You can take yourself away from them. Me, I've got 'em living in flats over my head and under my feet. And a damn German across the hall. Another reason not to ride those streetcars. Cars fill up with damn Germans. Oh, they claim to be displaced or claim to be Jews or claim they always lived here before the war but they're still Germans. They cook their food and it stinks, they rub against you in the cars and their clothes stink. Their breath stinks, ever notice that? Anyway, that's why I walk to work. Good exercise, too."

He stepped in front of McIntyre and put his basket on the checkout counter. After he had paid Mabel for the groceries he turned back to the ranger with what could have been mistaken for a smile in anyone else. He was a bitter man.

162

"Thanks for the tip," he said. "I'll find me a map and see about those places. I'd like to hike to that waterfall. What'd you say it was named? Something about a wedding?"

"Bridal Veil Falls," McIntyre said as he set down his own basket. "You can get yourself a map at the park supervisor's new office. It's there where Riverside Drive joins High Drive. Probably not far from where you're staying."

After the man left the store McIntyre lingered to explain to Mabel that he didn't want to buy all the groceries he had collected. Affable soul that she was, she set the shopping basket under the counter and said she would put the things back on the shelves as soon as she had time.

"That's another problem with this helpy-selfy grocery idea. People come to the counter with items they can't afford or don't need and I have to put them back on the shelves," she said. "That guy's a sourpuss character, isn't he?"

"He seems bitter. Probably the war made him that way."

"Is that how he lost his hand? What did he do in the war?"

"Didn't ask him."

"And what kind of job can a man do with one hand?"

"Something in Chicago. I didn't ask him where he worked."

"What's his name? Is he traveling alone?"

"I don't know."

Mabel shook her head and looked up at the tall ranger as if he was a species of exotic animal being exhibited in a cage.

"McIntyre," she said. "One of these days I want to go home with you."

"Your husband wouldn't like that," he said.

"I know, but I'd sure like to see which planet you live on. If a woman spent five minutes talking with that man, she'd know everything there was to know about him."

Back on the street, McIntyre watched the one-armed man walk away. There was one thing he would like to know: what did he do in the war? Any veteran can tell you that you don't up and ask a stranger whether he killed anyone or saw anyone killed. If they bring it up on their own, fine: if they mention combat experiences first, it means they're okay with the memories, however bad those memories might be. But if a man's mind had been twisted by combat and you ask him what he did in the war it could quickly set him off. He might clam up or he might start to rage and say all kinds of strange and incoherent things. For most

164

men, the war had been bad. Very bad.

McIntyre was still curious, though. In his experience, a veteran might not be able to shake off the pain and trauma of being in combat and go back to living as he had lived before the war. Some ex-soldiers kept looking for the enemy everywhere they went. Some became very quiet and didn't talk to anyone. Even worse, some began to silently drink alone.

McIntyre had started up the street when an idea made him turn into the nearest shop, which happened to be the shoe repair place. Mr. Vinter was in the back, hunched over a noisy huge sewing machine. He looked up when McIntyre came in, but didn't take his hands off of the shoe he was holding under the needle.

"Phone?" McIntyre yelled over the noise of the machinery.

Vinter nodded toward the tiny desk against the wall.

"Thanks!"

He gave the operator the number and after a moment or two a pleasant voice answered.

"Rocky Mountain National Park, Supervisor's Office."

"Dottie? This is McIntyre. Any messages?"

"No, nothing."

"I need you to do me a favor," he said.

"Okay. What?"

"A man might be coming in to pick up a map of the park. A man with one hand missing. And I need to warn you that he doesn't like women very much."

"Doesn't like women? Does he like fishing?"

"He didn't mention it, no."

"He's not a friend of yours, then?"

"You're a real hoot today. Listen. If he comes in, try to find out his name. And anything else you can find out about him, like what he does for a living, where he's staying, that kind of thing. I know he's from Chicago. We might want to know where he works. The name of the company."

"Is he a veteran?" Dottie asked. "Supervisor Nicholson lets us give veterans a complimentary car pass to the park, but they have to furnish their name and address and the name of their military unit. And their car registration number."

"That'd be perfect!" McIntyre said. "Could save me lots of time."

"More time to go fishing?" she replied. "A tourist came in this morning and said the trout were biting over on the St. Vrain. Said he caught three lunkers in five minutes."

"Dottie, it would take a cruel and sadistic

woman to tell me that."

"Goodbye, Ranger."

CHAPTER 7

McIntyre hung up the phone. He looked over at Mr. Vinter, still hunched over the clattering machine, concentrating hard on the stitching of a boot. Vinter probably wouldn't mind one more phone call.

"Number, please?"

"Oh-Eight-Oh-R-Four."

"One moment."

"Fall River Station."

"Jamie? McIntyre. Everything okay up there? I'm stuck here in town awhile."

"Been a more or less normal day here. Had a climber stuck yesterday evening, up on Hallett's Peak. But he was lucky. By coincidence a bunch of guys from the Colorado Mountaineering Club were practicing rock climbing at Bear Lake. They went and got him down."

"Good. They just happened to be there, huh?"

"It's gettin' to where there's people everywhere. You find a car parked on the road, owner might be up Hallett's or hiking the Mummy Range, y' never know. A guy could be way the heck and gone back in Forest Canyon and he'd run into a farmer from Kansas."

"I'll have to agree with you," McIntyre said. "Anything else to report?"

"Minnie March phoned for you. From Fall River Lodge? Seems like that snooty woman is back again. But not at the lodge. Minnie's breakfast cook, Howard, he said he overheard a couple of guests talking about running into her at Chasm Falls. According to Minnie, another couple at the next table, they said they'd seen her up there, too, a real standoffish kind of woman, expensive clothes, wandering around Chasm Falls like she was looking for something. One couple saw her on a Tuesday, the other couple saw her there on Wednesday. One more guest chimed in and said he'd seen her, too, only two more days after that. At least that's what Howard told Minnie."

"She's not staying at the lodge?"

"Minnie says not. But a few lodge guests have spotted her."

"You say Howard's back cooking at the lodge again?" McIntyre said. "The guy who makes those walnut and cinnamon waffles?

Makes his own sausage?"

"That's the guy."

"Maybe I'd better look into this," Mc-Intyre said. He could already taste the waffles and smell the maple syrup. "Anything else? Anyone been hanging around out in the moraine meadow?"

"I told the boys to keep a lookout, like you said. The other day they're emptying the trash can at the parking area. Where everybody stops to look at the elk herd? They seen a rider on a horse moving back and forth way out there in the willows, but couldn't tell who it was. Too far away."

The clattering racket of the sewing machine stopped abruptly. Mr. Vinter looked up and seemed startled to see the ranger still there, leaning on the small desk and speaking into the telephone.

"Gotta go," McIntyre told Jamie. "I think Vinter wants his phone back. By the way, I located the one-handed man and talked to him. Strange guy. He needs a friend, is what he needs. I think maybe he got a little shell shock from being in combat. But he says he only wants to be left alone."

"Tell him good luck with that. The park seems to be full of people tryin' to be alone with each other."

"See you later," McIntyre said.

McIntyre rang off and thanked Mr. Vinter. Vinter looked none too happy about having the U.S. Government use his business phone like a police call box.

As long as he was near the post office, the ranger decided to pick up the mail. Which involved walking across the Thompson River bridge. Which led him to notice that two or three particularly fine trout were surface feeding in a wide rill down-current from where kids had constructed a little stone jetty. He looked at his watch. He looked at the sky to judge how much time would be left before the sun dropped behind the mountain. He might have time to hurry back to his room at the inn, change out of uniform, make a few casts into that rill, and still be back at the inn in time for supper. The cook's evening special was going to be stuffed pork chops.

Tomorrow, maybe Howard's walnut and cinnamon waffles. And homemade sausage. He'd make an early start in the morning and see if Howard and Minnie could tell him anything else about the snooty woman who kept hanging around Chasm Falls.

As he had hoped, McIntyre found Minnie in the kitchen enjoying her early dawn breakfast at the little table outside the chef's

171

office. Chef Howard was already hard at work, going about his morning preparations with a kind of grim and determined efficiency. Minnie was one of those people who liked to be up with the sun long before any guests came in for breakfast, even before the waitresses and busboy. She invited the ranger to sit down and try Howard's waffles.

"Pour yourself a cup of coffee first," she said.

Never one to refuse a lady, McIntyre complied. Minnie looked him up and down as he selected a mug from the shelf. She couldn't figure out how McIntyre managed to stay slim, the way he liked to eat. This morning he looked a little different than usual: the riding pants, tailored green tunic and knee-high riding boots were the same, but today he was wearing a Sam Browne belt with a pistol holster. The butt of a Colt revolver showed under the holster's flap.

"You're back to wearing a gun," Minnie said. "Going hunting for the murderer? Or is it in case you find a chipmunk with a broken leg and need to shoot it?"

"I guess I'm supposed to find a murderer and arrest him," McIntyre said. "Supervisor Nicholson says I'm a cop now. It's my reward for solving that so-called 'accident' case last summer. And let's not overlook the case of the missing trash barrel. Nicholson thinks I'm Sherlock Holmes. Sheriff Crowell, he's doing what he can, of course. But the sheriff is nervous about whether his jurisdiction extends into federal land."

"Does it?"

"Nobody knows. The park is too new to have any precedents. The way it stands now, I can legally detain a person for the sheriff, but the sheriff has to make the arrest."

"How long can you detain them? Twenty-four hours? Legally, I mean."

"I don't know."

"Some cop. Here, have a waffle."

The waffles and sausage were warm and mouth-watering, every bit as good as he had imagined, and when it came to food McIntyre had a very keen imagination.

"Tell me what you heard about our mystery woman," McIntyre said.

Minnie handed her empty plate to a busboy who was passing by on his way to work. She leaned her elbows on the table. *When Mike was alive,* McIntyre thought, *she must have sat that way with him many, many mornings. Sharing early breakfast before starting a long day of keeping guests happy. Planning what they would do that day, maybe planning what to do once the tourist season was over. They had made a darn good couple, those two.*

"Like I told Jamie Ogg," Minnie said, "it started with a couple of dining room conversations about this rich-looking lady hanging around Chasm Falls. I knew you'd be interested. I kind of made a point of asking others about her. Often — not all the time — guests tell the front desk where they're headed when they leave for a day. We like to keep track in case there's a telephone message. Or in case they don't return when expected and might be stuck somewhere. Anyhow, the day book showed several couples had gone up to Chasm Falls. Next time I saw them I asked them about it. Interviewed them, like you would."

"Good work. Maybe you ought to wear the uniform."

"No thanks. I'm allergic to neckties. And guns."

Minnie reached into her pocket and brought out a slip of paper.

"I wrote down the dates people saw her, see here? She was there at Chasm Falls every day for four days. After that, nobody saw her again. Two of the people had seen her with a camera on a tripod taking pictures of the pool at the base of the falls, and two others who saw her thought they'd

174

caught a glimpse of a horse tied back in the trees. Oh, and one thought she heard a horse whinny but didn't see it."

"You'd still make a good detective," McIntyre said, impaling the last bite of waffle with his fork.

"Shucks. If you run a place like this," Minnie said, waving her hand to indicate the size of the lodge, "you're just naturally interested in people. Everybody who comes through here has a story. You see it in lots of little things they do. Like for example the guest we had last summer who wouldn't use the bureau in his room. The maids told me he stacked his clothing in tidy little piles, one for each day. Shirt, pants, underwear for the day, five, maybe six days' worth stacked in separate piles around the room. There's a story there, I bet."

McIntyre pushed back the chair and rose to his feet. He used his napkin to dust the front of his tunic before folding it neatly and setting it down. The powdered sugar Howard put on his waffles showed up something awful on a dark green uniform.

"Tim!" Minnie said. "How many times have I told you? If you're going to eat here you need to learn not to fold your napkin when you're finished. Leave it crumpled up so we know it's been used and needs to go into the laundry basket."

"Sorry," he said. He hung his head and tried to look like a contrite schoolboy being reprimanded. Had he succeeded in accomplishing such a look, it would have been a considerable accomplishment for a six-foot tall ranger wearing a uniform and a .45 caliber revolver.

McIntyre's next stop was at the lodge livery stable. Tom, the hostler who had been with Minnie and Mike ever since they built the lodge, was sitting in the morning sun repairing a bridle.

"Yeah," he said in answer to McIntyre's question. "Matter of fact, I did see that woman. Nice-lookin' lady but cold as ice."

"Did she have a horse? Or was she here to hire one?"

"Dunno. She didn't ask about no hirin'. I didn't see no horse, but the funny thing is, she was dressed up in ridin' pants and boots. Plus, she wasn't carryin' nothin' but a little shoulder purse. She had no coat or anythin'. It was like she'd left her stuff somewhere. Well, I figured she had a room here at the lodge, but I asked her and she said she didn't. Thinkin' about it later on, I thought she might've come in on a horse but left it someplace, see?"

"Or maybe she had a car?" McIntyre suggested.

"Dunno. I was workin' and looked up and there she was," Tom said.

"Did she talk to you? What did she want?"

"That's another funny thing. She had one of your maps with her. Wanted to know about the Lawn Lake trail. How far it was, what was up there, stuff like that. Dunno why she didn't go down to the entrance station and ask you guys. Anyway, when I told her about Lawn Lake and that ol' shelter cabin up there she acted very interested. In the shelter cabin, I mean. Oh, and I told her how a body could go on up from Lawn Lake and find Little Crystal Lake. Told her how it's such a small lake and how there's no trees since it sits above timberline so hardly nobody goes there."

"That doesn't seem too odd," McIntyre said. "You said it was a funny thing. Asking about a trail to a lake, that's not unusual."

"Wait a minute. I'm comin' to the good part. Remember, she's a lightweight, looks like she spent her time all indoors. You know those ads in the magazines showin' a woman in a tight evening dress posing next to an expensive car and smokin' a cigarette in a holder? She could pose for those. Classy, see? She ain't no woods-woman, for sure.

But what does she ask me? Why, she points to Lawn Lake on her map and says 'what's up north of there?' to me. She wanted to know all kind of details about what's beyond the lake. Hell, nobody goes beyond the lake, 'cept to go up to Little Crystal Lake. But anyways I told her how she could turn east over the ridge once she got to Lawn there and she'd find Potts Puddle and could follow the creek from there all the way down past Arrowhead Lake, or else cross Baum's Ridge and she'd end up ridin' down Willow Creek and eventually come to Bridal Veil Falls. But we're talkin' a two-, three-day ride. And a tough one at that."

"Anything else?"

"Lemme think. No, 'cept she wanted details. Oh, and she was interested again when I told her there's another shelter cabin at Arrowhead. You know the one that some gold miner built, only there's no gold up there? Had me tell her all about it, how it's small, has a low roof, made of stone instead of logs, that kind of stuff like she was gonna draw a picture of it."

According to the hostler, the mystery woman had asked him to describe landmarks along the route and marked them on her map. Every question she asked made him believe that she was planning to make

178

that long ride up to Lawn Lake and keep going until she ended up miles and miles from the National Park. She had thanked him and she walked away and as far as Tom or Minnie or anyone else could discover, that was the last that was seen of her.

"I thought you said you'd be buying me lunch," Jamie Ogg said.

Ranger McIntyre put the sardine can key over the little metal tab and rolled back the lid.

"I did," he said. "There's the bread, help yourself, and we've got a wee pot of mustard, plus lovely cold cuts, even a bottle of soda pop for you. And didn't I buy it all? Have a sardine. There's no forks, so you'll have to use your pocket knife."

The ranger stretched out his legs and relaxed against the back wall of the grocery store. The rustic bench and table were out of sight of the street, but faced the trout stream. Mabel and Murphy and the grocery employees sat there during their work breaks.

The rustic picnic table carried a memory for him, a memory of the day he had fallen in love on that very spot. She was on her break, and the table is where they first met. The next day he began teaching her how to fly fish in the stream behind the store. She shrieked when a trout broke the surface and grabbed her fly.

"Jamie, would you look at these surroundings," McIntyre said. "Better than being in some ol' café. It's God's own day out here. Not a cloud in the sky nor a breath of a breeze. Grand day to be alive, Jamie, grand day. Now, I need to ask you if you found out . . ."

"Aha! Here's where our government pays you loafers to hang out!"

The light feminine voice came from the corner of the building. It was Doris Killian.

"Doris!" McIntyre exclaimed, hurrying to untangle his boots and stand up.

"I was just telling young Jamie here that this day could not be any better, and here you show up out of the blue! Come on, sit down and share our sardines and mustard."

"Oh, thanks!" she said sweetly, seating herself at the picnic table, "but I'd rather eat a raw trout whole than put a sardine in my mouth. Or maybe I'd rather starve. How can you eat those things, and how do you do it without dripping oil on your uniform?"

Ranger McIntyre looked down at his dark green tunic to see if there were any spots. He shrugged his shoulders.

"I thought you were stayin' out in Wild

Basin," Jamie said.

"I am," she said. "I needed supplies, though, and I wanted to drop off my exposed film and buy new rolls."

"Taking lots of pictures?" McIntyre asked.

"Hundreds!" she said. "Every day, in every kind of wonderful light you can imagine. Twice now I've camped right next to a waterfall so I could photograph it in first light of morning."

"Then . . . you're nearly through? You've got enough pictures?"

"I hope I'm not through! I just want to keep going on and on. The further I go, following each little stream or creek, the more little waterfalls I find. Plus, I might not have the financing to ever spend this much time again. I can never be sure my photos will bring in enough money to come back next summer. I need a bunch of truly sensational shots. You don't have any more dead bodies, I don't suppose?"

McIntyre smiled that certain smile. At a recent church potluck supper, a cluster of females had pronounced it a "lovely" smile.

"Doris, if only we'd known you were coming!" he said. "But we're fresh out of corpses and there's no place to find any on such short notice. Unless the guys at the icehouse are storing a body we don't know about.

Jamie had a rock climber hung up in his own ropes on Hallett's Peak, but the mountain club guys went and rescued him before he died of exposure. Had we known you were coming, we could have left him hanging there so you could take his portrait."

"That would be a good opportunity," Doris said.

"Do you mind if we . . ." McIntyre said, indicating the meat and sardines and bread.

"Oh, not at all. I've had my lunch. You two go ahead and eat your sardines while they're . . . uh . . . fresh? But tell me about the murder case? Is it solved? Did Jamie find the vital clue and tie up all the loose ends?"

"Jamie? This young dowser? Tie up loose ends? He can hardly tie up his necktie, let alone a complicated mystery like this is."

"Bring me up to date," she said.

To McIntyre it was as if she had never been gone, as if he had always known her. It wasn't anything like the time he had fallen in love, of course. That was different. With his first love, his only true love, the very moment when they met it was like they had always known that they would. By the third time they met it was like two spirits rushing to hug one another, laughing with parted lips, each one bringing a bright spark to the

182

eyes of the other. It wasn't like that with Doris, although it made his heart smile to have her back where he didn't need to worry about her. And it seemed natural for her to be there, as if this kind of encounter happened between them every day, or should happen every day, Doris with graceful fingers reaching and tearing off a piece of bread, Doris taking up his bottle to steal a sip of his soda pop.

"Okay," he said.

Brilliant way to begin a conversation, he thought.

"Okay, let's see if I can remember what happened after you toddled off to Wild Basin. Paul Barrow, over at the stables on Mills Creek, he saw our mystery woman, the snooty one. Thinks she was wearing a wig. Apparently, she said something to make him think she carried a gun. Which reminds me: how can you tell if a woman's wearing a wig, anyway? Do you ever wear one?"

"Sure, I've got a wig. A nice one. Once in a while, a girl wants to look like a dark-haired flapper, you know, for a wild evening at a dance. Not that any park ranger ever invites a visiting lady *to* a dance."

"Hey! There haven't been any dances . . ."

Her light laugh cut him off.

"I'm kidding you, you kid!" she said, quot-

183

ing a popular song. "I guess the giveaway on whether a woman's wearing a wig would be the hairline. Especially over the forehead. Probably it would look too straight, too abrupt maybe. Or the color would look too even, too consistent. What else happened with this mystery woman?"

"Well, Barrow rented her a horse. Later on, she turned up at Fall River Lodge, asking the hostler about the trail up to Lawn Lake and beyond."

"Beyond?" Doris reached for another hunk of their bread and took another sip from McIntyre's bottle of pop.

"This is going to sound corny," McIntyre explained, "but the high country beyond Lawn Lake looks like another world. No trails to speak of. Keep riding north and eventually you'd drop into another river system, another drainage entirely. Heavy woods, old ponderosas. If you've got a good map and compass, you could find your way to where two different creeks run east. If you followed the first one you'd end up at Arrowhead Lake. Or if you went on over that high ridge and down the next creek you'd come to Bridal Veil Falls. You'd be six or seven miles from the nearest ranch, which is a long way off the Devil's Gulch road. I've done that ride myself, up from

Lawn Lake and down to Devil's Gulch. Took me three days and I kept moving at a steady clip. But it's rough, rough country. Risky for a lone person."

"Especially risky for a mere woman, would you say?"

"I would, if one weren't sitting where she could kick me in the shins."

"You wouldn't want me to kick you and smudge your shiny boots?"

"In truth," Jamie Ogg volunteered, "there's times in that country where your physical strength's all you got. If you ever climbed up a steep ridge with the scree crumbling under you, pulling a horse along by the reins, you know what I mean. For instance."

"Any more clues show up while I was gone?" Doris asked, skirting the issue.

"The family of our Chasm Falls victim, Ernst Snyder, says they don't think the fishing stuff belonged to him. The family thinks he was having an illicit affair and that's why he was in Estes Park alone in the first place. To meet her."

" 'Illicit affair'? What kind of books do you read, anyway?"

McIntyre ignored it. With the long winters, a man read whatever he could find. Usually dime novels left at campgrounds by tourists. Dottie often gave him books, but they were the kind she said he "needed to read" and so naturally he didn't. If he did, he didn't tell Dottie.

"I found the one-handed man," the ranger said. "He's a bitter war veteran looking for a remote place in the mountains where he can be all alone. But you know what? I don't think he would even be happy if he found it. I think he hangs around town in hopes that somebody will notice him. Maybe somebody might show interest in his story, you know?"

"What is his story? How did he lose his hand?"

"Didn't ask him."

"There you go again!" Doris said. "You men! You do deserve a prize, do you know that? I would love to know what two men do talk about."

"Tell about the mystery rider of Moraine meadows," Jamie suggested.

"Right," McIntyre said. "There's a hermit who lives on the ridge above the meadows. He spotted a person on a horse riding back and forth on a couple of the trails there. And they rode in and out of the willows like they were waiting to intercept another rider. Or maybe a hiker. It wouldn't seem too strange, except that I think that's what happened to Varna."

"Varna?"

"The other victim."

"Oh, right."

"Anyway, she might have been a random choice. A girl alone, heading into a place where few people go. Maybe the same horseman was down in the meadow waiting for another chance to kill somebody, see?"

"Ugh!" Doris said. "You make me glad I'm staying miles away from there!"

"Still," he said, "I want you to keep on your toes. Try to stay out of harm's way."

"I will. Although I'm intrigued by the name of Bridal Veil Falls. When I'm done with Wild Basin, if I have any time left, I might go and take photos of these falls. Or this fall. Whichever it is, fall or falls."

"It's one fall of water. Maybe I can go with you," McIntyre said. "Oh, and speaking of your photo article, there's another thing."

"What?"

"A theory. Or maybe just a kind of feeling. I feel like these two dead people were connected with photography. I think there was a camera tripod at the Cub Lake site that left pointy marks in the ground. Don't know. Like I said, it's a feeling."

McIntyre stood up, put the leftover cheese

and the little jar of mustard into his haversack, tossed the sardine tin and paper sack into the trash can, cast a lingering look at the river, and turned to give Jamie instructions.

". . . and if you have time, why don't you make a trip to Fall River Lodge and find out if anyone's seen our mystery woman lately. I'd like to know where she's been living. I'm going to check with the Livingstone Hotel and the two little hotels here in town. Maybe I'll ask Dottie to phone anybody who rents rooms in the village. Mabel thinks the woman came in for groceries, but it was her day off and Murphy only had a vague memory of a dark-haired woman who didn't talk. I'm going to check with the camera store next and the outfitters. If you hear anything, phone Dottie. I'll check in at the S.O. from time to time."

"If you're going to Kaplan's camera store," Doris said, "I'll tag along. I need to pick up a few rolls of film."

Fresh lettering a foot high on one of Kaplan's front windows advertised UNIQUE NATIONAL PARK VIEWS. The other window offered CUSTOM DEVELOPING AND PRINTING. When Doris and McIntyre entered, Doris gave an involuntary

188

start to see Mr. Kaplan with the one-handed man. Most of the shock came from seeing the way the man pointed at a mounted photograph on the wall, using the arm without a hand on it as a pointer.

"I like that one," the one-handed man was saying. "Where's that building?"

"Place called Arrowhead Lake. Used to call it Knife Lake, 'cause it's long and narrow. According to the story, there was an old prospector who built it because he'd found gold up there. Nobody knows why he went to the trouble to make it all out of stone. Once there was a rumor that the old boy had quarried a mine tunnel into the side of the mountain and used the rock to build the hut. But I've never seen such a mine. Never heard of anybody who has. The old stone cabin's a picturesque place, though. Isn't it?"

"You took that picture yourself?"

"Sure did," Kaplan said. "I took all the photographs you see here."

The one-armed man went on looking at the photo while Kaplan excused himself to wait on the ranger and the lady photographer.

"No," he told McIntyre, "your snooty lady hasn't been here. Haven't seen her anywhere, but business has picked up and I've been too busy to go anywhere except here and the sandwich shop up the street."

Doris bought her film, sweetly said "no thanks" to Kaplan's repeated urgings that she try out his latest expensive camera, then joined McIntyre in perusing Kaplan's gallery of framed photography. She had to admit that his work was very good. Good enough to hang in one's living room. Most of his pictures were of granite crags and rocky promontories, and unusual man-made things such as the Arrowhead shelter and abandoned mining equipment and old log cabins.

The one-armed man came up to McIntyre with a folded map he had taken from his jacket pocket. He opened it with one hand and smoothed it out on Kaplan's counter.

"Can you show me this Arrowhead place, where it is?" he said.

"Sure," McIntyre said. "It's what you'd call out of the way. There was a good trail to it once upon a time, but half the sections have either washed away or been grown over with brush. The trail was probably built by the same miner who built the stone cabin, thinking he'd be hauling gold ore out. Except there isn't any gold anywhere around here. The trail is more of a game track, but it's usable."

"How do I find it?"

McIntyre borrowed a pencil from Kaplan and drew a line from a point on the north road up along a little line on the map, a line that represented Knife Creek.

"That's where it is," he said. "The trail more or less follows Knife Creek up to the lake. It's a small lake. More of a long pond in the creek. In Scotland they'd call it a glen loch. It's narrow enough that the fish have to line up and take turns turning around."

Nobody laughed at his joke. Which for McIntyre was an all too common experience.

"Much of a walk?"

"Once you find the trailhead, which is off the road a little ways, I'd say it would take you about three hours on foot. Maybe four. If it was me, I'd plan to stay overnight. But I suppose a man could walk there and back in a day. Here: I'll draw a circle around the trailhead to show you where to find it."

"Looks shorter from this other direction. What's the trail like if I went that way instead?"

"Much harder," McIntyre said. "You'd need to drive to the Lawn Lake trailhead across the road from Fall River Lodge. The Lawn trail is steep and has lots of switchbacks. Once you got to timberline you'd have to bushwhack over the ridge. And after reaching the top of the ridge you'd find it dangerously steep going down the other side. A real ankle-breaker of a slope. On the map, it does look shorter, but it's actually a lot longer because of going up and down the mountain. That'd be a rugged way to go."

"Thanks."

The one-armed man folded his map and left the shop. After McIntyre politely refused Kaplan's camera sales pitch one more time, Doris and the ranger took their leave.

"The man with one hand isn't much of a talker," Doris observed as they were walking down the street.

"Nope," McIntyre agreed.

"Doesn't seem to like people much," she said.

"I think it was the war," McIntyre said. "He seems like one of those men who are always looking to belong somewhere. Once you've been a soldier, especially if you came out wounded or missing a limb, you feel like you need to still be part of a unit somehow. You made your sacrifice, you paid your dues. If you're a good soldier you fit in with the group and you know your job and you know why you do it. But one day they discharge you and you find yourself out on

192

your own and you don't quite know what to do. I think he's like that. Plus, he's talked himself into believing that women don't want anything to do with a cripple. Add in his general hate for Germans and you've got a guy who's going to be lonely a lot."

"Are you speaking from experience?" Doris asked.

"About being lonely for the old outfit? Yeah, as a matter of fact, I know the feeling. When I got out, all I wanted to do was to keep flying airplanes with other guys. Three or four of my pals joined up with flying circus outfits or else found jobs flying the U.S. mail. But like our friend with one hand I wanted time alone, too. It was a lucky day when I happened into this job with the parks department. I'm back in uniform; I work alongside a bunch of other guys. And if I need to be alone I can head for the woods. I consider myself a fortunate guy."

Doris was thinking about asking McIntyre why he didn't seem to have any ambition to rise in the ranks, didn't want to try for a supervisor position. He could make a good salary as a chief in the enforcement division. He was smart, he had oodles of personality, and he had all the makings of a natural leader. She was trying to think how to put the question to him when an excited young voice called out.

"Ranger! Ranger!"

A chubby boy of about ten years came running across the street.

"Ranger! Wait a second!"

The boy caught up to them, panting for breath.

"Miss Killian," McIntyre said, putting his hand on the boy's shoulder, "meet Ned. Did you say you'd met his mother, Dottie? Up the hill at the supervisor's office? Ned's mom is the lady who keeps the National Park operating smoothly. Anyway, Ned, what's the trouble?"

"Hiya," Ned said to Doris. "Ranger, Mom sent me lookin' for you. Jamie called in and said he'd been up to the Beaver Point store and ran into Paul Barrow and he said if you were interested, that snooty woman come back and got herself a packhorse and you oughta go out to Mills Creek and talk to him."

"Talk to the horse?" McIntyre never could resist teasing Ned about grammar, since the boy's mother was very particular about it.

"Nah, to Mr. Barrow."

"Thanks, Ned. Anything else?"

The freckled boy looked at Doris as if he was trying to determine whether she could keep a secret.

"Well," he said in more of a whisper, "the brookies are rising on Little Creek. Old Bo says a caddis hatch started there yesterday. I'm tellin' you in case you need to check it out and want me to maybe ride along in your truck, see. I could run home for my rod and meet you at the S.O."

"Sounds tempting, Ned," the ranger said. "But I'd better drive out to Mills Creek instead and see what Barrow knows."

"And I," Doris said, "I'd like to get back to Wild Basin before dark. I'd better make a start. I'll be back again in a few days."

"I'll be waiting," McIntyre said.

When he got to the Rocky Mountain National Park Supervisor's Office, McIntyre found Dottie in a cheery mood. She always seemed cheery.

"I heard you got caught fishing while on duty," she said as he strode in.

"Yup," he said, tossing his ranger flat hat on the nearest chair. "There's a rumor that they're building a new national park up at the Arctic Circle in order to have somewhere to send people like me."

"Well, if I know you," Dottie said, "before too long you'd be harpooning whales instead of doing any actual work. Here, I got the information you wanted."

195

She pushed a printed form across the counter to him. The heading on the form was PARKS PASS — MILITARY VETERAN.

"Not much there," she said. "Prying information out of him was like trying to open one of those hard black nuts we used to find in our Christmas stockings."

She was right. According to the form, the man with one hand was named John O'Reilly, his home address was Chicago, he had served with the 2nd Army Machine Gun Battalion, and he received a medical discharge in December of 1918. And that was it. No other contact information, no occupation, no affiliation with veterans' groups.

"He told me he had already paid for a pass at the entrance station," Dottie said. "I refunded him his money. What he really wanted, though, was a map. One of the good ones with lots of topographic detail. I give them to people when they ask me where they should go fishing. I take my crayon and circle all your favorite fishing spots."

"I've said it before and I'll say it again. You're a mean, cruel woman."

Ranger McIntyre borrowed Dottie's phone and rang up Fall River Station.

Jamie's voice was unusually energized.

"What's going on?" McIntyre asked. "You sound like you won an Irish sweepstakes."

"Almost!" Jamie said. "Almost! Y' know that girl I've seen a couple of times? Wilma? If I can get a day off she and me are goin' to Denver, to Elitch Gardens for the day! Whatta you think of that? Say, it's a swell place to take a girl. Can I have a day off, you think?"

"I think you mean 'she and I.' What are she and you going to do, take the bus?"

"It's all fixed! One of the summer temps has a car, a good one. And a girlfriend. We drive down t' Denver in the morning, she and me in the back seat, see? Have a picnic lunch, listen to the music, walk around, look at the gardens, ride on a few of the rides. We'll have a long drive home maybe in the moonlight. Whatta you think?"

"Your job already entails walking a lot, eating outdoors most of the time, driving roads in a park, and for your day off you do the same thing?"

"You forgot the girl part. Plus, it's Elitch Gardens! Lots of stuff to do and see. Ride the carousel, take the girls to the penny arcade, lots of stuff."

"Fine, Jamie. Go ahead and go. But first, do you and I need to have a talk about the birds and bees? Before you go with this girl, I mean?"

"Heck no. I know all about bees. And I'll betcha I can name mostly all the kinds of birds we've got in the park."

"Okay, Jamie. I hope you have fun at Elitch Gardens. But back to business, Dottie says you saw Barrow? Has he seen our mystery lady again?"

Barrow had seen her, but that's all Jamie knew about it. Barrow hadn't said anything except to tell the ranger that he'd seen the woman again. McIntyre rang off and gave Dottie her phone back.

"What was all that about?" Dottie asked.

"Jamie and his pal are taking a couple of girls to Elitch Gardens on their day off."

"And he wanted your advice about women?"

"No. On my planet, guys don't talk about that stuff. A guy has to figure them out all by himself. Trial and error. It's kind of like learning to catch wildcats. Learn from your mistakes and keep bandages handy."

McIntyre left the S.O. and walked back up the street to the truck. Consulting his watch, he figured he had enough time to drive out to Mills Creek and find Barrow, but it might mean missing supper. Nuts! The brookies in Little Creek were rising and he might go to bed hungry. The things he sacrificed in the name of duty!

Paul Barrow was there all right, up to his boot tops in the never-ending task of cleaning up after the horses. When he saw McIntyre drive up, Barrow jammed the scoop shovel into the steaming pile of manure and went to meet the ranger by the tack room.

"Y' got my message," Barrows stated flatly.

"Thanks, yes," McIntyre said. "Our mystery woman showed up again?"

"Yep. Came ridin' in as bold as you please. Didn't have her car, had that horse this time. I figure she rode the creek trail to get here, leastways that's the direction she come from. Did you put out them cards for me like I asked?"

"Sure did," McIntyre said. "In the rack, right in front of the entrance station with the others. For people who want to know where to rent cabins and such."

"Okay. Say, maybe that's what Crazy Alice oughta do, hire Kaplan to make cards for your rack. She ain't had but four or five renters all summer, she says. 'Course she don't talk much."

"Alice? Alice Reader?"

"The same. The Wigwam Lodge lady."

"I completely forgot about her place," Mc-

Intyre said.

"Most people do. Prob'ly the way she wants it. If you federal boys don't remember she's there, you won't try to force her out."

"No danger of that, not until the park has more money to buy private land with. You and Alice, you're kinda two of a kind. Hermits. Or semi-hermits, at least. Like Leon Counter up there on his ridgetop."

"Yeah," Barrow said. "We're thinkin' of startin' a club or a union. Federation of Hermits, maybe."

"If I didn't know better, I'd swear you just made a joke," McIntyre said.

"I did."

"Like I said, I know better," McIntyre said. "Tell me about our mystery lady. What'd she want, for instance? Did she tell you a name or where she's staying?"

"She didn't say. But like I told you, wherever she's from, she knows her way around a horse. It's a pleasure to see her ride, not like these damn dudes who ride like they're tryin' to hump the saddle horn. Her clothes, like I told you, they look expensive. But the saddle, it's plain. Like it's a livery saddle, see? I tried t' see a brand on the horse, but I don't think it had one. If that animal was from a livery I think she'd been workin' with it. When she got down,

200

she dropped them reins t' the ground and she says 'stand!' all sharp-like and that mare, she stood there the whole time."

"What happened next?" McIntyre said.

"She rented a packhorse, didn't she? She chose that short-legged little gelding of mine, plus she went through my tack and picked out the best packsaddle and a good bridle herself. Oh, and she bought a picket rope off'n me, a forty-footer. I tell you, Ranger, when it comes to horse stuff that lady knows her cabbages."

"She say where she was headed next?" McIntyre asked.

"Well, she asked about all that wild country north of Lawn Lake. Oh, and waterfalls. Was there any high waterfalls up in that country. She'd heard about Arrowhead Lake and I told her Bridal Veil Falls was just acrost the mountain from Arrowhead. She asked did I have a tarp I'd sell her, but I didn't. My best guess? She's lookin' to explore up there, maybe even in the Mummy Range. Seems t' have more time than Noah had water and don't seem to be scared of goin' alone."

"Doesn't sound like it," McIntyre agreed. "You still think she's left-handed?"

"No doubt about it. I think she's got a gun, too."

"Oh? How do you know?"

"She asked me, 'is it legal to have a gun in the park?' and I said you're supposed t' take it to a ranger station and they put a government seal on it but nobody ever does."

The rest of Barrow's information was as sketchy as before. The woman was of average height, maybe an inch or two taller, physically fit, snooty attitude, talked like a teacher or a minister, dark hair, nice clothes. She didn't give her name or say where she was from.

McIntyre went away more mystified than when he had arrived. But he was relieved by Barrow's theory that she was going to explore the Mummy Range region: if the horsewoman was the killer, she wouldn't be likely to find any victims north of Lawn Lake. It was rough country, too rough for chubby German men or skinny city girls. And Doris was at Wild Basin, many miles away in the opposite direction.

CHAPTER 8

The next morning, Ranger McIntyre woke up thinking about Alice Reader and her Wigwam Lodge, a haphazard collection of rustic cabins hidden in the forest at the far edge of Moraine Park. Even the road to the place was hidden. While asking around the liveries and lodgings, he and Jamie had overlooked Alice's place. Alice had no use for the park service, hated anyone who looked like a "cop," and never shared with others. Nothing. Especially information. She kept her mouth shut tight as a Scotchman's purse.

Dragging information out of Alice would present a genuine challenge, even for McIntyre, who had a natural talent for engaging people. When he talked to working men, either journeymen who brought their families to the park, or the livery hostlers, or the hunkies who worked on the roads, they regarded him as an equal, a guy who understood them, a guy who had been in the war and who knew one end of a shovel from the other. Sure, he was a ranger, but by God he wasn't afraid to roll up his sleeves and pitch in to do the job. With lodge managers and businessmen, McIntyre seemed like a businessman in a green uniform, a shrewd administrator like themselves, a man who would listen to their woes about profit and loss and nod his head in somber sympathy. Sure, he worked for the government, but that young man understood how hard it was to make money these days.

As for the ladies, his height and good looks and uniform seemed to do the trick, mostly. For instance, the time when he spotted a tourist lady standing on top of her automobile and stretching up to paint her initials on a rock cliff beside the road. She had no sooner seen the flat hat, the tailored tunic, and the polished boots than she climbed down and meekly put her hands out as if expecting him to put her in handcuffs. Another afternoon two other ladies, elderly traveling companions, saw him standing in a pullout and stopped to confess to him that they had been collecting rock specimens along the road, which they assumed was illegal.

But Alice Reader, she would be a different

proposition altogether. McIntyre sat at the table by the window, looking out at the village, finishing his pancakes and thinking about the snappish woman in the isolated cabin camp. Maybe he could put on his fishing clothes and pretend to be fishing the river near Wigwam Lodge. Maybe pretend that he "happened" to drop in.

Nah. Miss Reader was way too smart to fall for that. No, he needed to find a good pretense, a logical pretext. It couldn't be "government business," since she was scared to death that the Department of Interior was going to seize her property for the park. Still, he had better show up at her place in uniform; he didn't want it to look like he was trying to fool her into thinking he wasn't a ranger. McIntyre looked down at his badge and remembered his last encounter with her. He had gone to Wigwam Lodge to tell her to stop burning trash piles when there was a high risk of starting a forest fire.

"Know what, Ranger?" she said, raising her old .30-30 rifle for him to see, "that shiny badge pinned on that dark coat of yours, it'd make a helluva nice target for ol' Winnie here. Stands out real good."

Winnie? Oh, "Winnie" the Winchester. To McIntyre's way of thinking there was something deeply dangerous about a woman who gave her deer rifle a name.

As he was leaving the inn McIntyre remembered Kaplan's camera shop up the street, and those advertising postcards he printed for local businesses. Like the ones he had made for Paul Barrow to stick in the rack at the entrance station. If Kaplan would give him a couple of samples and a list of prices, he could drive out to Wigwam Lodge and tell Alice Reader he had come to let her know about the card rack at the entrance station in case she'd like to have her cabins included. Maybe she would talk to him.

The little bell hanging over the door jingled as McIntyre entered the camera shop. But instead of Kaplan emerging from the back room it was the schoolboy Kaplan had hired for the summer.

"Can I help you?" the boy asked, looking at the badge and uniform.

"I wanted to see Mr. Kaplan about publicity postcards. Is he around?"

"No, sir. He took the day off and he's up to his house gettin' ready to take a camping trip. Me and Mrs. Kaplan, we're the only ones here."

"Well, that's okay," the ranger said. "You know those advertising cards he makes? Any chance I could have a couple of samples? I might know a cabin camp owner who'd be interested in ordering a batch."

"Sure!" the boy said. "I know where he keeps them. They're right over here in a box."

He handed McIntyre four of the postcards.

"That be enough? Anything else?"

"I guess that's it," the ranger said. "Mr. Kaplan's off to photograph more mountain views? You said he was going camping."

"Yeah! I guess a customer was talking about Bridal Veil Falls the other day. And they talked about Arrowhead Lake, too — that's the lake in that photo on the wall over there — and he said he'd like to head up there and do some fresh new pictures. Different angles, that kind of stuff."

"I see. Are you learning the business, or is this a summer job for you?"

"Both, kind of," the boy said. "I'd like to learn all about it, the developing and printing and all. I got my own camera. Mr. Kaplan, he thinks there's money to be made in photography. Heck, just the other day, the same day he decided to go to Arrowhead, he said he got a telegram offering to buy views from him. A regular telegram! And from a buyer outa town he'd never met. I heard him telling Mrs. Kaplan there might be a lot of money in it for them. I'm figuring, hey! A young guy, you know, a young guy without many expenses, who ain't tied down, he could do okay for himself once he got started. Once people saw his stuff and wanted more of it, you know. What if they'd send me money in the mail and I'd send them pictures! What a deal!"

"You might be right," McIntyre agreed. "And there's magazines. Most magazines have pictures these days and I guess they've got to buy them somewhere. Interesting how Mr. Kaplan said he got a telegram offering him money for photos and he took off for the Arrowhead Lake country. Did you actually see this telegram?"

"Nah. He said he left it up to his house," the boy said. "Say! I wonder! Maybe after tourist season winds down and you ain't as busy, maybe you'd let me take photos of you in that uniform. And pictures of the ranger station. Maybe Mr. Kaplan would let me use the equipment to turn them into postcards or mounted pictures. For the tourists, you know. Tourists love that kind of stuff."

"I don't see why not," McIntyre said. "Tell you what, next chance I have I'll clear it with my supervisor. In case there's a rule against government employees modeling for photos. I'll let you know. Thanks for the price list and samples. I'll return them to you as soon as I can."

McIntyre patted the pocket of his tunic to be certain the postcards weren't making a bulge and opened the door of the S.O. He asked Dottie if there were any messages for him, but she said everything was quiet in the park. The summer temps were manning the entrance stations, nobody needed rescuing, no complaints from hikers finding clumps of horse manure on the trails or protesting because the chipmunks wouldn't pose for pictures.

"But what's up with your little friend, the cute photographer?" Dottie asked.

"What do you mean?"

"There's a man who's been trying to contact her. I've had two phone calls from a man with a weird voice. Long distance, but he didn't say where. Said she should call 'the office' but he said 'the office' like it was a code word. His voice had a kind of growl to it, like a man who smokes too many cigars. And sounded like he was breathing into the phone."

"What did you do," McIntyre asked, "phone Wild Basin Lodge?"

"Of course. They hadn't seen her or anybody who even looked like her. Same thing at the Old Owl Inn. Nobody like her had registered there or even had a meal there. I had the operator ring up the Tundra Tea Shoppe, too, but there wasn't any signal. The line's probably down again and those funny sisters who run the place don't even realize it. But I know they don't have any rooms to rent. There's barely enough room for themselves in that tiny place."

"Did you try the entrance station?"

"Same again. With the usual bad connection. I do wish they would fix that telephone line down there. As we both know, if dear Doris drove her car to the trailhead in order to hike into Wild Basin, she would have to go through the entrance station. Besides which, the car parking area is right next to the ranger cabin. But that nice young man Supervisor Nicholson posted there, he hadn't seen any attractive young woman on her own. Just his luck, he said. It's a lonely post for a young bachelor."

"It's lonely down there, but there's good fishing in that St. Vrain River," McIntyre observed. "I wouldn't mind spending my summer there. The breakfasts at the lodge aren't too bad, either."

"Timothy McIntyre," Dottie said, "you

are incorrigible. You ought to go to work as a game warden for the fish and game department. You could spend all day with trout."

"Don't think I haven't thought about it," McIntyre said. "But I'd hate the idea of giving out tickets to people for fishing. I don't approve of cars speeding along the roads, or littering, or illegal camping. Or murder, I'll arrest people for that. But I don't see why anybody needs a state license to catch a few trout in the National Park. It's not like the state stocks the streams or patrols them or anything. A man ought to be allowed to fish wherever and whenever. That's what I think."

"McIntyre?" she said.

"What?"

"Go away and let me work."

"Okay. In case anybody wants to know, I'm heading up to talk with Alice Reader at Wigwam Lodge. I'll probably swing by Moraine Park on my way back to the station. If Alice Reader doesn't shoot me."

"Moraine Park? You really mean you're headed for Stead's Lodge. Today's lunch special at Stead's is what? Pork chops? Or the meat loaf?"

"So long, Dottie."

Puzzles. Ranger McIntyre drove up the road

along the Thompson River. Ordinarily he would be watching the river as he drove, in case the trout were rising. Today, however, his mind was trying to arrange all the pieces. It was a puzzle that stretched from the St. Vrain valley to the south all the way to the north border of the National Park. For one thing, Doris Killian had set off to photograph waterfalls in Wild Basin, yet the people at the two main lodgings down there hadn't seen her, nor had the ranger at the Wild Basin entrance station. True, there was another place: it was a kind of settlement located on the St. Vrain River, little more than a bunch of scattered summer cabins and a wayside general store. McIntyre didn't know if anyone living there had rooms or cabins for rent. It was possible that Doris had found a place there, although it didn't make much sense. In theory, she could stay there and hike or ride horseback to the waterfalls. She would need to cross over the ridge into Wild Basin to avoid the entrance station. But why would she do that? McIntyre remembered that he had not spoken to the Wild Basin ranger directly. Dottie had talked to him over the phone, and the telephone connection to that station was undependable and often full of static. Maybe Dottie hadn't given the ranger a good enough description of Doris. Maybe Dottie had misunderstood the ranger's reply.

What about Mr. Kaplan? Other village storekeepers were working long hours and putting on extra help because the summer tourist business was good, but Kaplan decides to leave his shop and pack in to Arrowhead Lake. The mystery woman in the wig got herself a pack animal and headed in the same direction, but by a different route. A rough and dangerous route. Let's not overlook the man with one hand, John O'Reilly, either. He seemed to crave human company, but claimed that he needed to be away from people.

Could it have been O'Reilly who met Varna alone in the woods, tried to make love to her, ended up killing her in frustration? And was he now headed for Arrowhead, too?

Not that having several park visitors interested in the same location was anything unusual. A couple of weeks earlier McIntyre had been at Bear Lake when a tourist complained that his photographs of the lake and mountains were being spoiled by gaping individuals strolling into the view. McIntyre suggested that the man might hike up the trail a couple of miles to Dream

Lake, where fewer people go. Somebody overheard, however, and told someone else, and before you knew it, a half-dozen tourists were out to find this "Dream Lake" where nobody went.

The road along the Thompson River passed through Beaver Point, where a grocery store and gas station served the summer cabins scattered through the woods. The store owner was a 300-pound flesh vessel of smiles and pleasantries known as "Tiny" Brown. He was standing at the edge of the road outside his store and waved for McIntyre to stop.

"Hiya, Tiny," McIntyre called out, pulling off onto the shoulder of the road. He switched off the engine; talking with Tiny usually took awhile.

The large man leaned his arms on the open window, causing that side of the pickup truck to sag toward the ground.

"Ranger McIntyre!" he said, as if seeing the ranger was about the best thing that had happened to him all day.

"What's up?" McIntyre asked.

"Oh, you know. Anything that ain't down! But the reason I stopped you . . . your Dottie called from the S.O. She said you're to phone her, if I can catch you. Apparently, it's official, something to do with young

214

Jamie. Ain't he over at the Fall River entrance station?"

"Not today. Today he's in Denver, squiring Wilma around Elitch Gardens. His day off."

"Well," Tiny said, "you'd best park the truck and come inside and use the phone. I've been slicing ham for ham and pickle sandwiches, if you'd like one."

Dottie's message was indeed about young Jamie Ogg. The boy was at the county sheriff's office and needed McIntyre to phone him right away.

McIntyre rang off and tapped the earpiece cradle until the operator answered.

"Good afternoon. Number please?"

"Jane? That you?"

"Yes?"

"I guess you're back at the phone exchange for the summer? This is Ranger McIntyre. Official business. I'm at the Beaver Point store and I want to place a call to the county sheriff's office, long distance. Want you to put it on the National Park's account, okay?"

"Person to person?"

"I need to talk to Jamie Ogg if he's there."

"Okey-dokey, Ranger. I'll ring you back when I have a connection."

"Thanks, Jane."

■ ■ ■ ■

McIntyre had finished half of his ham and pickle sandwich when the phone rang again. Tiny answered and handed the earpiece to McIntyre.

"Jamie," McIntyre stated. "Don't tell me. Sheriff Crowell arrested you for speeding. Or did he catch you and Wilma parked in the boondocks, necking? Don't tell me I need to drive all the way down there to bail you out."

"No, Boss, I'm all right. Our fun day at the gardens, though, it got cut short. You'll never guess what happened. I didn't want to spend the money to phone you from there. I figured I'd better report to Sheriff Crowell anyway, 'cause he'd want to know about it. That's why we drove up here. We got the Denver police involved, too. I figured that's what you'd do, if it was you."

"Let me guess," McIntyre said. "You flipped a cigarette end into the wrong place and it set fire to the gardens?"

"No, but cigarettes is kind of what started it. See, we got to Elitch's okay and took a nice stroll around, looking at the gardens and stuff and waitin' for the rides and the shootin' gallery to open. The girls decided they had to go off arm in arm towards the restroom facilities, the way girls do, in pairs. Me and Phillip, we went in the men's. We came out before they did and we was lounging around smoking our cigarettes outside when this kinda slick-lookin' city dude came up to us."

"I'm with you thus far," McIntyre said. "But this call is costing the government money."

"Okay," Jamie said. "This flash character, he says 'I can see you boys is real sports' and he does more chatter like that, laying it on thick about how we looked like men of the world and boys who liked action and thrills and all that. I guess we did, all dressed up in our good suits and new straw boaters and all."

"Go on."

"The girls come out and saw we were engaged, as it were, with this city slicker. Wilma sort of waved and they strolled off toward a flower display to wait for us and this city clown, he winked a couple of times and started talkin' about how a man can put girls 'in the mood,' how to make sure they're stimulated and all ready to 'do it' and have fun. Directly he asks if we got any money and we said we had and he said maybe fifty bucks wouldn't be too much to pay for somethin' that would put the girls, you know, in the mood. And what's he doing, Boss?"

"I have no idea. Selling drugs?"

"No. He's sellin' picture postcards. Pictures of women naked or in nothin' but their underpants. Phillip passed some remark or other, I don't recall what, but it made this guy think we might like to look at pictures of naked men, too. He hauls out more pictures and one of 'em shows this guy lying there in undershorts but the gap in his shorts is showin' his, well, you know. The huckster, he said lookin' at it would excite most any woman."

"You turned this guy in to the Denver police?"

"We didn't have enough cash to pretend to buy his merchandise. We said we'd go look up a friend of ours and borrow some more. I think he tumbled to that, because by the time we found a city cop and brought him back with us the smut merchant was nowheres in sight."

"And that's it?" McIntyre asked.

"No! Boss, it was the pictures! The ones he showed us! His postcards? At least one of them was that same dead guy from last summer, up at Chasm Falls. And one of the other ones, it was that girl in her knickers you found up at Cub Lake. I'm sure of it. Dead certain. Looked a lot like the pictures that you took, in fact. First thing I thought was that he'd found a way to steal those pictures you had."

"Wait a minute. This slicker you met, he was selling pictures of dead naked people including our murder victims?"

"That's what I'm telling you, Boss. He said there were 'collectors' who paid big money for blowup shots of the same pictures, but we could buy the postcard version for just twenty-five bucks apiece. Phillip said those collectors must be deviants, and the guy winked and said 'sure they're deviants but their money's as good as yours.' "

McIntyre told Jamie that he had done the right thing in letting the sheriff know about it. If anyone could find out who was making those postcards and selling them to "distributors" it would be Sheriff Crowell. He had connections with lawmen all over the entire region.

The ranger walked out of the Beaver Point store and back to the pickup, leaving half a sandwich and a bottle of root beer behind. His visit to Alice Reader would need to be another day. This was a whole new twist to the puzzle. Jamie made it seem certain —

absolutely certain — that an unknown person also had pictures of the two dead bodies and had turned them into bizarre photos to sell to sex perverts.

McIntyre sat motionless in the truck, absentmindedly tracing the wood grain of the varnished steering wheel with his finger. The puzzle. How many ways could he make the pieces fit? What were the possibilities? First possibility, the killer made those photos himself. Maybe the dead man at Chasm Falls started out dry. Maybe the killer clubbed him, undressed him, made photos of the body, and shoved it into the water. Maybe they took his clothes up to the top of the falls and stacked them to make it look like he had stripped down and dived in. They rigged up his creel and his rod and threw them in the pool to make it look like that's why he dove in. They rode away and then that other tourist, Blackman, came along and discovered the corpse. Somewhere, somebody was running a racket selling thrill pictures to perverts and this is how they got them. They ambushed people all alone in the woods.

Or.

Or the entire puzzle might have a different explanation. Maybe somebody somehow intercepted Doris's photos. Or his own negatives, for that matter. Maybe they were stolen during developing or taken out of the mail. Maybe the person worked at a developing shop and sold dirty pictures on the side. He'd seen Doris's pictures, made copies. Now that McIntyre thought about it, it seemed likely that several people would have had access to the negatives and the prints. Maybe selling pictures had nothing to do with the murders.

McIntyre started the engine and drove more slowly than usual all the way back to the village, his mind turning each fact one way and another, trying to find how the pieces would fit. Several pieces were still missing: for instance, he didn't know exactly who could have handled the rolls of camera film. He remembered that Doris had taken hers with her and she must have had them developed because she sent him back the prints. It hadn't occurred to McIntyre to find out what Kaplan did about developing film, but it stood to reason that he had a darkroom and printer in his shop.

However, McIntyre thought, *there's still the possibility that the underwear photographs might not have anything to do with the murders.* While it's true that a person has to be sick in the head to be a dealer selling pictures like those, he'd have to be really,

really sick to murder strangers in order to take their clothes off for photographs.

Maybe it was a coincidence that photographs of Varna and Snyder after they were killed showed up in the hands of that sick-minded pornography pusher in Denver. Might be two different murderers. Might be one murder and one accident. One thing was certain: it was coincidence when the huckster approached the wrong pair of boys at Elitch's. Jamie saw it as a major break in the investigation, of course, but maybe it was nothing but chance. Nothing to do with killing anybody. Simply coincidence, like having three people who all seem to be headed toward Arrowhead Lake on the same weekend. Three who were interested in cameras. The one-armed man, John O'Reilly, who had been curious about self-timers. Van Kaplan, who develops film and makes his own postcards. And the mystery woman with her expensive camera.

All three going toward one very lonely mountain lake to take photographs.

"You do move around, don't you Tim?" Dottie asked sweetly.

Ranger McIntyre was sitting on the edge of her reception desk at the supervisor's office, enjoying a cup of Dottie's coffee and eyeing the last piece of fudge brownie. It looked lonely, sitting in the middle of the plate like that.

"That's why they call me a ranger," he said. "I'm supposed to range around. Cover a wide range. Be at home on the range. I even cook on a range. But what are you talking about?"

"What I'm talking about is a 'who.' That cute little flapper who works at Maguire's Ranch. The one with the short skirts and the bucket hats? How many hats does that girl own, anyway? And those high heels. Supervisor Nicholson took one look at those high heels and those legs — he took more than one look — and said he ought to arrest her on suspicion."

"Suspicion of what?"

"Just suspicion."

"She was here?"

"Looking for that tall, good-looking ranger, she said."

"Well, that would have to be me."

"Yes, wouldn't it?"

"Did she say what she wanted? Other than the obvious, I mean?"

"McIntyre, you've got to work harder on your self-esteem. She said that *you* said you might help her choose the fly fishing equipment she needed — she fluttered her eyelashes when she said it — and she said now seemed like a good time, since your girlfriend was out of town for a while. I didn't even like the way she said 'good time.' "

"I've got a girlfriend?"

"Doris. Doris Killian?"

"How does whatshername know Doris is out of town? Wild Basin is miles in the other direction from Maguire's place."

"Apparently Doris isn't at Wild Basin. Remember how we couldn't find anyone who'd seen her there? Miss Whatsername said that Doris showed up at Maguire's Ranch yesterday and took a room. Rented one of Maguire's horses, took off early this morning headed toward the Bridal Veil area. When little flapper whatsername realized how lonely and despondent you would be without Doris she took a day off, put on her flouncy little frock and strappy heels, and came dashing into town to cheer you up. Oh, McIntyre, you are such a sheik with the shebas!"

Dottie was enjoying this banter much more than Ranger McIntyre was.

"Let's be serious for a minute," he said. "You're certain she said Doris Killian had taken the trail west from Maguire's toward the Arrowhead and Bridal Veil country? You're sure?"

A tingling sensation raised the little hairs on the back of his neck. Too much coincidence. Four people going in the direction of a remote lake in a remote valley. One because of a suggestion, one because he overheard another person mention it, one apparently trying to lose herself in the mountains, and now Doris Killian made four. One of those . . . it stood to reason that at least one of those was not a coincidence. One of those knew at least one of the others and was going to Arrowhead on purpose. Deliberately. Across his mind there flashed images of the nearly naked man at Chasm Falls, then the body of the girl in her underpants lying on the log at Cub Lake.

The ranger put down his coffee mug and picked up his flat hat.

"See you later," he said.

"Where will you be, in case we need to reach you?" Dottie asked. "Fishing?"

"Thinking. Fishing is a way of thinking. I'm going back up the road by the Beaver Point store," he said. "After that, I don't know. Probably headed toward the Fall River entrance station."

225

CHAPTER 9

Ranger McIntyre took off his neatly pressed tunic. He tossed it into the cab of the pickup truck and reached behind the seat for his wrinkled, stained fishing jacket. And his fly rod. Any other lawman would be rushing toward Arrowhead Lake, but McIntyre needed to stay calm, think it through, consider all the options before doing anything. It was like fly fishing: you don't simply walk up to the river and start flailing around with the fly rod. You analyze the currents in the river, the way the shadows are lying; you anticipate the trout striking and make certain you'll have a clear stretch of water in which to play the fish.

Everybody in the area had driven the dirt road that went south out of Beaver Point and crossed the Thompson River before winding up a steep hill and on toward groups of summer cottages. What most people didn't know was that the bridge over the Thompson River concealed a long, deep pool that sheltered several large and wily trout. The overhanging bridge and the arching willows downstream of the bridge made each fly cast a puzzle, a problem in logistics of wind, distance, and hazards.

McIntyre dropped over the end of the bridge and crept like a cat toward the river's edge. Quietly he released the clicker on his fly reel and stripped off enough line to attach a fly.

He opened his fly wallet and his finger lightly stroked the top row of dry flies, each one a #12 Rio Grande King. Six of them in a row, five of them never used. She had tied them for him and he had laughed because it was the only pattern she had ever really mastered. Now they were just about all he had left of her. Six Rio Grande Kings and a hundred memories.

He considered using a #14 Mosquito, the dry fly that seemed most logical. But a little voice in his head kept whispering "#12 Black Gnat." He argued with himself that it would look unnatural for the time of day, like a deer fly drifting in the water. But maybe under the bridge, maybe in those dark shadows, maybe deer flies would hang out there and sometimes drop into the water. Worth a try.

It had to be done carefully. These trout didn't grow to that size by being stupid or by being easy prey. One bad cast, one splash, one near miss if you didn't set the hook hard enough, and the pool would be spooked. The little ones might resume feeding, but the lunkers would head for the bottom and stay there for who knows how long.

Everything had to come together. The line had to float invisibly, the Black Gnat had to look real; even the way it drifted on the current had to look natural. He knew the fish were down there under the water; he could predict almost exactly where they would be lying and how they would react to the sight of an artificial fly drifting above them. If he made his cast very, very carefully the fly would not snag on the bridge timbers over the stream and would not catch on a willow branch. The Black Gnat would drop lightly a few inches upstream of a trout and the trout would see the slight movement and would believe it to be a bug that had fallen into the water. If everything came together.

If not, well, there was always another pool. Always another day. That's how the murderer had it figured, McIntyre thought. That guy riding back and forth waiting for someone to come along. That guy who did the murder at Cub Lake and then disappeared. Have a plan, take advantage of knowing the scene, scout the hazards, do it where you won't be interrupted, make it seem natural, and if the victim doesn't rise to the bait, wait for another victim and another day. That must be how he did it. Heck, maybe he's been doing it in another place, a city or maybe another national park, and McIntyre hadn't heard about it. It might be worthwhile to drive down to Denver and have a look through the files at the newspaper building.

He drew his mind back to imagining what kind of strategy the killer would use to persuade his victim to undress before he killed them. Any temptation he offered, whatever the inducement might be, would be like picking the dry fly to cast for a trout. It had to look right and it had to be presented right.

Those photographs had to be the key piece in each puzzle. Either the killer murdered the victims in order to take pictures of their bodies, or he took pictures of them and needed to murder them afterward. Maybe there was an argument about money. Maybe both people agreed to pose in underwear for a certain fee and when the pictures were finished they asked for more. The problem with that theory is that the smut merchant could simply pay up. Or destroy the pictures and not pay for them at all. Why risk going to jail for murder? And then there was the physical appearance of each crime scene to consider. There had been no obvious signs of a fight, especially in the case of the girl. If you're arguing about money you don't lie down in your underwear to do it. You'd put your clothes on, you'd stomp your feet, you'd throw things.

McIntyre watched a little dark shadow detach itself from the bottom of the pool. It was a trout, coming up to investigate the floating insect. But a larger shadow appeared from nowhere and frightened the first one back to the bottom of the river. Apparently, the bigger fish wasn't hungry: it ignored McIntyre's dry fly, swimming slowly away into the cold, dark waters instead. It didn't want the insect, but didn't want to share.

Money, McIntyre thought. *Money for pictures.* Whoever murdered Varna must have offered her money to pose for him. And maybe offered Snyder money, too. Once the job was done he killed them so he wouldn't have to share his profits. And that way they wouldn't be able to tell anyone that he was out there in the woods taking dirty pictures. Money, greed, and protecting his identity all the way. A triple motive. The greed for money did not stop with the murderer, either. It stood to reason, especially considering Jamie Ogg's discovery at Elitch Gardens, that there was a top buyer and distributor for smutty photographs of dead people. McIntyre had no trouble in believing that such perverts existed, men who collected photos of women — and boys — doing all kinds of unmentionable acts. He had been in France. He and his buddies had explored the grubby corners of gritty old French towns where weasel-eyed men opened the folds of their filthy raincoats to display dirty postcards for sale.

McIntyre hauled in the slack line while raising the tip of the rod and picking the spot for his next cast over the pool. His mind, however, wasn't actually working on catching trout.

Okay, he thought. *Let's imagine the worst.* Let's imagine that the killer is headed for Arrowhead Lake. A victim is heading up there, too. And the killer knows the victim will be there. It's like this place in the river right here. I come because I know fish will be moving upriver and will stop to rest and feed right here. I'm going to wait for them and kill them. What's important to me? Equipment. Having the right equipment.

231

Second, having nobody around to watch me. Third, having a plan. A plan to catch a fish and kill it. To kill something, is that my motive? Do I get a thrill out of killing? Or do I intend to fry those fish and eat them. Maybe I'm killing in order to keep from starving, to stay alive.

The killer doesn't have to know the victim, McIntyre realized. All he needs to know is where the victim is. This particular killer also has to know about photography. The killer finds out where the victim will be. He goes there, too, and puts the bait in front of the victim. If they don't take the bait, if the thing doesn't go right and they get suspicious, he needs to break it off and vanish. Nobody has ever reported any such encounter to us, but why would they? What would they report, that someone with a camera came up to them and said he was taking pictures and would pay them to pose for him? Nobody would report it. Like a trout. If a' trout looks at a floating bug and figures it has a hook in it, he doesn't go tell other fish. He just goes about his business.

Let's imagine that the victim does accept the offer. What happens next?

Let's see. If Old Man Trout comes up and bites on my Black Gnat, I set the hook and I try to reel him in while he tries to escape.

If I've set the hook good and hard, I've got him and he's a goner. It's all over. All I need is a sharp knife and a hot frying pan. What does the murderer need next? He needs a way to get those pictures developed and a person to buy them.

He couldn't sell them unless the buyer could see what was in them. Nobody would buy an undeveloped roll of film just because a guy said it had dirty pictures on it. That would be buying a pig in a poke. This was the puzzle piece McIntyre had almost overlooked. The killer had to be either a person who could develop photographs or else who knew a very discreet place to get them developed. Maybe this piece of jigsaw puzzle had been under his elbow all the while. The safe way to have pictures developed with absolute discretion would be to do it yourself. McIntyre knew everyone in the village and knew their hobbies. He knew who was a coin collector, who did woodcraft, who painted watercolors and tinkered with old timepieces. However, he didn't know anyone who had a darkroom except Van Kaplan.

He was the one person who had everything needed to develop pictures and make prints. He was the person who showed up at the start of tourist season, opened his shop, and sold views of the National Park. He closed the shop in September and went away for the winter. Where he went and how he made his living during the next eight months nobody seemed to know.

The boy at Van Kaplan's shop had said Kaplan was going to Arrowhead Lake to make photographs. And flippy little whats-hername from Maguire's Ranch said that Doris Killian had headed in the same direction. What if Doris had stopped at his store, to buy film, and had told Kaplan where she was going? Maybe she noticed that framed photograph of the stone shack at Arrowhead and told him she wanted to go take pictures of it herself. Maybe Kaplan figured he would arrive ahead of her.

"I'll be back," McIntyre said to the trout pool. "You fish just keep on feeding and I'll be back to catch you."

Borrowing Tiny's telephone at the Beaver Point store, McIntyre rang up Fall River Station.

"Fall River Station," the voice answered. "Jamie Ogg speaking."

"Jamie, this is Tim. I'm at Beaver Point. I'm heading your way. I'll be there in twenty or thirty minutes. Want you to do me a favor."

"Sure thing," Jamie said. "What's up?"

"Just a hunch. I think I'd better ride up to Arrowhead Lake tomorrow. I'll drive to Maguire's Ranch tonight and start up the trail at first light in the morning. May have to spend a couple of nights up there. Could you catch Brownie for me and make sure the horse trailer's ready to go? Maybe you could throw in a bag of oats for Brownie, my saddle, my bedroll and mess kit. If you have time you might find a flour sack and stick a couple of cans of beans in it. Maybe a chunk of bread, some tea. A little jerky if there is any. Tin of sardines, and a can of tomatoes?"

"I'll take care of it," Jamie said. "Want me to go ahead and pack it all into the saddle-bags?"

"Yeah. Throw in my camera, extra roll of film, handcuffs. Oh, and there's a half a box of .45 shells on my desk, put it in. Anything else you can think of. It'll sure save me time."

"See you soon," Jamie said.

"Bye," McIntyre said. He rang off, hung up the earpiece, and turned to the store owner.

"Tiny," he said, "we'd better gas up my truck. No telling where I'll be going from here."

235

■ ■ ■ ■

Jamie was helping McIntyre load the saddle and saddlebags into the pickup when he bent over with a cramp in the gut, muttered "back in a minute," and hurried behind a tree next to the hay shed. True to his word, he was back in a few minutes.

"What was that about?" McIntyre asked.

"I've been drinking a lot of tea today."

"Probably for the sugar."

"We've got an outhouse you could use, you know."

"Ah, a tree will do. So long as there's nobody around, of course."

Jamie's need to go behind a tree reminded McIntyre of the day he drove Doris Killian up to Chasm Falls.

"I just now realized something," he said, checking the safety chains on the trailer hitch.

"What?"

"Doris. Doris Killian? She can't be Ernst Snyder's killer. We can take her off the list of suspects."

"How come?"

"When we were driving up to Chasm Falls, I stopped to put some water in the radiator and she went 'up the hill' into the trees. For the same reason you just did."

"So what?"

"If she had ever been up that road before, which she would have had to do in order to push Snyder off the waterfall, she would have known that we would be at Fall River Lodge in a few minutes and they have public toilets. Instead of going up into the woods, she would have waited until we got to the lodge."

While driving to Maguire Ranch, Ranger McIntyre kept worrying about the possibility that Miss Whatsername would intercept him. She was one of those clinging types who would take hold of a man — literally — and not let go. This evening he was lucky: he drove quietly past the ranch office and reception lobby without being seen. Behind the building, near the kitchen door, there was a walled stockade where the garbage cans were kept away from prowling bears. He maneuvered the truck and trailer around the stockade and into the trees out of sight. With a sigh of relief he opened the trailer and unloaded Brownie. She would graze on Maguire's grass while McIntyre's supper consisted of ham sandwiches from Tiny's store plus a bottle of milk and two apples. As a meal it was cold and uninteresting, but better than going to the dining room and running into whatshername.

The sun dropped out of sight early at Maguire's, thanks to the wall of high mountains west of the place. As the evening darkness came creeping down the valley, McIntyre arranged his bedroll on the grass next to the truck and put Brownie on a picket rope. He stripped down to his skivvies, slid into his bedroll, and lit his candle lantern to read awhile before going to sleep. The book he had with him was Jack London's *Son of the Wolf.* Now that London was dead, McIntyre felt a need to read everything he had written. But if anyone had asked him for an opinion he'd have to say that *Son of the Wolf* didn't really grab his imagination as much as London's other books.

He didn't know what woke him, whether it was the predawn clatter of the cook or the galley jack slamming the lids of the garbage cans or the aroma of fresh coffee drifting through the pure mountain air. That coffee smell. To McIntyre that aroma was always as irresistible as the splash and spreading riffle of a trout rising in a beaver pond. Surely that girl wouldn't be an early riser and wouldn't be in the kitchen at this hour of the morning. She looked more like the type of woman who slept until midmorning and spent an hour arranging her hair. He decided to take the risk; he would put on his clothes and lace up his boots and stroll into the kitchen wearing his most engaging smile. McIntyre didn't know the cook at Maguire's Ranch, but he had never met a cook who couldn't be talked out of a mug of coffee and a bite of breakfast.

Brownie watched him lace his high boots. Next would come that itchy saddle blanket on her back and the cold steel of the bridle bit in her mouth. With the crafty indifference of her equine breed she sidled away from the trailer as if she had noticed a tempting tuft of grass a bit farther on.

The cook looked around when he heard the screen door of the kitchen bang shut. He didn't seem surprised to see the tall, uniformed ranger wearing high riding boots and packing a revolver.

"Good morning," the cook said. "I saw you were camped out there when I went to take out the garbage. Ace, he would've given you a room for the night, you know?"

Ace Maguire was the founder, owner, manager, and semi-professional full-time western character of Maguire's Ranch. A man of theatrical charm with costume to match. Tourists never seemed to tire of taking his photo and hearing his wild tales about hunting and pioneering.

"Didn't want to bother anybody," McIntyre said. "Any chance of a cup of coffee? It sure smells good."

"Sure thing. Sit you down at the little table there. Push Kitty off onto the floor. She's supposed to be hunting mice anyway, not lounging around on the furniture."

He brought McIntyre a steaming hot mug and turned to the stove to load a plate with strips of thick bacon and hot, fresh biscuits.

"Start with them belly anchors while I fry you up a couple of eggs," the cook said, indicating the biscuits. "So, what brings you out this way?"

He slid the butter dish and jar of jam where the ranger could reach them.

"Got poachers in the park? Or maybe you're here to give one of those ranger talks. I heard one at Yellowstone once, mostly interesting. It's kind of early in the day for a lecture, though. What was it you said brought you out this way?"

McIntyre was still trying to sort out which question to answer when the batwing doors from the dining room swung inward to announce the arrival of Miss Whatshername, all bright and sparkly and starched and ready to start serving breakfast. The bright

240

red rouge on her lips seemed to come into the room ahead of her; at least it was the first thing someone saw. She spotted McIntyre sitting there and her eyes went wide with pleasure. Acknowledging the cook with a nod of her head she pulled out the chair opposite McIntyre's and sat down on the edge of the seat like a hawk settling itself on a branch to watch a mouse.

"Good morning, Miss . . ." McIntyre thought he'd better start by making it formal.

She giggled.

"Nobody remembers. This name of mine, nobody can remember who speaks English! Now listen closely: it is 'Aninia Freudkovak,' not hard to remember. Now, are you here for the entire day? Do you want to question people about the killing, is that why you have come? You want to question me. So. We have breakfast, you and I. I am off duty at ten o'clock when we can talk more."

McIntyre looked at his watch. If he was going to be at Arrowhead Lake by noon he needed to make a start. After breakfast.

"See what you think of these," said the cook, sliding fried eggs from the frying pan onto McIntyre's plate. "I'll fetch the pot and refill your coffee."

"Well, Aninia," McIntyre said, digging

241

into his eggs, "do you happen to know Mr. Kaplan? From the village?"

"Oh, yes!"

"And has he been here, like yesterday for instance?"

"Oh, yes! He is here yesterday and he always likes to see me and say hello. But yesterday he is in a hurry. He was to go have a love meeting, I think. With that woman."

"Woman? What woman?"

Aninia tilted her head back with her nose pointed to the ceiling. She made a sneering face as if she had bitten into a lemon.

"That one. You know, what is the word for her? The nose in the air."

"Attractive? Well dressed?"

"Snooty?" the cook volunteered.

"Yes! Snoot! The same woman as two summers before, and I think the last summer also. Except she wears a wig now. But the same."

"Okay. Same? You saw her last summer? And earlier than that, too?"

"Two summers before. I am working for Livingstone Hotel. That man of last summer, the one who . . ."

She joined her palms and thrust them into the air as if diving from a platform into a pool. McIntyre didn't understand at first, but when she did it again it dawned on him what she meant.

"The dead guy we found at Chasm Falls? He dove off the waterfall?"

"Yes, him. Two summers before now and I am cleaning rooms for Livingstone Hotel. That dead guy and that woman, they are having good time. Very secret, keeping in their room by themselves. Two rooms, but in his, the bed is not used. In her room, the bed is a mess every morning."

"And you saw her this summer, too?"

"My day off. Last week. I am off tomorrow. You will be back? We might do something."

"I can't say for sure," McIntyre said. "Where did you see her?"

"This time? Fall River Lodge. I am friends with Fleurette who works there. From here I ride to village with a guest to have a picnic day with Fleurette and her friend. Very nice, beautiful day. We are at those aspen where the road goes through, in the trees. The woman rides by us on her horse and she is leading a horse with a pack. I say to Fleurette, 'Look! It is that fine lady again!' and Fleurette says yes, too."

"And she had a love affair with . . . with the dead guy," McIntyre said.

"Oh, yes!"

Aninia had little more to offer in the way

of information, other than to repeat that Mr. Kaplan seemed to be on his way to a meeting with "that woman." It was in something he said but she could not remember. Aninia understood from him that he was going somewhere up the long valley that led to the junction of two trails, one leading to Arrowhead and the other to Bridal Veil Falls. Aninia had seen the man with one hand, too, John O'Reilly, talking to the stable foreman. She repeated her description of the young woman who was on her way to the valley trail; it was, without a doubt, Doris Killian.

While saddling Brownie the ranger imagined a jigsaw puzzle of Arrowhead Lake and the narrow valley in which it lay. The picture included Van Kaplan, the mystery woman, Doris, and O'Reilly. All of them in the picture, but what were they doing? If it wasn't coincidence, and it sure didn't seem like it, what was going on? Were the four of them in cahoots, maybe? Maybe smuggling drugs? Maybe they were Chicago gangsters having a secret meeting. But why in such a remote place as Arrowhead Lake? If they were rumrunners or smugglers or killers, surely they could just meet at a restaurant.

He chuckled at an image that had jumped into his mind. Doris Killian in a silk dress and lavender cloche, holding a Thompson submachine gun. Equally silly was another image, meek Mr. Kaplan chewing a cigar and holding a .45 automatic pistol while pouring himself a shot of Who-Hit-John.

Ranger McIntyre had no sooner settled himself in the saddle when who should appear from the kitchen door but Aninia. She came trotting toward him holding a folded napkin from the dining room. When she put it in his hand, it was warm.

"Apple turnover," she said. "One for the road like they say."

"Thanks," he said. "That will be nice. Thanks."

"I wish for you a good trip. You find what you look for! Oh, if my day off was here! I could go with you! What a beautiful day for two to ride, yes?"

"Yes. But I'm on duty, see? I need to be in a hurry. No time to enjoy the scenery. We'll see you in a few days, okay? Thanks again for the pastry. And thank the cook for me, will you?"

When McIntyre looked back, Aninia was still standing by the horse trailer, merrily waving bye-bye like a young wife sending her husband off to work.

"Whew!" was the only thing McIntyre could think to say.

Brownie echoed the ranger's sentiment with a loud snort and settled into her businesslike hard trot. Within the hour, the sun would be growing warm and both horse and man wanted to be in the shade of the canyon among the pines. And away from the odd-smelling woman with the annoying voice.

Ranger McIntyre finished the turnover and stuffed the napkin into the outside pocket of his saddlebag. He'd return it to the dining room when he could be sure that Little Miss Whatshername wasn't there. She was a persistent flirt. Her interest in men was lucky, though, because now it had given him another piece for his jigsaw puzzle. A summer romance between Van Kaplan and the mystery woman! Well, well. As the nudist said after sitting in the wicker chair, that's a new wrinkle.

Of course, summer romances happened all the time, especially in resort towns, fresh settings where everything seems different and exciting. Or maybe there's a romance ingredient in the mountain air that seems to sharpen . . . what did that psychologist call it? . . . the sex drive. Men weren't the only ones who started thinking about romance the minute they got off the bus, either. Women appeared to be livelier, more forward, had more of a gleam in their eye once they were out of the office and dressed for picnics and hikes in the mountains.

A memory of another woman and another picnic stabbed his heart and fled as quickly as it had come. Like a screen image in a magic lantern show it flashed and vanished, followed by a picture of Doris Killian in white shirt and riding pants. It took an effort to drag his thoughts back to the Arrowhead Lake puzzle.

Assembling a puzzle is made easier by having the picture on the box. Individual pieces don't look like anything at all until you look at the picture. The trouble was that he didn't have a picture for this puzzle. He had a dead girl, undressed. He had a dead guy the previous summer, also undressed. He had a missing pistol. He had a few little holes in the ground that might have been made by a camera tripod. And he had Jamie's report that photos of the victims were being sold under a raincoat by a pervert in Denver, photos that the sheriff believed to be traceable back to Sioux City.

"Finding a moonshine still would be a whole lot easier," McIntyre said to Brownie. "Or a poacher. Finding a poacher, that's relatively simple."

Brownie flicked one ear back toward her

rider to indicate that she was listening. As long as they had nothing to do but keep moving up the trail she might as well let him indulge in one of his monologues.

"I know what a moonshine still looks like," he continued. "Evidence is in the smoke, places where they cut trees for firewood, places where they camped near a creek for the water. And poachers? Poachers make it easy. They hunt close to a road where they can load their kill into a car or truck. You see their jacklights moving in the woods at night. Or you notice coyotes are unusually interested in a particular thicket or rock pile where animal guts were dumped."

Brownie flicked the other ear.

"With those kind of details, you can form a picture of what happened, see?" McIntyre said. "But with this deal, I don't know. All I can see is a bunch of people moving around. Like watching a child playing with a chess set, moving pieces at random. But I think maybe Kaplan is our man. I should have asked if he carried a gun when he went camping."

The sun was rising above the mountain tops and the day was warming up. McIntyre wished they had started earlier in the day. But he wouldn't have run into Aninia and wouldn't have found out about Kaplan's love affair with the snooty woman. Do you suppose they really were intending to meet at Arrowhead? That was one picture the ranger could visualize, at least. Heck, he had already experienced a mental fantasy about the same kind of rendezvous, only it was a picture of himself and Doris Killian over the ridge at Bridal Veil Falls. The tent at the edge of the woods, the campfire in the chill of evening, the solitude. That picture he could see.

McIntyre laughed. Brownie glanced around to see what was funny. She shook her bridle and went on walking up the trail.

"What if," he asked the horse, "what if the man with one hand and Doris Killian were going to meet up at Arrowhead Lake for the same reason? Sure, that would make a picture. Kinda funny, right, Brownie? I mean, one couple showing up to do a little private horsing around — nothing personal — and another couple moving in on them, a couple that just happened to have the same idea. Boy, what a balled-up mess that would be!"

However, a tiny grain of doubt continued to drift around in McIntyre's mind. There was another reason, another explanation for two people wanting to meet at a remote lake. He couldn't shake the conviction that there was a common link connecting all four people. What or who would make a link between them? Not the mystery woman. She and O'Reilly had nothing to do with one another. She had nothing to do with Doris, as far as McIntyre knew. But the mystery woman and her expensive photo equipment having a rendezvous with Kaplan, who sold photos and equipment? Cameras. Kaplan and cameras. What about Kaplan and the mystery woman working in cahoots? Could they be partners?

McIntyre had never considered the possibility that two people had killed Varna Palmer.

Kaplan . . . and cameras. Maybe that was the link. Doris bought film from Kaplan. He developed pictures for her. Mystery lady had an expensive camera. O'Reilly asked Kaplan about camera timers. Maybe O'Reilly was the centerpiece, the key to the puzzle. If he was the reason, what had he done or what had he said that would cause the others to start moving toward that one remote lake? Never mind. What he had said or done didn't matter. What mattered was that something was going to happen up there, and Ranger McIntyre would bet his shiny brown boots that he would find Kaplan and his photo studio at the bottom of it.

"C'mon, Brownie," he said. "We need to keep moving right along."

Brownie flicked both ears. Move along? What did McIntyre think she had been doing all this time? Maybe they could make a little better time if one of them would lay off the sausages and turnovers.

CHAPTER 10

"Sorry! I thought I was all alone up here!"

"Oh, that's okay. You wouldn't have seen my camp. My tent's back behind those trees over there, behind the stone hut. The truth is, I heard you come in before dark last night but I didn't want to say nothing. Didn't want to make you nervous, having somebody else already here. Thought it would be better to wait until daylight."

"Sure. I guess we both figured this would be a good place to be all alone."

"I won't be very long. I'm trying to catch the morning light on that stone wall. You can see all the little cracks and moss and everything. Lots and lots of texture. This camera has a fine lens for detail. Want to take a look?"

Show him the camera. Yes. He's interested in the camera. Interested to know what you're taking pictures of. Oh? There's plenty of stone walls close to town? Well, sure. But it's about

252

the privacy. The trees and mountains and all. He's becoming interested. Keep it up.

"I hope to be packing up by noon. Right now, I'm just waiting for my model to show up. He was supposed to be here before this. In fact, he said he might arrive last night so we could catch the first morning light for photos. I don't know what's happened to him. Good thing I didn't pay him in advance, huh? He probably figured it wasn't worth a hundred bucks, riding all the way up here and back again. Nuts. I need to get back to the city day after tomorrow, too. Darn it. Well, I guess I need to find myself another stone hut someplace. And somebody else to model for me. Dammit, I'd like to get the photos off to my publisher, too."

Keep up the chitchat. Fiddle around with the camera, trying different angles on the old stone wall. He's a standoffish sort of guy, but he's thawing out. Ask him to stand in the shot a few times, but don't click the shutter.

"I prefer having someone stand there as I sight through the lens. For reference. To save time in case my model shows up? Would you mind helping? Stand there next to that old tin washtub. Right. Yes, right there. I want to see how to frame the shot, if he ever shows up. But I don't think he's coming. He'd have been here by now. Move a little to your left? No, the other way. There. That's perfect. Could you make a scratch in the dirt with your toe right there? Yes, an X for a reference point? Great. Thanks."

"Where's this model supposed to be coming from? Town?"

"No. He was going to drive up from Edgemont and hire a horse at Maguire's Ranch. Maybe he figured it wasn't worth a hundred bucks if he had to spend his own money on gas and a horse. But I could be wrong and he will be here. I hope he will, because I don't think I'd find anybody in the village who would be willing to model for me."

"A hundred bucks for one day? That's a lot of money. Heck, that would pretty much pay for my whole summer lodging."

Do a few more setups. Look at the horizon like you're calculating where the sun will be when it rises over the mountains. Stay casual. Look calm.

"I think my little kettle's on the boil. Want a cup of coffee?"

"I don't mind if I do. I'll go find my tin cup."

While he's fetching his cup, you slip the little envelope of sodium oxybate into your pocket ready to dump into his coffee. Let's hope he takes sugar in his coffee. Sugar hides the taste better. And here he comes, ready to sit and sip and chat. Perfect. Couldn't have planned it better.

"I make my coffee kinda strong. Would you like some sugar?"

"Sure, if there's plenty."

"Give me your cup."

"Can you tell me more . . . damn, that's hot! . . . more about this photo business? You sell pictures? Much money in it, if you don't mind me asking?"

"Well . . ." *Keep him interested.*

"Sorry. Didn't mean to be nosy. I know what it's like to have people ask you questions. Same with me. People see that I lost my hand in the war and they ask me does the government pay me extra veteran benefits because of it. None of their business."

"No, no, you're not being nosy. No, I don't mind that. The thing is . . . well, like in your case, lots of people don't understand what I do. You see, I make special pictures for collectors. Nudes."

"Oh."

"Right now, for instance — and this is why I needed a male model, see? — they're paying me to make risqué cover art for classic books. Classic adult books? Like *Fanny Hill* or *The Yellow Book.* Ever hear of them? Or

The Way of a Man With a Maid?"

"Hey! I read most of that last one. One of the boys in my army outfit owned a copy. The cover was damn near wore off from guys passing it around. But it didn't have pictures."

"There you go, see? This publisher pays big bucks for pictures to put in books like that. And I don't mind taking the money."

There it was again, that little glint in his eyes when money was mentioned. This guy might be the next fish. If played right.

"Why here? If you don't mind telling me. Besides privacy and all. I mean, you'd obviously want privacy."

"Privacy's important. You won't tell anyone? See, there's at least one other photographic artist in town and I'm sure they know about this publisher. The publisher back east I mean, the one who illustrates books for special customers. Some of this publisher's pictures are very, very special. I don't want people to find out that I'm taking that kind of photos. It's good business to keep it secret. See?"

"Sure."

"It's like finding this particular location. I want to use it before another photographer discovers it because it's a perfect backdrop for an illustration to put in a 'special' edition of a book called *Lust of a Lady.* In one scene, the lady goes for a walk and comes upon a man outside a stone hut, washing himself."

"I see why they'd want an illustration. If it's that kind of book, I mean."

"He doesn't know she's there. He's washing himself without anything on. Not a stitch. Seeing him like that gets her all excited. When I heard about this stone hut in an isolated setting I suspected right off that it would be perfect for that scene. All I needed was a model willing to take his clothes off for a few minutes. A hundred dollars for a few minutes seemed fair to me. I guess he's not coming, though."

"Oh."

"Too bad. It's private here, isn't it? Look how the early morning light shows the texture of the stone wall. Almost perfect. The light is excellent this morning, too, darn it."

Time to fuss with camera again. Change angle a little. The sodium oxybate doesn't seem to be working very fast. Didn't use enough, probably.

"Well, I guess I'll have to pack it in. Maybe I can take a few postcard pictures on the way back down the trail. Why don't you have another cup of this coffee? Finish it off and then I can pack up the kettle and break camp. Boy, I feel like a fool coming all the way up here for nothing."

That's it. Have more coffee. Sure, take all the sugar you want. Now sip and think about it. Think about it . . .

"What about one-fifty?"

"What?"

"Maybe I could model for you. Maybe only the shirt off, you know? Only you don't show my face. For one-fifty. Cash."

"I never show a man's face." *Not a live one, anyway.*

"What do you say?"

"One-fifty's a high price. I'll do it, except that everything has to come off. All of it. It's cheaper than hunting around for another setting and another model."

"Okay, it's a deal."

"Let's get started before the sun gets too high in the sky."

"Want me to stand in the same place as before?"

"Sure, that'll be great. Drag that old washtub over to the corner of the hut. No, on second thought, can you set the tub on that tree stump right there by the corner? That's good, right there! Now, I'll set the camera. You stand by the washtub like you're getting ready to wash yourself. It won't take but a few minutes to shoot the pictures. I don't know how to thank you for this!"

That's it, unbutton the shirt and slip it off. Now strip off your undervest.

"Wait! Could you hold that pose like that, pulling the vest over your head with one hand? That's beautiful against the stone wall. Beautiful! Hold it . . ."

Aha. He's doing a little muscle flexing. He's tucking in the tummy. He's posing for me and I think he likes it.

"That was fine. Go ahead and take the rest off."

Sitting down to unlace the boots and strip the socks. Standing up to unbutton the pants and let them drop. Now the shyness hits him again, but that's all right.

"All right. You have a good-looking torso! Very manly! Now bend over the tub, turn your face away, but make it look like you're dipping up water in your hands. Yes, like that. Oh, I wish you could see how nicely the sun makes your muscles stand out on your back."

Was he looking wobbly? It was hard to tell from behind the camera. There! It looks like he lost his balance for a moment.

"Time to try the hard shot. I know how I want it to look, but I'm not sure we can

259

manage it. I want you to step around the
tub but stay against the stone wall. No, the
other way. No, keeping your back toward
me. That's it. That's it. Now the skivvies
need to go. For a moment or two. Step out
of them."

*He looks wobbly. No question. He's wobbly
and now he's naked. How many shots are left
on the roll of film? Take two more. Beautiful.
Maybe two, three thousand dollars' worth of
shots in this roll. I'll need to ask that book
seller for . . . what do they call it? . . . a royalty.
Ask them to pay me a royalty on how many
they sell. Now calm down. Enough pictures
while he's alive. It's time to finish it.*

"Hold it a moment! Don't move! I need
to go get a roll of film out of my pack. I'll
be right back."

Stupid.

*Should have had the gun on me all along.
Damn it, he's watching me walk to my pack.
He's blinking, but he's watching me. No way I
can hide the .22 in a pocket. Okay, carry the
gun behind my back. Now look nonchalant,
smile. Walk toward him. Not to the camera,
straight to him. The time has come to do it.
Feels awkward to walk with one hand behind
the back like a kid trying to hide something.
Heart is pounding hard. I'll bet my face is*

flushed. Same excitement as before. Such a rush, only better! Look at that body! I'm shaking all over.

"Stand there a minute. I've got an idea for another photo, one with the both of us in it. Okay? What's that? Well sure, more money. How about instead of a flat one-fifty I give you fifty per shot? How would that be? Fifty dollars a picture for these, and they are going to be special."

He looks really groggy. Good!

"Move that tub out of the way and sit down on the stump."

Now for the ultimate excitement. This is better than all the booze and drugs in the world. I'm going to take my own boots off. But keep the gun hidden! Now take off the socks. Necktie and shirt next. Drop my trousers and kick my feet free of them. He's watching me undress! He's trying to say something, except his mouth won't work right.

"What am I doing? I'm going to be in the photos with you. My friend, together we're going to make pictures that will pay for both of our vacation trips. The publisher will pay a lot for these, believe me. I'm going to be wearing only my underpants, see? Two of us."

Okay, good. He doesn't comprehend. He's sitting on the stump and looking down at the

261

washtub. He'll go to sleep any minute now. That smut seller will pay thousands for the pictures I'm going to show him. This will be the freshest set of murder photos ever made. Ever! I'll do a lot of them, too. Set the timer, put one little bullet in the head, and I've earned a year's wages. I'll keep my face turned away from the camera when I shoot him. I'll take more pictures of him dead with me in them. After I put my clothes back I'll do more photos of his body. After that I'll cover him with a sleeping bag or tarp and ride away to "report" the death. I'll tell how I was camping and he was camping in the same spot and one morning I found him like that. I was asleep, but maybe it was the gunshot that woke me. Somebody must have come in the early morning and shot him, that's what I'll tell them. I'll tell them I heard a horse running away.

"Okay, ready? I'm going to start the timer on the camera. Now, I'm the lady and I've discovered you washing yourself. And I'm coming to join you. I'll be pretending to wash your back first. Afterward we'll come up with another pose. Two of us in one photo. See? The timer on the camera will do it all. No, don't try to stand up. No! Stay there! Sit down! Don't back away! Why won't you sit down! Be still! I'm not going to bite you!"

"What's . . . what're you doing with . . ."

"Oh, the pistol? It's a prop. It's to, uh, to make it look like I'm afraid of you and I have a gun to protect myself, see? Okay, the timer's running. Let's get ready."

His eyes are glazed. He has his head tilted, listening. He hears the timer clicking off the seconds.

"Now, I'm going to stand behind you. Like this. No, don't look around. I'm washing your naked back but I've got the muzzle of a .22 automatic against the back of your head, see? Won't that make an exciting picture? Now hold very, very still until the shutter goes off."

O'Reilly's drugged mind struggled to send him an alarm but the back of his head tingled like his brain was swelling up. It was like that horrible time in the trenches at Arlais when he was trying to raise Corporal Ordway out of the mud and his head got numb with that same kind of heaviness in the back of the skull and he turned in time to see a German looking down over the edge of the trench at the two of them. The German was pointing an automatic pistol.

"No!"

O'Reilly's left leg seemed to collapse as he tried to stand up, but he still managed to

263

grab the wrist of the arm holding the gun. Now he was heavy against her, using her to support himself, his stub arm clamping her body to his. With his good hand he twisted and twisted at the gun.

Her finger jerked the trigger. With a "pop!" the .22 went off. The bullet went harmlessly skyward, but pain ripped across the web of O'Reilly's thumb when the gun's receiver snapped back and forth to chamber the next round. The pain was sharp and awful but he held fast. If he let her point the muzzle at his head, he'd be killed.

A jumble of thoughts filled his mind: *Awful dizzy. Might pass out.* O'Reilly could only keep clamping her hard against him, could do nothing but keep squeezing her hand holding the gun until she let it go. *Probably going to fall down. Better make sure I land on top of her. Gotta grab that gun, gotta shoot her or she'll shoot me. Can't . . . can't let her loose now or I'm a dead man. She's screaming in my ear. My hand hurts like hell. Bleeding. Stop screaming! She's gotta be insane. Must be! Stay on your feet, O'Reilly, stay on your feet. Don't go down. Twist the gun out of her hand. Break her wrist, rip her hand off. Everything spinning now. Head pounding like hoofbeats. Hoofbeats pounding. Stop screaming. I'm try-*

ing to hear the hoofbeats. Too dizzy, can't stand up! Dizzy . . .

CHAPTER 11

Brownie's ears flicked forward. Ranger Mc-
Intyre heard the shot too, the pop of a small
caliber gun going off, instantly followed by
the screaming of a person in pain.

"Brownie, go!"

Village taxpayers loved it when they
caught McIntyre having midmorning breakfast or prowling the river with his fly rod.
They loved to tease him about being a lazy
ranger who drove around in a government
truck telling tourists to be careful with
campfires. What those villagers never saw
were the hours McIntyre spent practicing
with his revolver in case he ever had to
dispatch a crippled animal at a distance.
Few knew that McIntyre dedicated even
more hours to Brownie's training. The time
spent had been worth it: the tall mare would
stand like a statue in a crowd of schoolkids;
she could open a gate latch, pick up his hat
from off the ground, open almost any

unlocked door or window. At the ranger's command she could intimidate bullies, no matter how big and tough they seemed, by crowding them with her broad chest. Or she could take a child by the shirt collar and gently lift him out of harm's way.

"Brownie, go!"

The mare broke into a racing gallop up the rock-strewn rutted trail, stretching neck and legs like a cow pony after a runaway steer. In less time than it takes to tell, the old stone hut came into view.

The trail, the forest, the old stone hut, and even Brownie's plunging head seemed to go out of focus for McIntyre and all he saw clearly was the two figures locked in a struggle. One was obviously Doris Killian, naked except for her ivory-colored knickers. She was struggling to break free of O'Reilly's grip. O'Reilly was wearing absolutely nothing. His stub arm was clenched around her, crushing the breath from her body. She had a gun in one hand, but O'Reilly was twisting her wrist to take it from her.

O'Reilly!

Not Kaplan, but O'Reilly! There was the camera on the tripod and over there was the pile of clothing. O'Reilly was the killer! He made his victims undress at gunpoint and took pictures of them.

McIntyre's brain flashed a warning: where was Kaplan? Maybe Kaplan and O'Reilly could be in cahoots. Kaplan could be hiding anywhere, could show up without warning. There was no time to look for him. Right now, he needed to separate Doris and O'Reilly and get that gun before it killed somebody.

"Brownie!" the ranger said. "Break it up, Brownie! Break it!"

It was a maneuver that Brownie and the ranger had practiced by using a couple of summer workers as tackling dummies. Hardly slowing down, Brownie ran straight into Doris and O'Reilly. The horse kept her neck arched and her knees high, forcing the two people apart, shoving them off balance. As Brownie slammed between the two naked people, McIntyre leaned from the saddle and tore the pistol from Doris's hand.

The ranger hauled up on the reins and leapt to the ground. O'Reilly was down. Down and out; he looked either unconscious or sleeping. Maybe he had struck his head when he fell. He looked ridiculous, sprawled on his back unconscious and stark naked. *Doesn't look much like a dangerous killer,* McIntyre thought.

Doris had dropped to her knees and was shaking all over, but she looked unharmed. McIntyre slid the ammunition clip out of the automatic pistol and jacked the live round out of the chamber, then dropped the clip into the pocket of his tunic and tossed the gun out of reach where he could find it later. He'd need it for evidence. It was a Colt Woodsman.

Varna's gun.

He helped Doris to her feet. She held onto his lapels with both fists. Her nakedness embarrassed him and he wanted to take off his tunic to cover her with, but her trembling hands were clamped on his lapels and would not let go. She looked up into his face and he looked down into hers. He saw the wild, wide-eyed stare, the fixed pupils, the same look he had witnessed during the war in men who woke up dreaming they were shooting Germans. Same wide-eyed staring expression.

"You all right?" he said.

Stupid thing to ask. The woman is naked in the middle of a wilderness, she's been attacked by a man with one arm, run over by a horse, and I ask if she's okay. Stupid.

"What happened?" she said.

"The cavalry arrived," he said. "In the nick of time, from the look of things.

O'Reilly had you in a bear hug. You had hold of a gun and he was trying to wrestle it away from you. Now he's out cold. I guess Brownie hit him too hard. I apologize if we hurt you. I think maybe O'Reilly hit his head on a rock when he fell back. He's out for the count, anyway."

Doris seemed to rally when she heard that O'Reilly was unconscious. She still held onto one of the ranger's lapels; her other hand stroked down the polished leather of his Sam Browne belt until it touched the flap of his holster. The two of them stood there holding one another until she stopped shaking, although having her body against him and his arm around her had gotten awkward and embarrassing.

"It was the photos, see?" he told her. He avoided looking down at her as he spoke. "Thanks to Jamie Ogg we found out there's this outfit that makes obscene photos to sell. Apparently, there are men who pay well for the risqué stuff, like naked dead bodies. Or girls taking their clothes off in the woods. God knows what these sick creeps will use those photos for. I knew a guy like that in the army. He couldn't leave it alone. He had dozens and dozens of pictures of women. When he heard about a spy camera you could hide in a suit pocket, he spent weeks trying to find out where he could buy one to take secret pictures of girls. Maybe O'Reilly had the same sickness and when nobody would hire him for a regular job he connected with a dirty picture dealer. Maybe it was peephole pictures to start with and escalated all the way to photographing naked dead people."

"O'Reilly?" Doris said.

"It sure looks like it. Plenty of evidence. The camera, Varna's gun, attacking you, everything. At first, I thought it was Kaplan who killed that girl, since he's got the darkroom and develops pictures. Speaking of which, Kaplan is supposed to be here. That's mostly why I rode up here."

Doris looked up into his face. One of her hands was still holding his lapel; her other hand rested on the flap of his holster.

"Maybe you ought to put your clothes on," McIntyre suggested.

Doris stepped back and looked down at herself as if she had forgotten that she was in her underpants. But instead of going toward the pile of clothing next to the camera tripod she walked to where her sleeping bag and backpack were lying beside a pine tree. This puzzled McIntyre. Maybe she was a little woozy yet. Maybe she had other clothes in her pack, or maybe she needed some female thing, and it was in the pack. Being a gentleman, or because her nudity embarrassed him, he turned away. Instead, he would turn his attention to O'Reilly and see how he was doing.

At least he wouldn't have to search the one-handed man for a concealed weapon. O'Reilly wasn't concealing anything.

The unconscious man's breathing was regular. He wasn't bleeding from a head wound. He was merely asleep. Brownie was grazing near the stone hut; McIntyre walked over to her, still keeping his eyes averted from whatever Doris was doing, and took a pair of handcuffs from the saddlebag. The trouble with handcuffs, though, was that O'Reilly had only one hand. Luckily there was an exposed tree root not far from where the killer had fallen. McIntyre snapped a cuff on O'Reilly's good arm and dragged him until he could fasten the other cuff to the root. It would keep him out of trouble. Or from making trouble, once he woke up. McIntyre gathered up the man's shirt, pants, and jacket and spread them over his nakedness.

"That should take care of him," McIntyre said loudly, still avoiding any glance in Doris's direction.

"I'm going to look around for his campsite," he said. "There should be another horse around here, too. I oughta make him walk all the way back to Maguire's Ranch, but I guess it would take too long. I'd better find his horse for him. Are you okay now?"

"You can turn around," she said.

Ranger McIntyre turned, smiling his charming smile to cover his embarrassment. He saw that in addition to her knickers she was now wearing a short, clinging, very thin little silk camisole. He also noticed that she was pointing a revolver at him.

"That," he said, nodding at the gun, "would be the .32 Smith and Wesson you wrote about in your letter."

"Correct," she said. "Please take out your own gun. Hand it to me."

"I'm not sure exactly what you think you're up to," McIntyre said, "but to make things clear, how about if I tell you that I'd never surrender my weapon? Maybe you'd tell me what's going on. It looks like I got things wrong. I guess I never really believed that O'Reilly could be the killer. And Kaplan, he doesn't seem the type, either."

"Hand me your gun."

"No. Tell me what's going on."

"I'll shoot."

"Fine. But first tell me what's going on."

273

"Why? If I told you, would you even understand? You've always had your life the way you want it. Roam around in the mountains all day, go wherever you please, talk to anybody you meet without worrying that they'll follow you home. What if you were a woman? Where would you be if you were female? What if you liked to dress nice, and live in a city, and go traveling, who do you think would hire you and pay you enough? You scrape up the money for one trip to Colorado to take photographs in hopes of selling them. Guess what happens? Up pops a handsome park ranger and you help him take crime scene pictures of a naked man. You take them to a place to be developed. A couple of days later, out of nowhere comes a man willing to pay for those negatives, more money than you could earn in four months. And he offers even more money, much more, if you came back with photos of a girl who looked like she was lying in a forest dead and naked. Understand? I've told you everything you need to know. Now take out your gun and give it to me!"

"The answer's still no," McIntyre said. "What the heck do you expect to do next, anyway? If you had my gun, would you shoot me with it?"

"Me? Little me? Why, Mr. Ranger! No. I wish you would listen! Listen! No! It's all about money for photos, don't you understand? Lots and lots of money."

Her voice dropped to a conspiratorial whisper. McIntyre saw wildness staring out of her eyes and the way her hands were trembling. He'd seen it in France that afternoon when a French pilot climbed out of his cockpit following a ferocious dogfight. The man gazed at them without seeing them. He trembled all over, then turned and walked into a spinning propeller.

"You have to give me your gun, Tim," she said. "I need to have it. Don't be silly. Do you see? You give me your gun, then I point both guns at you because I want you to strip naked like your friend O'Reilly there."

"What did you say?"

"Oh, yes. See? Now you understand why I need to have both guns. You see? It's another opportunity for me. This situation has become another opportunity. Now, you be a good boy and hand it over. Or I have to shoot, see? I have to. Except it will be more trouble to undress you if you're already dead."

"But why? You think you can run away like you did after you killed the girl at Cub

275

Lake? You plan to vanish like you did before?"

"Silly. We're not talking about running away now. No. I tell you and tell you, don't I? I need more money. I need to make more photos to sell. And this, this is a chance I cannot pass up. A private place way back in the mountains, two naked men?"

Doris gave him a very sly look, a look she probably intended to be naughty. To McIntyre it looked as if her mind had slipped even further.

"What if it was the other way around and you had a camera and two nude girls?" she asked. "Hmmm? What pictures would you make, if a man was willing to pay you bags full of money for salacious photos? Now, Tim, try to listen to me: first, I want you to toss me the key to those handcuffs. Then very carefully take off your hat and your belt and put them on the ground. No tricks! Next you sit down and take off your boots."

"You're sure you want to do this?" McIntyre said. "You think you have all the consequences figured out?"

"Oh, I'm very sure. Very. I can already see the kind of photos I'm going to make. They are going to bring me a pile of money. And I don't have to share, so there."

"You're going to take photos of me naked,

276

after which you're going to kill me and take more pictures? If that's your plan I might as well try to take your gun away right now."

"You're still being silly. I won't kill you! I won't kill you at all, if you cooperate. I'll give you my special coffee, Tim. It will relax you and you won't mind becoming a photographer's model like O'Reilly. It'll be very nice, Tim, I promise you. O'Reilly, he drank my coffee and he was beginning to enjoy acting as my model until he became crazy and attacked me. I think he went nuts when he saw me in these little panties. C'mon, Ranger. Undo the belt and have some coffee. You'll like my coffee. It makes you all calm and sleepy. When I have enough photos, I promise I'll handcuff you to Mr. O'Reilly. I'll pack up and I'll take all three horses and I will be gone. So there! There's your consequences! If you're a naughty boy, though, I might burn your clothes first. By the time you and Mr. O'Reilly free yourselves and hike back to the ranch you two will be too embarrassed to ever tell anyone what happened. Either way, I don't care. You won't know where to find me. I'll be several states away before you can even decide what to do about it. I'm very good at planning, you see."

"You expect me to believe your blarney?

You do, don't you?" McIntyre said. "I'm supposed to trust you after you killed two people? And did it to sell pictures of dead people for a bunch of warped perverts to drool over? You don't have any intention of leaving me and O'Reilly alive. I'll tell you one thing: your pictures of me are going to show bullet holes in my body, because I'm not giving up that easy."

"I didn't kill two people, Tim! I didn't plan to kill anybody! Varna was an impulse. Oh, I had thought about it ahead of time, sure. In a general way. Kind of a fantasy, you might say, that I'd meet a good-looking gal, or a guy, on the trail. That I'd have my little sleeping drug with me, and my rubber helmet and maybe there would be a chance to knock them out and pose them to look dead in photographs. Then I saw her on that log and I had the urge to suffocate her. I don't know where the urge came from. I knew that after she . . . passed out? I'd be able to put her in any pose I wanted. Anything I wanted! You wouldn't understand. It was a rush, see? Like the first time you try cocaine. A rush."

McIntyre thought he heard a noise, very faint, like a layer of pine needles being crushed under a foot. Could've been a deer out there in the trees. Or even a mountain lion. He glanced around to see where Brownie was. She could have done it, but she was nowhere in sight. Probably wandered off looking for fresh grass when he needed her to help disarm Doris. *Too bad I didn't teach Brownie a command for this situation,* he thought, *a word to make her come charging in and disarm a villain.* Then in the other direction and out of the corner of his eye he caught a glimpse of her large brown shape, so he knew where she was. The footstep noise had come from another direction, from among the trees.

"The waterfall guy, was that another rush like cocaine for you?" McIntyre said. "How'd you manage that? Kill him first? I'd like to know how he got undressed and went over the falls."

"I didn't kill him, you dumb palooka. Why can't you figure it out? Why? What do you think I did, wake up in the dark that morning, go all the way up to Chasm Falls, happen to run into him there, kill him, take pictures, and drive back to town in time for breakfast? Listen, I didn't even see him until we drove up there in your truck. I'd never been there before, remember?"

Her anger flashed like an electric spark, then subsided. Her eyes took on a sly and secretive look.

"But that's where I got started, see? They paid me a lot of cash for the pictures I took of him. I won't tell you who paid me. You can't make me tell. But it was a lot of cash. But I didn't kill him. If you think so you're being ridiculous again."

"Then who did kill him?"

"Look," she said with exasperation in her voice, "I'm tired of talking. You throw the key for those handcuffs to me. And right now."

She brought the gun up and pointed it at McIntyre's chest.

Ranger McIntyre began fumbling in his trouser pockets. He kept his eyes on her while going through the pantomime of hunting for the key, calculating his chance of making a grab for the weapon. He had another reason to stall: looking past Doris, he'd seen a shape move among the trees like a shadow moving in shadows. A curious deer? It didn't seem to move like one. More like a person, maybe Kaplan. Whoever it was, the shadow silently crept forward. At the edge of the trees it materialized into the figure of a tall, slender woman dressed in riding pants and jacket. She was armed with a tree branch the size of a baseball bat and was cautiously creeping up on Doris.

"Right now!" Doris repeated. "Right now!

Find it!"

"Take it easy," McIntyre replied. "I'm looking for it. I dropped it into one of my pockets but I don't remember which. Darn handcuff keys are too small. They can lose themselves in a man's watch pocket. Give me a minute. And let me warn you, don't be angry with me if it's not the right key. Jamie put two pairs of cuffs in the saddlebags and one of them doesn't use the standard key. Stay calm. I want to live through this, you know. I ought to check on O'Reilly, see how he's doing. What the heck did you hit him with, anyway?"

"My coffee. He drank my special coffee. With a tiny little bitty bit of sleeping drug, that's all. You'll try it, too. You'll like the feeling. Now you'd better find that key."

McIntyre again told her to stay calm as he searched his trouser pockets, his watch pocket, the pockets of his tunic, all the while mumbling and cursing like a man will do when he can't find what he's looking for. He knew he was making a dramatic production of the search, but he had to keep Doris's attention on himself. He didn't want her becoming aware of the tall woman creeping up behind her.

"Ah! Here it is!" he said.

He drew the small key from his tunic

pocket and held it up for her to see.

"Catch!" he said, pretending to toss it in a high arc toward her. As Doris looked up into the sun for the key, her hand with the pistol in it drooped toward the ground.

Ranger McIntyre had heard the word "conked" before. He had even seen it on a movie screen — *"Conk!"* — during a Mutt and Jeff cartoon when the boxing kangaroo clobbered Jeff atop the skull. Until the thick club made contact with the back of Doris's head, however, he had assumed it was a word that a scriptwriter had made up. But the hollow echo of the branch against the skull was definitely a "conk," like a baseball bat hitting a coconut. Fortunately, Doris had not cocked the hammer on her .32 revolver, otherwise it might have gone off when the club hit her. Without a murmur, she sagged to the ground like a deflating rubber doll.

The ranger wasn't in the mood to take any more chances: he hauled his service revolver from its holster and aimed it at the mystery woman who was still holding the pine branch club in her left hand.

"Drop it," he said. "Good. Now put your hands in the air. Turn around, all the way around, very slowly. No sudden moves."

She stood stiff as a statue while he patted her pockets and looked for any bulges under the arms or on the calves, anything that might be a concealed knife or gun. Satisfied, he stepped back and let her put her hands down.

"But stand there and do not move," he said.

Keeping his gun ready, he crossed over to O'Reilly and removed the handcuffs. He rolled Doris onto her stomach, bent her arms behind her, and applied the cuffs to her wrists. He took her .32 revolver and put it in his pocket.

"Sit there," he told the tall woman, indicating a fallen log.

She complied without protest.

"I need to warn you," McIntyre said, "that I haven't had a very pleasant morning and I'm likely to be kind of cranky with people who come at me with guns and clubs. I want you to tell me who you are and what you're doing here and I want you to do it without saying anything that might upset me. No tantrums, no screaming, no threats. Okay?"

The woman crossed her legs gracefully at the ankle, accentuating the riding pants and high boots. Her hazel eyes regarded the ranger with calm curiosity.

"Aren't you going to say thank you?" she said.

"Maybe later," he replied.

She smiled. And a very nice smile she had.

"Very well. My name is Mari, with an 'i' on the end, Mari Canby."

"Related to Abe Canby who lives down along the Thompson River?"

"Probably not. I live in Denver. Formerly New York. And Europe before that. I moved to Denver about the time the war in Europe broke out. I live alone there; I love to hike, and ride horses, and camp in the mountains. In winter, I love to ski. Another of my hobbies is photography. Oh, and fly fishing. I understand from the locals that you are an expert with a fly rod? You have a reputation, you know."

"Sure. But let's keep on the subject. Several people have reported seeing you behaving in ways I don't understand. But I'd sure like to."

"Ways? Such as?"

"Such as being seen in and out of the park, yet not being a guest in any lodge or boarding house anywhere. Or such as hiring horses and making trips into the mountains alone. And such as the people who noticed you searching around Chasm Falls. Let's start by explaining all that."

She smiled that very nice, very classy smile again.

"I see. All right, to begin with, I'm employed as an executive private secretary, which gives me a month off each summer. Secondly, I knew Mr. Snyder, the man who died in the park last summer. I knew him very well. A summer romance, you would call it. I have been grieving over his death and decided to use my vacation time this summer to revisit the places that he and I had shared. Plus, I've been looking for solitude to think. As simple as that, you see. Well, nearly that simple."

"Go on," McIntyre said.

"You were surprised to see me walk out of the forest. Imagine my own surprise when I came upon a park ranger being held at gunpoint by an unclad female. I had been riding down this canyon — or perhaps you call this a valley? — when I heard what sounded like a gunshot. I rode ahead slowly and carefully and thought I could hear people talking. Having been camping and hiking alone as much as I have, I have learned to be very cautious. I dismounted. I tied my horse and pack animal back in the trees. I came ahead on foot. In time, apparently, to save you from being shot by that young woman lying over there in her undergarments. You haven't yet thanked me for that. At first, I thought you two might be playing a naughty game. You know, lovers pretending to be the policeman and the frightened maiden. For excitement?"

"Where were you going?" McIntyre asked. "Before you came across us, I mean. I don't understand what you are doing up here in the first place."

"Ah. This will be the difficult part to confess. It goes back to photography. You know Mr. Kaplan at the camera shop, I assume? I was admiring his photos of Bridal Veil Falls. Frankly, Ranger — McIntyre, is it? — I do not remember which of us suggested it, but Mr. Kaplan and I agreed that we would meet today, this afternoon, at Bridal Veil Falls and he would show me how he got his photo angles. I suspect, of course, that he had more in mind. More 'angles.' He seemed quite eager. However, we are both adults and the idea of a summer tryst in a lovely private valley near a waterfall is not without its appeal. In short, I agreed to meet him there. According to my map I could get there by coming down this valley to where it joins Bridal Veil creek and then follow the creek up to the falls. I had come as far as this when I encountered the lingerie woman pointing a gun at you. My first thought was to hurry back to my horse and get my own gun; however, I'm not that good a shot. I might have missed her and hit you, if things came down to shooting. Therefore, I found a sturdy stick and decided to creep up on her. If she had heard me approaching, at least it might have been a distraction to help you gain an advantage. May I add, by the way, that you still have not expressed gratitude?"

"All right," McIntyre said. "Thank you for not shooting me. And for rescuing me from whatever she had in mind. Thank you."

"You are welcome."

Doris groaned. Her legs twitched. She moaned again.

"It looks like she's starting to come around," McIntyre said. "Maybe you'd help me dress her? She's going to jail for murder. You probably heard about the dead girl they found at Cub Lake."

"Of course. You think she did it?"

"She confessed to it a little before you arrived. I think she killed your friend Mr. Snyder, too. I only need to figure out how she did it. She likes to use a sleeping drug on people, so don't drink coffee or anything else you might find around here."

The ranger and the lady wrestled the sleepy girl into her white shirt and jodhpurs.

She tried to kick when he began to put her boots on, but McIntyre solved that problem by sitting on her legs while he did up the laces. She did go on resisting and complaining, but her efforts only served to increase the sharp pain of her splitting headache. McIntyre put the handcuffs back on her and brought her a bandanna soaked in cold water.

"Don't move," he said. "I'll put this on your forehead."

Doris lay there moaning but motionless. In the interval, Mr. O'Reilly had recovered sufficiently to stagger to his feet and put his clothes on.

"The poor thing," Mari Canby said, looking down at Doris.

"Poor thing?" McIntyre said. "I'm sorry she has a headache, but she killed two people. Two that we know of. I'm certain she would have shot O'Reilly and me, too."

"No," Mari Canby said. "She had nothing to do with Mr. Snyder. I believe the time has come for me to tell you the truth. You seem very trustworthy, and, frankly, I'm extremely tired from carrying the guilt and hiding from it at the same time. Can we walk over to that large boulder and have a talk?"

"Okay," McIntyre said. "Sure. I don't

think Doris will go anywhere. There's nowhere to go. But why would you trust me? You never met me before."

The woman led the way to the flat rock, which was out of earshot from Doris and O'Reilly. She gestured for the ranger to seat himself and sat down next to him. McIntyre felt like a priest about to hear a confession.

"I think the word is 'corny.' It sounds corny, but your uniform and your face and the way you carry yourself inspires trust. As I said, I'm tired of the guilt. The time has come to rid myself of it, all of it. I might go to jail, I might lose my job, but I cannot face the thought of another winter with the guilt upon me. I very much need to trust someone. This is an ideal spot for it. When we get back to town there will be law officers and questions and confusion, but up here I can think clearly and say what I have to say. I think I can trust you."

"Okay," he said. "Go ahead and say your piece."

"That girl didn't kill Ernst last summer."

"She didn't?"

"No."

"Were you there?" he asked.

In his mind, Ranger McIntyre heard the "click" of a puzzle piece snapping into place. This Mari Canby must have been the mysterious love affair that Ernst Snyder's family said he was having.

"Were you?" he repeated.

"Yes. You might say it was an accident. But still you are going to want to charge me, I know. And I'm glad. It will be a deep relief to have it all known, to have it over with. That's what I've been doing this summer, you see, trying to clear my mind and conscience. I've been going over it and over it. I've been going back to where it happened and I've been riding up into the mountains where he and I had gone. In a way, I suppose I've been looking for him, hoping to find out what it is I must do in order to put it behind me. I hired a tiny cabin on the outskirts of the park and I've been avoiding people. I didn't want to be social, you see. Didn't want to be cheered up. That probably sounds strange."

"You said a cabin. At Wigwam Lodge?"

"No. Where is this Wigwam Lodge?"

"Edge of Moraine Park, but never mind."

Her voice was no longer snooty and cold. The woman had thawed considerably. McIntyre had an urge to put his hand over hers.

"Let's get back to Ernst Snyder," he said. "How he died. You two were . . ."

"Lovers, yes. The same old story. A man whose wife has stopped loving him, so he said. Or whose wife has stopped being interesting to him. They were 'estranged' according to Ernst, but a divorce would distress his family. As I said, it's a very old story. However, I had cooled to the idea of continuing our affair. He was getting almost strangely fearful of being found out. At times, he would rage about the frustration, about needing secrecy. I added to his frustration, I suppose, when I said I wanted to have more fun than we were having. Dancing, parties with other people, walking together. I agreed to meet him again last summer, one more time, but only in order to tell him our affair was over. I couldn't go on with it."

"Suicide? Is that what you're leading up to?" McIntyre asked. "You told him it was over and he killed himself?"

"No. I caused his death."

"Be careful what you say. I might be a ranger, but I'm also a policeman."

"I know. I have to tell someone. I don't want to live with it any longer. And look where we are. This is such a nice place in which to explain everything. It's as peaceful as a church. Do you mind?"

"I guess not," McIntyre said. "Go ahead and get it off your, uh, conscience."

"Thank you. Well, Ernst and I arranged

our summer rendezvous as we had done before, arriving separately and taking separate accommodations near the village. This time I thought it best if he had a room at Fall River Lodge while I hired the small cabin at the edge of the park. A man named Thorton owns it."

"I know the place," McIntyre said.

"I thought that if Ernst and I were in the same lodge, and our emotions got the better of us . . . well, it would be too easy for us to end up in the same room. Maids and housekeepers would know what was going on. As I said, he was becoming more and more fearful of discovery, of unexpectedly encountering a friend, or an acquaintance of his family. On that terrible morning, the morning he died, we were to meet at Chasm Falls very early, before anyone was up and around. He would be pretending to be fishing while I would pretend to be taking early morning photographs. From there we would look for a lovely secluded glade or grove in which to spend the day together. I rode my horse to the top of the falls before sunrise. A beautiful mountain morning."

She sniffled and took out a hankie to dab at her nose.

"Well," she continued, "Ernst arrived after sunrise. We sat on a log near the top of the falls and it was very private. There wasn't anyone around. He wanted to make love right there. He became insistent. That's when I told him that I wanted to end the affair. I gave him all my reasons, but he wouldn't listen. All he wanted was to make love, to rekindle our passion of the previous summer. He kept pawing at me, trying to unbutton my clothes. I kept pushing him away. It was difficult, of course, but I was determined not to give in to the feelings of the moment. I knew I had to end the affair. I hope I am not embarrassing you?"

"You are," McIntyre said. "But go ahead."

"His frustration got the better of him. He called me cold, accused me of not loving him and said he thought I had found another man. 'Last summer you teased me that I was getting pudgy. I worked all winter to get in shape,' he said, 'all because of you! For you. Since it was all for you and since I've come all this way you may as well see the results. Look, look at this!' He stood up and took off his coat and shirt to show me his muscles. 'Hours and hours at the YMCA, working out with the Indian clubs and chin-ups and push-ups! All to impress you!' I said I was impressed, trying to calm him down. He came at me again, and again I pushed him away. 'The stationary bicycle, too!' he said. 'Hours! I did it all for you. And you may as well see what you're throwing away!' He removed his boots, trousers, and vest and hurled them at me. It was a very silly attempt at seduction, showing me his body like that, but he was so serious about it that I didn't dare to laugh."

She paused and seemed to lose some of her poise, staring at the ground but seeing the memory in her mind.

"He went on and on, showing how he hardened these muscles with the medicine ball and those muscles with the Indian clubs, flexing his back to show what chin-ups do to muscle. It was as if he was ranting to himself about it. I didn't know what to do. I had never seen him like that. All I wanted was for him to calm down and act rationally. I began picking up his clothes, which were lying all around. I suppose I absentmindedly folded everything into a neat pile. It's what I do when I'm nervous, arrange anything I find around me. I found his fly rod on the ground, along with the creel he had bought, and I picked them up and took them to him. He had gone quiet standing near the edge of the waterfall, sulking. 'Here,' I said. I handed him the rod and creel. 'Come back to the stream and let me watch you fish. You cast a line so beautifully. Look, I've fixed the harness on your new creel for you. You look very fine, very muscular. I'm proud of you. Now let's get dressed and do some fishing, all right?' I seem to remember saying something to the effect that we could still find the spot we had talked about and have a nice day and forget what had just happened.

"He snatched the rod and creel from my hands. 'Stupid woman,' he said, 'you fastened the harness on the wrong side!' And he hurled rod and creel over the falls into the pool below. He came toward me with blood in his eye and his hands reaching like talons, like a madman, like someone I did not know at all. As he reached for me I slapped him, then slapped him again. He bent and reached down for a rock lying near his feet. All I could think of was that he was going to hit me with it. That's when I grabbed up a stick and hit him. I hit him on the head. He turned away to shield his face and I hit him across his bare back.

"He went quiet again. So quiet. Frightening. He climbed up onto a rock at the lip of the waterfall. 'If you don't want me I may as well jump,' he said. 'Maybe you don't think I will.' I dropped my stick and hurried to take hold of his arm to pull him back, but his foot slipped. He went over the edge.

295

He screamed. I think he struck his head. By the time I climbed down to the pool he was lying in the water facedown and not moving at all."

Mari Canby took out a hankie and dabbed at her eyes.

"I was shaking all over. His body was in focus, but everything else seemed all blurry. I started to wade into the pool, but pulled back because the bottom dropped off so abruptly into deep water. I looked around for a long stick or something to pull him to the bank. He was too far out of reach. He floated out there, slowly going around and around with the current."

"And you ended up doing nothing," McIntyre said. "Probably nothing you could do."

"He might have still been alive. But I froze, you see. I only stared and watched him float around and around in the pool. I think I was dazed. Eventually I climbed up and got on my horse, I think with the idea of trying to find somebody. I still see it in my nightmares, Ernst's body turning around and around. Accident or not, he died because of me. It was my fault. I knew he was married, I shouldn't have allowed our affair to go forward. I shouldn't have agreed to a meeting in a secluded spot. I handled

296

everything in the worst possible way from beginning to end. I killed Ernst as surely as if I had put a gun to his head."

Silence. She put both hands to her face and bent over until her face was resting on her knees.

The sun's warmth on the evergreen forest released an incense of pine and spruce. Softly, the mountain stream hummed its melody of ripples and bubbles to the rocks. A rising trout broke the mirror surface of the lake, hung in the air like a silver rainbow, dropped again in a circle of jeweled water. Back in the trees one of the horses nickered to another.

Doris moaned in her pain. McIntyre wished he had an aspirin or brandy to give her.

Mari Canby, McIntyre's mystery woman, raised her head and wiped at her eyes. She went on speaking.

"She is a poor thing, that girl. Because I know what it is, taking a life. Murdering another human, it becomes a canker in the mind, a kind of malignant weight. It seems to lie on top of all other thoughts and emotions and memories, smothering everything. Unless you are a monster you cannot shake it away."

"I know," said Ranger McIntyre. "I know."

His mind was flashing images of the Great War like a magic lantern show. He saw three young German soldiers in a machine gun emplacement. With cold eyes he was squinting along the steel barrel of the Nieuport's deadly machine gun, maneuvering for the gun to bear on them as his plane flew on and on, wheels so close to the ground as to nearly snag on the barbed wire. He remembered the sensation of pulling the trigger, the clattering staccato of the gun, the dust and smoke of his bullets hitting the ground ahead. Afterward, he flew away and never knew whether they were dead, wounded, or uninjured.

"Now what would you like to do?" she asked.

"Do?" McIntyre said. "Oh, do. If I had my rod and reel I'd make a cast into the lake for that lunker who's doing all the splashing. That's what I'd like to do. I'd like to go fishing. I'd like to turn my back, then turn back around and see that all of you had gone away and left me to my mountains. That's what I'd like."

He stood up and sighed and adjusted his uniform.

"But. Always the but. You're not going to run away, are you?"

"No."

"And you have a gun?"

"Yes, in the saddlebag of the riding horse."

"According to the damn rules, first thing I must do is disarm everyone and 'apply appropriate restraints,' which means handcuffing you. For the time being I'm going to treat you as a prisoner, since you have admitted being at the scene of a death. If Mr. O'Reilly feels strong enough to help me, we'll organize the horses and camping gear, pack it up, and start down the trail. We can make it to Maguire's Ranch before dark. Before we leave I'll write out a simple statement saying you were present at the death of Ernst Snyder and I'll ask you to sign it."

"I don't mind writing it myself. I know what it needs to say. There is paper and pen in my other saddlebag. Perhaps I could do that?"

"I suppose it would be all right."

"What about Mr. Kaplan? He'll be at Bridal Veil Falls by now. He'll be wondering what happened to me. I could not face him now. It would be like the affair with Ernst all over again. What is wrong with me, anyway?"

"We can't take time to ride up there. But you might write him a note and we'll leave it at the hut where he can see it. Stick it on the wall somehow, in case he comes looking for you. I expect, though, that before night-fall he'll give up waiting at Bridal Veil and return to Maguire's. There's not much else he could do, other than make the detour up here to Arrowhead in hopes of finding you here. We'll leave him a note, just in case."

The tableau in the mountain clearing was a curious one to see. A park ranger in flat hat and green tunic, loading horses with camp-ing gear. A young woman, her hair in much disarray, handcuffed and tethered with a short rope to a tree, complaining over and over about a headache and about money she had lost, shouting about the money that McIntyre's interference had cost her. An-other woman, mature, more sophisticated, wearing handcuffs, kneeling by a tree stump, using it as a writing desk. And a man with one hand missing, staggering a little and blinking into the bright sunshine while try-ing to help the ranger with the packs and saddles. The scenario gradually took on a semblance of order as the prisoners were mounted and handcuffed to their saddles. The man with one hand mounted his horse and took the lead down the trail. As for the park ranger, he brought up the rear where he and Brownie could keep an eye on the caravan. Mari Canby's gelding shied at a fallen tree branch and looked as though he might take off running, but Brownie lowered her head at the other horse and nickered as if to say "try running away, buster, and I'll turn you into a buffet for scavengers."

Brownie seemed testy as a matron who's missed her nap and Ranger McIntyre was even grumpier. He had not had any lunch; he had seen fine trout rising in the lake and hadn't been able to even moisten a dry fly; in short, he was in no mood for foolishness. The ride to the Maguire Ranch would be long, steady, and silent.

CHAPTER 12

Ranger McIntyre stepped from the Fifteenth Street trolley and straightened his suit jacket for the tenth time. He wished he knew why the FBI had asked him to come to Denver and why he had been asked to wear civilian clothes. His double-breasted business suit made him self-conscious; it seemed like he was always reaching inside the jacket to straighten the inner lapel — which never needed it — or else smoothing down a pocket flap. The Homburg hat was equally foreign to him: no matter how he adjusted it, cocked left, cocked right, sitting square, brim up, brim down, he never looked like the men who modeled hats in the newspaper ads. He didn't even resemble the mannequins in the haberdashery store. Wearing a Homburg, McIntyre looked like a man wearing a hat.

He adjusted the Homburg for the umpteenth time and went up the stone steps into the office building. A directory board on the wall inside the double doors told him what he needed to know: Federal Bureau of Investigation, Denver Office, Room 240. Up the stairway and down the hall was a door with a frosted glass panel bearing the same information: Federal Bureau of Investigation, A.T. Canilly, Agent in Charge.

There was no one in the reception area. Against one wall were three wooden armchairs, centered and evenly spaced. Hanging on the wall above the chairs were three evenly centered photographs, group pictures of men he assumed to be FBI agents. Probably somebody's graduating class from the academy.

On the adjoining wall, hung one photograph and two framed maps above three additional evenly spaced chairs. The reception desk was furnished with three items: a pad, a calendar, a pen holder. The office was clean enough that a dust mite would starve in it.

The ranger held his hat in his hand, adjusted the knot in his tie, and coughed.

"One moment, please," came a woman's voice from the other room.

The voice was followed a moment later by the woman herself, coming straight at him with her hand extended so artlessly and so

303

graciously that he wasn't certain whether to shake it or lift it to his lips and kiss it.

"Violet Coteau," she said.

She gripped McIntyre's hand; it felt like she was drawing him toward her or like she was going to lead him away with her. And McIntyre wasn't going to object.

Her voice was as soft and as enveloping as her face. She had a smile and a way of looking at him that made the ranger feel the two of them were sharing a private moment in a special place. A place that was becoming awfully warm. His eyes took in her crisp white middy blouse, the black hair cut straight across the forehead in the fashion of the day, bangs down to her arched eyebrows. Her lips were shiny red but neither too shiny nor too red and when they parted in that smile of hers it seemed as though her eyes smiled, too. He would never be able to explain why, but her smile made him feel like she approved of him. And it seemed important that she should.

Thus far the ranger had been speechless.

"Violet?" the woman repeated. "Violet Coteau? Receptionist, secretary to the agent, office manager? And you are the ranger with the appointment?"

"Yes," he managed to say.

Ranger McIntyre searched in his inner

coat pockets for his NPS identification card.

"Can't find my card. Anyway, I'm McIntyre. Ranger Timothy Grayson McIntyre, how do you do. Park Supervisor Nicholson sent me?"

"Yes," she said. "I know. And we very much appreciate the help."

"Glad to be here," he said.

"Agent Canilly has been called away. Unexpected development. A counterfeiting case. For the next few hours you'll have to settle for me."

Too bad, the ranger thought.

"Why don't we have lunch," she suggested, "and I can brief you concerning this dirty picture distributor."

"The supervisor said something about crossing state lines? That's why the FBI got involved?"

"That's right," she said.

She was already on her way toward a corner of the room where there were exactly three things: a coat rack with three hats on it, a wall mirror, and a tall potted plant of a variety McIntyre didn't recognize. He was surprised to see that the plant had more than three branches to it. The lovely Vi Coteau selected the navy-blue hat, one of those bucket hats popular with fashionable young ladies, a blue windbreaker, jacket and a pair of dark gloves.

"And it's more than dirty pictures," she continued. "We can talk about it over lunch. Shall we go?"

Lunch? Mentally he counted up how much money he had in his wallet and added the change from his pants pocket. Judging from her swell clothes and classy bearing, this was a woman who would require an expensive meal.

To a forest ranger, the sidewalks of Denver seemed exotic and even fascinating, in a mundane kind of way. Like those markets in France. They were commonplace to the natives but to a foreigner they were exotic with fresh and fascinating details. On Denver sidewalks, he was constantly aware of details. The black flat blobs of discarded chewing gum, the iron grates of the storm drains, the pieces of paper litter that skittered along the concrete even when there was no breeze, the crippled men hunched in sun-warm corners with their tin cups held out. The sound of leather heels striking the pavement, the electric trolleys giving off a mixed smell of ozone and hot axle grease. Being on the sidewalks of Denver reawakened memories of an earlier time and another woman, one he would never be able to stroll with again. The very special woman. She had loved having leisurely, elegant luncheons at the Brown Palace Hotel.

Vi Coteau stopped in front of Walgreens.

"Here we are," she said, pushing the door open before he could reach it.

Even wearing a blindfold McIntyre would have recognized where they were; there was a Walgreens atmosphere that greeted the nose the moment the door opened, a signature aroma compilation that included chocolate, inexpensive perfume, tinned tobacco, and antiseptic bandages. Just walking into a Walgreens gave him the urge to buy a tin of Prince Albert tobacco and a package of Black Jack chewing gum.

"Wonderful, isn't it?" she said.

Vi Coteau's red lips were smiling a beautiful smile as she inhaled deeply.

"Can you smell them?" she asked.

"What?"

"Nonpareils! I have three weaknesses and one of them is for nonpareils. Absolutely cannot resist them. Not good for the figure, however."

McIntyre very nearly passed a very brash and clever remark about her figure, but bit his tongue instead.

"Come on!" she said. "The lunch counter

is over there. That's my other weakness. I love egg salad sandwiches and a milkshake for lunch. There goes the figure again, right? But what the heck. Come on."

They took the two stools at the end of the lunch counter. It was amazing to McIntyre: Vi Coteau looked absolutely natural on a soda fountain stool, showing a nice bit of silk stocking as she crossed her ankles, every movement and each angle of wrist suggesting that she was there to model for a Coca-Cola ad. She drew off her gloves and folded them on the counter.

A bored-looking waitress slid two menu cards across the marble countertop and Vi reached for one and held it up as if was a list of gourmet dishes, a catalog of fantastic things to eat. As McIntyre was to learn — was already learning — Vi's enthusiasm for life in general was apt to bubble over at the most ordinary things. Or things that seem ordinary to most people. On their walk to Walgreens she had laughed at a little breeze that teased her skirt; when they passed a wounded veteran selling pencils she gave the man a smile that no doubt made his entire week better; when a trolleyman clanged his bell at her, she waved back; and each store window seemed to contain wonderful treasures to delight her eye.

Ranger McIntyre felt energized as if her vivacity was contagious, but at the same time he feared that it could be exhausting. Pleasantly exhausting. He wondered how it would be to be FBI Agent Canilly and have this creature for an assistant. Overwhelming, most days, probably.

They both ordered egg salad sandwiches (Special Today: Potato Chips and Pickle Spear, No Additional Charge) and sipped at their milkshakes while they waited.

"So," she began, "Agent Canilly has been in touch with the Omaha field office, and Omaha thinks the operation is based out of Sioux City."

"Distributing dirty pictures?"

"More than that. Omaha seems to think it's a case of using dirt to cover dirt. A few of the pictures we have recovered are simply pictures of naked or nearly naked people, men and women alike. A few others are sheer pornography. Omaha, though, alerted us to the fact that there are other pictures in which the background seems more interesting than the half-naked woman. There's no doubt that the pervert photographer is selling very twisted pictures to twisted men, no doubt whatsoever. And it's crossing state lines. But somebody seems to be using him

309

to distribute pictures of military bases and factories."

"You're pulling my leg," he said.

Vi Coteau leaned over on her stool to look down at McIntyre's leg.

"Nope. Wasn't me. Must've been someone else."

"Who would want to do that?" he said.

"Pull your leg?"

"No! Sell pictures of military bases and factories?"

"You've been working in the woods too long, Ranger. Much of what we know is classified intelligence, but it's general knowledge that certain European and Asian countries are interested in learning all they can about the United States military potential. When we cranked up our production and jumped into the war it took the world by surprise. Any country that had designs on its neighbors wouldn't want the U.S. to intervene. How's your sandwich? Good, huh?"

"Best egg salad sandwich I've had this week," McIntyre said with a broad smile. "We need to eat here more often. Maybe splurge and order the meat loaf special. It could even be my treat."

"You think this isn't your treat?"

He smiled again. And watched with unabashed masculine interest as her red lips closed around her soda straw.

"Any idea why the FBI called me down out of the mountains," he asked, "other than to watch you eat lunch, I mean?"

Before answering, she took a long draw of strawberry shake and dabbed her lips with a paper napkin.

"Before I tell you, promise me you won't be offended," she said. "Agent Canilly interviewed your assistant, Jamie Ogg, who told him how he and his friend Phillip had been approached by the man selling dirty pictures."

"Yes. And?"

"Agent Canilly doesn't think it was accidental. Two young men, young men from out of town, let us say, judging by their clothes and demeanor."

"Hicks looking for action in the city, in other words?"

"Precisely."

He loved the way those lips formed the word "precisely."

"Two rubes with two girls. The girls leave them at a certain spot in the park. The boys light a couple of cigarettes. The man with the pictures approaches them. Jamie Ogg expresses interest in certain photos, but then something about his behavior puts the seller on the alert. The seller makes Jamie a price he knows he couldn't possibly afford."

"I'm starting to see the picture," said Ranger McIntyre, "so to speak."

"Hah-ha that's a good one," Vi Coteau said flatly, forcing a fake smile.

Puzzle pieces again. McIntyre nibbled on his dill pickle spear while his mind began arranging pieces. The guy with the pictures had been on the lookout for a certain person doing certain things. He wouldn't need to know the courier, and the courier wouldn't need to know him. He offers the stranger deeply offensive pictures, expensive pictures of dead nude people. If the stranger was the courier he would show interest and pretend to "buy" the photos showing . . . what?

"Showing what?" McIntyre said aloud.

"What?"

"These pictures. Besides naked people, what do they show?"

"Take the three cities I mentioned, for instance. Each city has a rubber plant where they make tires and belts. Fan belts, conveyor belts, drive belts. Vital to any war effort. Each city has an extensive natural gas storage farm, gas needed in order to make rubber and steel. Even better, these cities have air bases where the Army trains pilots to fly the newest bombers and fighters. We acquired several postcards showing scantily clad girls posing in the foreground and very sharp images of hangars and security towers in the background. Same with the parking lot of the tire factory. And a footbridge over some railroad switching yards. The boys in Washington said that both places would be ideal spots to set off a bomb, something like a car packed with TNT."

"Wow."

"Well said. Are you going to have a piece of that pie you've been ogling?"

"Can't resist. Will you have a piece?"

"I don't think so. But you go ahead. As I said, I have three cravings. Day-old pie at a five and dime store is not one of them."

Back at the FBI office they found Agent A.T. Canilly waiting for them. *Now*, McIntyre thought, *I might find out why Supervisor Nicholson offered my help to the bureau.*

Canilly came around his desk and stuck out his hand.

"Man," he said, grinning broadly, "look at that suit! That's exactly what I hoped you'd look like. Fantastic, isn't it, Vi?"

"Agreed," Vi Coteau said. "He seems perfect."

"Is my suit wrong?" McIntyre asked. "I've

got another one. A National Park official business suit. Back at the hotel."

"No!" Canilly said. "No! Don't change a thing! It's perfect. Your small town haircut, that outdoorsy deep tan, that suit from four or five years ago, that necktie that's a little too wide, it's all perfect."

"Perfect," Vi agreed again.

"Now here's my idea," Canilly continued. "First, we don't know if we're dealing with porn merchants, spies, saboteurs, enemy agents, or just a guy with a weird hobby. But the job of the FBI is to find out, okay? What I want to do is this. I want to replicate the same situation as before, when your assistant ranger was offered dirty pictures, and see if your photo smut merchant will take the bait. In other words, I want you to dress up like an out-of-town boy trying to make city folk think he's a sheik looking for a good time at the park."

"So far so good," Vi Coteau said. "He already looks like a farm boy dressed up to go to town." Her dimpled smile showed she was teasing him and enjoying it. McIntyre didn't mind.

"Stop it, Vi," Agent Canilly said. "Don't pick on our pigeon. Ranger McIntyre, I figure you and an attractive lady could go to the park. You go through that same routine. Look around, buy something to eat, so forth and so forth. At one point she goes off to the girl's powder room while you loiter outside the men's room smoking a cigarette. I figure you could repeat the routine maybe twice, three times in one visit, see? With any luck, our guy with the dirty pictures will approach you."

"And I nab him for questioning," McIntyre stated.

"You, or Vi. She's very professional when it comes to making arrests. I originally thought of shadowing this clown home, see where he goes. But if we can catch him in the act and he's carrying dirty pictures from out of state we'll have cause to search his rooms."

"But we could follow him. Like hunting mountain lion," McIntyre said. "Instead of shooting the first one you see you can follow it and maybe find the lair."

"But," Canilly said, "I think once we have him under arrest we can sweat it out of him. We're good at it. We obtain a warrant, search his place, and with any luck we'll find evidence leading us to the rest of the dirty bunch."

"It sure sounds more interesting than ticketing tourists for littering. But I've got a question. Why me? Why not use one of your own agents for your decoy?"

"You're looking at half of my manpower," Canilly said. "We have two other agents and both of them look like agents. We kicked around the idea of bringing in a private detective or an off-duty cop, since it might be necessary to make an arrest. While talking to your supervisor, he said you might be ideal. I'll admit that the sabotage and spy theory is thin, but at the very least we'll catch a smut salesman and maybe put them out of business for a while. Are you willing to give it a try?"

It was McIntyre's turn to try a little teasing.

"This attractive female I'm supposed to be squiring around the park. Where can I find one of those?"

CHAPTER 13

"I think we have a fish interested in the bait," Vi Coteau said softly. "He's standing over there by the candy floss wagon. He's been giving us the eye."

"I noticed him. There's two of them," Ranger McIntyre whispered. "The other one is on the park bench across the lawn. If they're spies they're not very clever ones. The one hasn't got any reason to hang around the candy floss wagon and the other one's been looking at the same garden brochure for ten minutes. Maybe it's time. Do you need to use the women's toilet?"

"No," she said. "Not that it's any of your beeswax. But you're right. It's time to pretend that I do. Have you got your fags?"

"Right here," he said, patting the pocket with the pack of cigarettes in it.

"Okay. Now I'm off to the ladies' room. See if you can draw that cowboy away where the other one can't see him. I'll be watching

317

the other one and follow him. Maybe we can nab the both of them."

"Are you sure you're only a secretary? You act like you're a commando. I'm finding it harder and harder to figure you out. You know that?"

"I've heard that you like puzzles," she said with a smile. "But forget me and go into your act. If he tries to sell you naughty pictures, arrest him."

Their strategy was impromptu, but as an entrapment scheme it worked to perfection. McIntyre stepped out of the men's room and took a cigarette from his shirt pocket. As he reached into his trouser pocket for a book of matches he sensed the first man casually approaching him. McIntyre opened the matchbook and sidled along the lattice fence as if looking for a place out of the breeze where he could light his smoke. He went along the fence feigning interest in the ivy and climbing roses until he had lured the man out of sight of his confederate.

"How ya doin', buddy?"

"Okay. Nice day for it," McIntyre replied.

"The gardens are lookin' good."

"Yeah."

"Got a match?"

The stranger had shaken a cigarette from

a pack and tapped the end of it on his wrist watch. McIntyre handed him the book of matches.

"Thanks."

"Sure."

"I couldn't help noticin' your lady friend. Lucky guy. I'm here on my own."

"Looking for a pickup?" McIntyre asked innocently.

"It could happen. I'm ready."

"Ready?"

"You know what I mean. I can tell. You look like a sport who's been around the block and back. With a lady who looks like that, wow. I'm hoping to hook up with a doll like that and I got my insurance policy right here."

The stranger tapped his jacket indicating that his "insurance" was in the inside pocket.

"Booze?" McIntyre said.

"Nah. Oh, booze is easy. I can get you booze in five minutes. No, what I got is pictures. Pictures guaranteed to put the lady in a loving mood. One look and she gets curious to see more, see? Two looks and she wants to talk about sex. And, my friend, three looks and a slug of good booze and her duds start to come off, I guarantee it."

He slipped a long envelope from his inner

pocket and opened it to give McIntyre a peek at the photos.

"Those don't look legal," McIntyre said, leaning closer to see the pictures better.

"Hell, no, they're not legal. That's part of the beauty, see? All you have to do is tell the Jane you've got illegal pictures and pow! She can't resist. Gotta have a look, know what I mean? Next thing you know you're in the hay. Slick as a whistle."

"You're sure they're illegal?"

By pretending he wanted to move in order to see the pictures in a better light, McIntyre maneuvered his prey to the corner where the lattice fence met the building.

"They're expensive as hell," the man said, "and guaranteed illegal."

"You'd sell me some?"

"That's why I singled you out, pardner. I got extras and I'm selling them."

"I'm glad to hear you say that," McIntyre said.

He opened his lapel to show his badge. The stranger's mouth gapped open in surprise and before he could close it McIntyre had him by the wrist. It took less than ten seconds before the seller of dirty pictures was handcuffed to a steel railing. McIntyre left him there and hurried to Vi's assistance only to find that she didn't need his help.

Here she came, strolling toward him with her man in cuffs and her .38 snub-nose revolver pressed into the small of his back.

The Denver police were waiting outside the main gate, as arranged. Ranger McIntyre was not surprised to hear them address the FBI secretary as "Vi". After seeing the porn panderers safely locked in the back of a paddy wagon and on their way to jail, Vi and McIntyre strolled back through the floral displays toward her car.

"That went slick," McIntyre observed.

"Yes, it did!" Vi agreed. "But now I'm hungry. What say we don't go straight back to the office? How would you like to go down to Curtis Street and have a hamburger? I know a really good lunch counter. Anyway, there's only an hour left until quitting time."

"Eating while on duty? My kind of gal," McIntyre said with a smile.

"Tell you what," she went on. "I know the lady isn't supposed to ask the gentleman, but they're showing a new Chaplin film at the Isis Theater. It's called *The Pilgrim* but I don't know what it's about. Part of a double feature. How about you take me to the movies after we eat?"

"I'd like that," McIntyre said. "Don't know when it was that I last saw a film."

But he did know. It had been before she went away forever, before he lost her. Laughing at the comic cops, her hand clutching his arm for the car chase, going to a soda fountain for lime phosphates afterward, kissing in the back seat of a taxi on the way to the railroad station. He knew. He knew every detail.

McIntyre and Vi Coteau sat side by side in the dark movie theater like teenagers on a second date. They shared a bag of popcorn and experienced those quick tingles of excitement whenever their hands accidentally touched. As the first feature drew to a close McIntyre wiped his palm on his pants leg and took Vi's hand. The lights came up while the projectionist changed reels and neither of them moved.

"That was good," McIntyre said. "I wonder where they found all those covered wagons. They sure looked real."

"I want to know where they got the buffalo," Vi said. "That stampede scene was terrific! I wonder if the real pioneers were ever in danger from buffalo herds. Have you ever worked with buffalo in your National Park?"

"No, thank goodness. We don't have any. I did help round up a bunch of elk once and that was enough excitement for anybody. Want me to buy more popcorn?"

"Thanks, no. But I do wish I had a bag of nonpareils!"

"Let me check my pockets," he said cheerfully. They both knew he didn't have any, but the act of patting his coat pocket gave him opportunity to take his hand away. He liked holding hands with Vi Coteau, but at the same time it was becoming a little awkward.

The lights dimmed and the clatter of the projector resumed. And there on the screen was Charles Chaplin, playing the part of an escaped convict and doing double-takes each time he encountered anyone in a uniform. In the story his escape takes him to a Texas border town.

In the film, the Chaplin character isn't really a crook but a sensitive young man. When he spots a thief lifting a widow's savings from a bureau drawer he chases the man down and recovers the money. But as luck would have it, the sheriff catches up with Chaplin as he is returning the money to the widow's fair daughter. The sheriff has recognized him from a wanted poster. He has done a noble thing and a brave thing in restoring the widow's life savings, but he must go back to prison. The daughter pleads with the sheriff, but to no avail.

In the final scene, however, the sheriff has a change of heart. As he herds his prisoner along a dirt road they come to a signpost marking the border between Texas and Mexico. The sheriff pauses. He looks thoughtful for a moment before pointing across the national boundary line. "Go pick me a bunch of those flowers over there," he says.

Vi Coteau reached over and put her hand on McIntyre's. He had been acting rather different since making the arrest. She noticed it while writing their report at the police station, and now she suspected why. The Chaplin film had given her a clue.

In the movie, Chaplin picks the flowers and returns across the line, not comprehending that the sheriff has no jurisdiction in Mexico. Sending Chaplin across the state line is the sheriff's way of releasing him, of giving him freedom to go. The sheriff tries again and again until in the end he has to physically shove his little prisoner across the line. He orders him to stay there in Mexico while he rides away.

As the scene closed, Vi squeezed McIntyre's hand and looked into his face. He was biting his lower lip. So her guess had been correct.

Outside, back on the brightly lit evening sidewalks of Denver, they walked hand in hand toward the trolley stop.

"Sorry," she said.

"What about?"

"The end of that film. It made you think about your friend Doris, didn't it? Made you think you wished you could let her go, that she wouldn't go to jail."

"No, not really," the ranger replied. "I'm sure they'll take care of her. They'll find psychiatric help for her and a prison or asylum where she can live. She shouldn't be free to risk any more lives, though. No, it was the other woman the movie scene made me think of, Mari Canby. I've got to figure what to do that would help her."

"Have you got a thing for your prisoner, Mr. Ranger? She is an attractive woman." Vi was trying to lighten up the conversation.

"No, it's not like that. I think she just found herself in one of those man-woman situations and an accident happened. I don't think she'd wander around killing people if she was free. Sure, she told the attorney that she was responsible for Snyder's death. But a murderer? A murderer wouldn't have jumped in to rescue me the way she did, up there at Arrowhead Lake."

McIntyre managed to smile once again,

later on in the evening as he walked Vi to the lobby of her apartment building. Not only did he smile: he let a little chuckle escape.

"Something funny?" she asked.

"Just thinking," he said.

"About?"

"Well, here I am, helping you on and off the trolley like you were weak and might fall down without me, and then walking you safely home on the streets of the big city while all the time you're packing a .38 revolver in your purse. Plus, you tell me you've had FBI training with the Thompson submachine gun."

"Naturally. A girl never knows when a wiseguy might make a pass at her and she needs to ventilate him with twenty or thirty rounds from her own personal Tommy gun!"

The doorman slumbering in his chair snapped awake at the sound of their laughter. He watched with a doorman's disinterest as Vi lightly kissed McIntyre on the cheek before stepping into the elevator. He watched the tall man in the uncomfortable-looking suit leave the building and went back to his evening nap.

Several weeks went by before McIntyre returned to Denver and Vi Coteau. And seeing her again was well worth the long drive: he walked into the courthouse hearing room and there she was, seated at one of the attorney tables with her steno pad in front of her. In her blue pleated skirt and sailor blouse she looked as though she might like go to the park for a picnic instead of sitting through a wrongful death hearing.

The judge explained the complicated problem of jurisdiction in the Mari Canby case. Although the arrest had been made in Larimer County, the arrest was not officially legal until the accused had been turned over to the county sheriff. However, the accused had been detained initially by a qualified and credentialed officer of the federal government — one Ranger Timothy Grayson McIntyre — within the legal boundaries and on the property of a United States federal possession, namely the Rocky Mountain National Park. Moreover, the judge continued, the incident in question did occur within the same aforementioned boundaries and on property of the National Park and could therefore be considered a federal matter. However, since the aforementioned ranger had surrendered the arrested parties to the custody of the county sheriff, it could be argued that the federal government had thereby waived and abandoned all and any claim to the case. None-theless, the involvement of the Federal Bureau of Investigation in events subsequent and considered contributory must take precedent and provide cause for federal court jurisdiction.

All of which only goes to say, McIntyre thought, *that this hearing is being held here instead of the Larimer County courthouse.*

Mari Canby's lawyer introduced two character witnesses, both of whom testified that she was a caring and outgoing woman of quality who would never intentionally harm anyone. Van Kaplan's name was never mentioned.

The judge took testimony from a witness for the family of Ernst Snyder, a cousin, who said that Snyder had a quick temper and at times had seemed irrational when enraged. Next, Snyder's brother was called. He confirmed and described some of Snyder's raging outbursts. The almost empty courtroom echoed until McIntyre could barely understand any of the words that were being said.

The hands on the courtroom clock crawled as if molasses had been poured into the mechanism. When they reached the twelve o'clock position, however, the judge did not call for a lunch recess. McIntyre glanced at Vi. She looked up from her notes to return his look. She winked and he found himself thinking about egg salad sand-wiches.

Jamie Ogg was called to testify how he had found the deceased man and summoned Ranger McIntyre. McIntyre confirmed, under oath, everything he had written in his report about the deceased, the condition of the body, the discovery of the clothing and fishing equipment, and his subsequent attempts to find out what the victim had been doing at Chasm Falls. The judge seemed satisfied; instead of calling for a lunch break, however, he instructed McIntyre to give the facts concerning the "subsequent happening," as he put it.

"I was a long ways back in the mountains without any other ranger or law officer to assist me," McIntyre explained. "I was arresting the woman who killed the girl at Cub Lake and admitted the same to me. She pulled a gun and threatened to shoot. Miss Canby was on her way down the valley and happened to see the woman pointing the gun at me. She quietly came up behind the murderer and knocked her down with a tree branch, undoubtedly saving me from being shot. I was able to secure the weapon and handcuff the suspect. Miss

Canby could have ridden away at that point, but she waited in case I could use her help and she even assisted. I needed to keep an eye on the suspect while I attended to her victim, who was regaining consciousness after she drugged him. Like it says in my report, the victim was too groggy to travel, as was the woman who tried to shoot me. While waiting for them to recover, I took the opportunity to ask Miss Canby how she happened to be there. That's when she told me about witnessing the Chasm Falls accident and her subsequent visits to the scene. She had been experiencing deep guilt about not being able to help him, and had come back to the park this summer in hopes that seeing the place again would help purge the bad memories. It reminded me of how soldiers will return to a battlefield after the war, to lay their demons to rest, if your honor understands my meaning."

"Indeed. I do. Did Miss Canby tell you how Mr. Snyder came to be undressed?"

McIntyre's version of what she had told him appeared to satisfy the judge, who was now glancing at the clock every few minutes. As everyone waited, he read several pages of the testimony, leafed through the official reports, consulted a thick book, and finally announced that, in his judgment, there was insufficient reason to incarcerate Miss Canby. Instead, she would be required to undergo a period of probation and keep the court informed as to her whereabouts.

Mari Canby came out of the courtroom to find half a dozen friends waiting for her in the foyer, but she looked in vain for the tall ranger.

"He went off with that classy doll in the sailor blouse. They had their heads together, talking about something," one of Mari's friends said. "I didn't catch what he said, exactly, but it sounded like he said either 'excellent lunch' or 'egg salad lunch.' "

CHAPTER 14

The telephone rang. He pulled it across the desk and lifted the earpiece.

"Fall River Entrance Station. Ranger McIntyre speaking."

"I still say you're a softie."

"Hullo, Vi. How's everything going with the FBI?"

"Oh, nifty. If it wasn't for counterfeiters and bootleggers we wouldn't have a thing to do all day. And it's too darn hot to do much. You could fry an egg on the Denver sidewalk."

"I'll pass. I've seen your sidewalks. You ought to come up to the mountains where it's cool."

"Don't think I haven't thought about it. Why don't you cook up a federal case we can come up and investigate?"

"Well, I did apprehend a foreigner doing sabotage to federal property."

"How's that?"

"A guy from France was feeding marshmallows to a chipmunk."

"I bet you let him go. Like Mari Canby."

"That was different. It's like fly fishing. With certain fish you seem to know that you need to release them back into the water. After putting up an honest fight they deserve another round."

"Softie. What's new up there in your mountain paradise, anyway?"

"You remember O'Reilly, the man with one hand?"

"Certainly."

"Well, he turned out to be the real Mc-Coy, a straight-up kind of guy. We found out — that's me and Supervisor Nicholson found out — that O'Reilly knows his way around these shortwave radios. And he's handy with telephones. We hired him and he's going to string wires to various places for us so we can have emergency telephones at spots like Chasm Falls. Next summer, if the S.O. can find the money for it, he's going to supervise building a fire lookout. We need to figure out where to put it, but O'Reilly will probably become our first full-time summer fire warden."

"That's good news. I bet he's happy. What about that other man, Van Kaplan?"

"Closed up the photo studio for the

season and left town. He'll be back next spring, but I don't think he'll be trying any more flings in the forest. Anything new in the dirty picture case?"

"We got the wholesaler and proof that he was sending his merchandise all over the country. Plus, the sick jerk who developed and printed the pictures, plus a list of the names of other photographers he had used. A kind of inventory. But the espionage thing, that went phflooey."

"Phflooey?"

"Phflooey. Nothing to it. We had to put it all down to an overly zealous FBI desk agent and a nervous investigator in Washington. I guess you heard that Doris Killian was remanded to state custody. She'll spend the next few years confined to the mental hospital. Maybe longer, if she doesn't show any improvement."

"So I heard. It was in the newspaper."

"What else is happening up there?"

"Not much going on. Fishing is okay, tourist traffic is slacking off. Up at the Beaver Point store I told Tiny Brown to be sure he had the ingredients for egg salad, in case you come to visit. He doesn't have nonpareils, though, so you'll have to bring your own. Which reminds me: what IS your third craving anyway?"

Her laughter over the telephone brought a broad smile to his face.

"Maybe I'll let you find out when I see you again," Vi said. "Which is why I called. I want you to let me know when the aspen begin to turn color. And when the tourists have gone home. I'd like to come up and have you show me your National Park in autumn. If you're not too busy."

"Well . . ." McIntyre hesitated. "Fishing is awfully good that time of year, once the stream levels start to drop. I'll be busy with that. And there's hunting season. I need to keep an eye out for poachers. Plus, we do a lot of maintenance work in the fall. Painting the station, fixing fences, lots of work to be done. Not much time to rest, let alone take ladies for tours of the autumn aspen."

"McIntyre?"

"Yes?"

"Stop it. You're not too nifty when it comes to kidding a girl. You'll have time to show me around and you know it as well as I do. Listen, when the aspen trees start to turn color, you give me a call. You can reserve a room in the village for me at that inn. We'll have breakfast."

"What about this third craving of yours? When are you going to tell me about it?"

"Ranger, if you don't know by the time

we have breakfast, you probably never will."

Just great, McIntyre thought as he hung the earpiece back in the cradle. *Great. Another puzzle, and this one's named Vi Coteau.*

The telephone rang again. With an audible sigh he answered it.

"Fall River Station, Ranger McIntyre speaking."

"Nicholson here. Why the long sigh? Never mind. There's no particular hurry, but I've got another job for you."

"Enforcement again?" McIntyre asked.

"It might turn into an enforcement problem. Which is why I called you. You know the little lodge at Blue Spruce Lake, the one called Small Delights?"

"Sure. Never been inside, but I understand it's an older couple running it. They've got four or five rooms. What's the trouble?"

"That's what I want you to find out. Either the old folks are the most unlucky people you ever heard of, or . . ."

"Or what?"

"Or somebody's out to kill them."

GLOSSARY:
THE LANGUAGE
OF THE LOCALS

"Altitude": up high enough in the mountains to brag about it, as in "we were hiking at altitude," or as in "we were camped at altitude." Usually above the treeline (see "timberline"). "Relative altitude" is one of two things heavily stressed by real estate salesmen, the other being "view." As in "Sure, your yard is mostly rocks and steep as a barn roof, but it sits above the village and has a great view!"

"Cabin camp": this was originally intended to be a step up from a tent camp. A slight step. A typical cabin camp consisted of five or ten one-room non-insulated 10 x 12 cabins furnished with one or two beds, a wood-burning cookstove, a single light bulb hanging from the rafters, and a small table with two chairs. If advertised as "rustic," the cabins had an outhouse "up the hill"

337

and a water tap in the middle of the parking area. "Semi-modern" meant there was a central bathhouse with hot and cold running water and possibly a water tap inside the actual cabin itself. "Modern" got you a cabin with a bathroom inside, unless that particular cabin had already been rented, in which case you got semi-modern.

"Chinook": a warm wind, often called "the snow eater." Saying "chinook wind" is regarded as redundant and makes you sound like a tourist. It is permissible to say "it's chinooking" even if it makes you sound like a non-English speaker. A chinook becomes most noticeable in winter when warm air sliding down from the Divide turns the snow into sloppy mush. Skiers do not like chinooks.

"Chipmunk": countless scientific man-hours have been spent cataloguing the characteristics of this point-nose little rodent. Thanks to all those generations of intrepid biologists and illustrators, we can now say with confidence that a chipmunk is not a ground squirrel, gopher, prairie dog, or marmot. Some tourists, however, have yet to appreciate the difference and gleefully send Junior to give peanuts to the "chipmunks," which actually turn out to be brown bears.

"Creek" [pronounced "krik"]: any dribble of water that appears to be moving. The rule is that a creek must have an unimaginative name. Thus we have Willow Creek, Beaver Creek, Rock Creek, and Pine Creek. If those seem too daringly descriptive, we resort to calling them North Fork, Middle Fork, or Miller's Fork. Fork of what, does not need explaining. Any dribble that becomes too deep, wide, or turbulent to wade across is termed a "river," much to the amusement of out-of-state visitors who live near the real ones.

"Crevice, crevasse": being primarily granite and suffering extremes of heat and freezing, the Rockies are prone to cracking. Any crack may be called a "crevice," mostly for dramatic effect as in "wow, would you look at that crevice." The exception is any crack in those ice fields. which locals erroneously refer to as "glaciers" when they (the cracks) become Frenchified into "crevasses." If your foot slips and you become lodged in one, you don't care what they are called. You only want somebody to come get you out.

"Clearing": for reasons no one has adequately explained, forests sometimes have expanses of open grass, usually flat and fertile, where no trees, or only a few trees, grow. Some clearings are created with chainsaws and bulldozers but will revert to forest if left alone long enough, for reasons I cannot adequately explain.

"Divide": the Continental Divide, an imaginary line running along the top of the Rocky Mountains but not always at the highest points. It is called the Divide because creeks and streams on the west side (known as the Western Slope) flow toward the Pacific Ocean, while those on the Eastern Slope of the Rockies drain toward the Atlantic.

"Dry fly": an emblem of fruitless hopes consisting of some feathers, thread, and chenille wrapped around a hook, which the fisherperson is convinced resembles an actual insect. The dry version is intended to float on the surface of the water and attract trout. The wet version is intended to sink beneath the water and fool the fish into thinking it is an emerging insect. Samples of both versions may be seen festooning willows, aspen, pine, dead logs, rough logs, and articles of clothing, not to mention certain protruding appendages such as noses, ears, and fingers.

"Elk": local jokers have a story about a tourist who asked, "What time of year do the deer turn to elk?" hah hah hah. Elk are taller and heavier than deer and have longer antlers and can run faster, which is good to remember if you are ever tempted to send Junior out onto the meadow to pose with one of them. Local lore also believes that "the Indians" (whoever they were) called the elk "wapiti," a word no one could pronounce until a ranger with nothing else to do came up with the rhyme "hippity hoppity it's a wapiti."

"Front Range": I don't know about other states the Rockies run through, but in Colorado the long line of high mountains dividing the state into two halves is itself divided up into "ranges." To the north we have the Mummy Range, so named because the collection of peaks resembles either a reclining mummy or a severely constipated boa constrictor; the Never Summer Range, in which there actually is summer every year; then the Front Range (for which there is no correlative Side Range or Back Range); then the Arapaho Range, named for the Indian tribe we stole it from (sometimes referred to as The Indian Peaks, but God help any Indian who would try to claim any of it).

"The gate": as in "who is manning the gate" or "I'm only going up to the gate and back" or "they will give you a map at the gate." The term refers to one of the automobile entrances to the park, where there are no actual gates unless that's what you call orange traffic cones.

"Lichen, krummholz, and scree": crusty moss on rocks, stunted and twisted trees at altitude and loose sliding stones where you want to walk. It's either that, the name of a pop music group, or a story of three squirrels. Hikers have other names for krummholz and scree but we aren't allowed to print them.

"Lodge": a large private home made of logs chinked with ten-dollar bills and credit-card receipts; a tiny summer shack with a grandiose name like Nest of the Eagle Lodge or a silly name such as Wee Neva Inn, Dew Drop Inn, or Lily's Li'l Lodge; a big establishment with a few rental rooms inside and a dozen or more cabins outside, plus a livery stable upwind of a dining room and a volleyball court no one has ever used.

"Moonshine": illegal alcohol. According to folk legend, it was distilled by the light of the moon in order to avoid the authorities. Also known as "shine," "hooch," "popskull," "varnish remover," "Who-Hit-John," and even "beer."

"Moraine": few terms confuse visitors as much as does the term "moraine." Locals use the term sparingly, because they don't understand it, either. Some say it means a big ridge of rocks that looks as if it was dredged up and stacked by huge machines — it was actually done by a prehistoric glacial flow — while others say it refers to a big treeless clearing. Locals sometimes take visitors to Moraine Park and point at the distant ridge, the flat meadow, and the campground and say "that's the moraine." Residents along Fall River Road live on no fewer than three moraines and none of them knows it.

"Mountain sickness": also known as "altitude sickness." Do you feel clammy, yet feverish? Dizzy and diuretic? Have a hangover-size headache? Nausea, aching joints, death wish? Have you been bitten by a wood tick lately, or have you sipped water from the stream? If not, you probably have mountain sickness. Go home.

"National Forest": an usually vast area set aside and under the protection of the U.S. Department of Agriculture and managed "for the greatest good of the greatest number in the long run." Land within National Forests is used for logging, mining, grazing, and recreation.

"National Park": a usually vast area set aside and under the protection of the U.S. Department of Interior and managed so as to preserve and protect it in its natural state for the benefit and enjoyment of future generations. The principal ideal is expressed in the slogan "take nothing except pictures, leave nothing except footprints." (Which, by the way, would get you arrested in The Louvre.)

"Park": a flat open space in the mountains, often named for a pioneer and ranging in size from a few acres (Allenspark, Hermit Park) to hundreds of square miles (South Park, North Park). Locals joke about tourists who arrive in Estes Park Village and ask where to find the roller coaster and Ferris wheel, or the caged animals. No one in human memory has ever laughed at that joke.

"The Park": Rocky Mountain National Park, the only important industry of Estes

Park and the only reason for the village's existence. Villagers speak lovingly of trails and peaks and lakes in "The Park" but roughly seventy percent of them have never ventured off its blacktop roads.

"Pass": (1) a slip of paper allowing you to bring your car into the park. But you already knew that. (2) In local parlance, a "pass" is a route over the mountains. There are more of these than you might assume, most of which are inaccessible. Foreigners to Estes Park might be confused by the fact that El Paso del Norte in New Mexico lies south of the village, while South Pass crosses the Wyoming Rockies to the north.

"Ranger": there are two kinds, and woe to him who confuses them. In the USFS a ranger is an important chieftain in charge of a very large district of the National Forest. In the NPS a ranger might or might not be a temporary summer employee, i.e., a schoolteacher wearing a uniform and badge. A National Forest symbol shows Smokey the Bear wearing a flat ranger hat, which National Forest rangers don't wear but National Park rangers do. Park rangers are known locally as "flat hats" and sometimes "tree cops." National Forest rangers can jerk your permit for grazing, mining, logging, or commercial recreation and thus are known locally as "sir" or "Mr."

"Sam Browne": in addition to the iconic flat hat, park rangers used to wear iconic Sam Browne belts (presumably invented by the iconic Sam Browne), a wide leather belt with had a narrower leather belt that went over the shoulder. Some say the function of the shoulder strap was to support a heavy pistol and holster. Some say it was left over from WWI, when the shoulder strap was used to drag wounded soldiers out of harm's way. Some say the function of the shoulder strap was just to make the uniform look cool.

"The S.O.": Supervisor's Office, or the central administration building from whence flows a relentless stream of orders, regulations, recriminations, requests, and regrets. For some reason, employees seem to like pronouncing "S.O." with a suggestive pause after it as if a letter were missing.

"The S.O.P.": a manual of Standard Operating Procedures. Updated on a weekly basis until no office shelf is sturdy enough to hold it, the S.O.P. dictates How To Do Everything, from what to tell people in the event of nuclear holocaust (pray) to how to install the toilet paper (roll from the top, not the bottom). Temps in search of answers to questions ("I just saw a bear climb into a visitor's car, what do I do?") have been known to disappear only to be found years afterward as desiccated corpses hunched over the S.O.P. Equally useful is The Compendium, revised almost annually, which tells everyone how to do everything and what not to do. It has been said that the flat hat rangers live in fear of offending it and won't even visit the restroom without taking The Compendium along.

"Summer hire": with more than a million visitors traipsing through the National Park each year, the park depends heavily on summer employees to keep everything (particularly restrooms) clean and functioning. They maintain hiking trails, clean toilets, paint signs, clean toilets, direct traffic, clean toilets, answer questions, clean toilets, pick up trash, and sometimes the rangers help them clean toilets.

"The Canyon": there are two major highways between Estes Park and "The Valley." One of them follows the Thompson River and is always called "The Canyon" as in "I'm going down The Canyon to The Valley to pick up some toilet paper at Sam's Club if you need anything." The other route, Highway 36, doesn't have a name. It also doesn't have much of a canyon.

"Timberline": 10,500 feet above sea level. Or thereabouts. Early settlers discovered that at that altitude the trees would not grow large enough to be cut down for lumber. And "timberline" sounded more euphonic than "lumberline." Some modern fussy little know-it-all decided that it should be called "treeline" instead, which confuses things because stunted, runty little trees can be found higher than 11,000 feet in some locations. Which, like having a word like "timberline," doesn't matter in any imaginable way.

"Up top" or "Up on top": locals who say they drove "up top" or took guests "up on top" are referring to the highest section of Trail Ridge, where they can see snowbanks in August at two miles above sea level. They can also enjoy driving a two-lane highway that (a) has almost no guardrails and (b) drops off more than a thousand feet from the edge of the pavement to the bottom of Forest Canyon. Restrooms are available Up Top. Sometimes for a reasonable gratuity, a local high school student will agree to pry your fingers from your steering wheel and drive you back down to your lodgings.

"The Valley": one Estes Parkian might say "I'm going down to The Valley" and another will ask "which one?" and the reply will be "Longmont." This may confuse those who don't know that "The Valley" may refer to any town or city between Loveland and Denver. However, one goes "up" to Fort Collins and "over" to Greeley, both of which are approximately two thousand feet lower in elevation than Estes. You also go "over" to Grand Lake, which is on "the other side," and you go "down" to Allenspark, which is higher than Estes Park (unless you're looking at a road map tacked to the wall, in which case it is below Estes). I hope this clarifies the matter.

ABOUT THE AUTHOR

James C. Work grew up in his parents' cabin camp a mile from one of the entrance stations to Rocky Mountain National Park. He was a little boy with a bicycle and more blessed freedom than can be imagined. Sometimes the RMNP rangers at "the gate" would put his bike in the back of their patrol pickup and give him a lift up the road. Sometimes a ranger would take winter lodgings at the cabin camp. These clean-cut, upright men were his heroes, the National Park his playground. By the time he finished high school he knew every trail, every stream and lake, and every ranger in the park. While in college he earned summer money with the trail crew, the fire crew, and eventually by presenting campfire programs for the U.S. Forest Service.

James is author of Five Star's Keystone Ranch series, a collection of stories from the 1880s with themes from the King Arthur chronicles. *Unmentionable Murders* is the first in a planned series of novels featuring NPS Ranger T. G. McIntyre. In the next book, *Small Delightful Murders,* Ranger McIntyre takes on some Chicago gangsters and a vandal who is out to frighten people — if he doesn't kill them first.

The employees of Thorndike Press hope you have enjoyed this Large Print book. All our Thorndike, Wheeler, and Kennebec Large Print titles are designed for easy reading, and all our books are made to last. Other Thorndike Press Large Print books are available at your library, through selected bookstores, or directly from us.

For information about titles, please call:
  (800) 223-1244

or visit our Web site at:
  http://gale.cengage.com/thorndike

To share your comments, please write:
  Publisher
  Thorndike Press
  10 Water St., Suite 310
  Waterville, ME 04901